DB

D0350371

THE VALLEY OF THE SHADOW

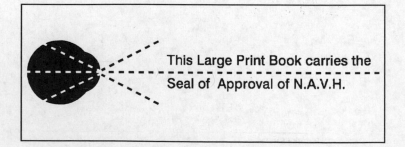

This Large Print Book carries the
Seal of Approval of N.A.V.H.

THE VALLEY OF THE SHADOW

CAROLA DUNN

THORNDIKE PRESS
A part of Gale, Cengage Learning

GALE
CENGAGE Learning·

Detroit • New York • San Francisco • New Haven, Conn • Waterville, Maine • London

GALE
CENGAGE Learning®

Copyright © 2012 by Carola Dunn.
Thorndike Press, a part of Gale, Cengage Learning.

ALL RIGHTS RESERVED
This is a work of fiction. All of the characters, organizations, and events portrayed in this novel are either products of the author's imagination or are used fictitiously.
Thorndike Press® Large Print Mystery.
The text of this Large Print edition is unabridged.
Other aspects of the book may vary from the original edition.
Set in 16 pt. Plantin.

LIBRARY OF CONGRESS CATALOGING-IN-PUBLICATION DATA

Dunn, Carola.
  The valley of the shadow : a Cornish mystery / by Carola Dunn.
    pages ; cm. — (Thorndike Press large print mystery)
    ISBN-13: 978-1-4104-5650-2 (hardcover)
    ISBN-10: 1-4104-5650-1 (hardcover)
    1. Cornwall (England : County)—Fiction. 2. Large type books. I. Title.
  PR6054.U537V35 2013
  823'.914—dc23   2012047161

Published in 2013 by arrangement with St. Martin's Press, LLC

Printed in the United States of America
1 2 3 4 5 6 7 17 16 15 14 13

ACKNOWLEDGEMENTS

My thanks for their invaluable assistance to Sue Stone; Sue Curran; Pam Gotcher; Sheila Roth; Jane Heydecker; Annette Dashofy; John Johnson; John Szostak; Ron Henderson, BSc, SR (Para); Jinx Schwartz; D. P. Lyle, MD; Captain Jackson; Malcolm of the Telephone Museum; Beth Franzese; Councillor Roy Abraham; Severn Boating; Tony Pawlin, Head of Research, and Peter, volunteer, National Maritime Museum, Falmouth.

AUTHOR'S NOTE

Port Mabyn is a fictional village in a fictional world lurking somewhere in the 1960s and '70s, between my childhood memories of Cornwall and the present reality. No computers, no cell phones, no GPS, no nose or navel rings; female police detectives were an anomaly; the Beatles were top of the charts, not golden oldies; instead of the Mediterranean or Caribbean for their summer holidays, the English still flocked to the Cornish Riviera, leaving it to the locals in the off-season.

For the most part, I have used the irresistible names of real places. Rocky Valley is very much as I've described it, as is Bossiney Cove in general, if not in the details required by my story.

The Constabulary of the Royal Duchy of Cornwall (CaRaDoC) has no existence outside my imagination.

For information about the real Cornwall,

I refer the reader to countless works of nonfiction, or, better still, I suggest a visit.

The "Old Squire" of Boscastle was a real person. His descendants as depicted in this book are entirely fictional.

ONE

"Yip?" said Teazle hopefully.

"You're not supposed to beg at table," Eleanor reminded her.

The Westie's ears flattened and she subsided to the floor, but her nose and her short white tail continued to quiver.

"Oh, all right." Leaving the last bite of chipolata sausage on the side of her plate, Eleanor finished the salad.

As she put her plate and coffee mug in the kitchen sink, just a step away, she glanced out of the open window. Though the schools' autumn term was well under way, plenty of tourists unencumbered by children still came to Cornwall. After yesterday's drizzle, today they were being rewarded with a day as bright and warm as summer. Even the usual cool sea breeze had stilled.

On the other side of the narrow street, a couple were coming out of the bakery, which stayed open at lunchtime till the end of September. The man carried a brown paper bag with twisted corners. He opened it and sniffed, whereupon the woman took it from him and firmly rolled the top. Hot pasties, Eleanor guessed. The couple turned down the hill, no doubt making for one of the benches overlooking the harbour.

"Wuff," Teazle reminded her.

She transferred the piece of sausage to the dog bowl. As she straightened after putting the bowl on the floor, the phone rang. A few steps took her across the sitting room to her desk by the window at the back of the cottage. She picked up the receiver and gave her number.

"Aunt Nell, it's Megan. It's such a gorgeous day, if you're taking Teazle for a walk, I'd like to join you. I didn't get to bed till three — we just wrapped up a big burglary case — and if I don't get out, I'll doze all afternoon and not sleep to night."

"Of course, dear. Shall I drive over to Launceston and pick you up?"

"No, that's all right. You won't believe this, but the DI has not only given me the afternoon off, he's said I can take a CaRa-DoC car — plain, not a panda — in case he has to call me back unexpectedly."

"Mr. Scumble?" Eleanor, though in gen-

10

eral inclined to believe the best of people, had clashed more than once with the detective inspector and mistrusted his apparent benevolence. "Are you sure you didn't misunderstand him?"

"I'm sure. He said I looked peaky."

"That sounds more like him, managing to combine an insult with a favour. Are you not feeling well, dear?"

"I'm fine, just a bit tired. We've been working long hours for a couple of weeks. I'll be over in about an hour, if that's all right."

"Why don't you meet us at Rocky Valley? Nick wants to do some sketching and photographing there, and I promised to take him this afternoon. It's a lovely place to walk."

"Nick Gresham? I don't know if I —"

"Don't be silly, Megan. It's months since he was arrested and he doesn't hold it against you. He's my next-door neighbour, you can't avoid him forever."

"I've managed pretty well so far! It's very embarrassing when you've had to question someone about his . . . personal life. Oh, all right, I'll be there. It's between Tintagel and Boscastle, isn't it?"

"Yes, dear. There's a lay-by on the east side of the coast road. Or it might be the

11

south side at that point, come to think of it. Never mind — It's just on a sharp bend, and there's a footpath sign on the sea side. We'll see you in an hour or so."

Eleanor was glad Megan had agreed to come but disappointed by her reluctance. She was very fond of Nick and her niece. They were both about thirty, the perfect age for settling down, and both free of romantic entanglements. What could be more natural than that they should become fond of each other? Unfortunately, the artist and the detective sergeant rarely saw eye to eye. Eleanor sighed.

Teazle, having heard the magic word "walk," was waiting impatiently by the door. Now she cocked her head, whining. Eleanor heard footsteps running up the stairs, followed by a knock.

"Come in," she called.

The door opened. "Ouch!" said Nick as Teazle's back paws danced on his bare, sandalled feet. "Down, girl." She rolled over on her back and he crouched to pet her tummy, his long brown ponytail flopping over his shoulder. The sleeves of his blue shirt were rolled up above the elbow. The shirt was spotless, but a splotch of turquoise paint on his arm had eluded him. "Ready to go, Eleanor? Shall I go and get the Incorruptible?"

12

"Yes, dear, would you?" Eleanor's pea-green Morris Minor (named after Robespierre, the "sea-green Incorruptible") lived at the bottom of the hill, in a shed she rented on the only flat piece of ground in Port Mabyn. The one and only street was too narrow for parking. "The keys are on the hook — oh, no, they're not. In my handbag? No, they must be in a pocket. What was I wearing last time I took the car out?"

Nick grinned. "I don't know, but it hasn't been this warm and dry for a couple of weeks, so try your coat pockets."

"Aren't you taking a mac? The sun may be shining now, but it is September, after all, and you never can tell."

"My anorak's in my satchel."

"Here are the keys. But there's no hurry. Megan's going to meet us there in about an hour."

He raised his eyebrows. "Detective Sergeant Pencarrow intends to grace us with her presence? I was under the impression that I'm out of favour. You did tell her I'll be there, didn't you, Eleanor?"

"Of course. It's not that she dislikes you, Nick."

"She just disapproves." He laughed. "Well, I like your niece, but not enough to be shorn like a copper. As for keeping my clothes and my person paint-free, it's just not possible. If it's all right with you, I'd like to get going. I want to reach the inlet while the sun's still high. You could let me out and go begging in Bossiney or Boscastle till it's time to meet Megan."

"Requesting donations for LonStar is not begging," Eleanor said severely. The London Committee to Save the Starving had employed her for decades as a roving ambassador, travelling all over the world. After retiring to Cornwall, she had dedicated her ground floor to a charity shop and now spent much of her time travelling the countryside, picking up donated goods to sell. "As a matter of fact, I did miss a couple of farms last time I was up that way. I'll change my shoes while you fetch the car."

Nick departed, his long legs making short work of the stairs.

The Incorruptible's aged engine did not make short work of the hill out of Port Mabyn. It groaned upward, past the newsagent's and Chin's Chinese, the Trelawny Arms and the mini-supermarket, then between hedge-banks bright with ragwort and garlanded with red and orange bryony berries and the white fluff of old-man's beard. This stretch of coast was all cliffs, two or three hundred feet high. The lanes wound about some distance inland, so that for the most part the sea was invisible.

Directed by Eleanor, who knew the maze of lanes like the back of her hand, Nick left the B road and drove through tiny hamlets, Bothiwick, Trewarmett, then cut across country to avoid Tintagel, where the street was often a tourist traffic jam. At one point, a stretch of higher, open land allowed occasional glimpses of a dark blue line of sea meeting the pale blue of the sky on the far horizon.

Beyond the small village of Bossiney, the road wiggled through a patch of woodland. The dark green footpath sign was easy to miss, but Nick spotted it. They pulled over and he got out. Teazle was about to jump out after him, but as she scrabbled over the gear lever from the backseat, Eleanor grabbed the end of the lead. Not that there was much traffic, but cars tended to come much too fast round the blind corner.

"She can come with me," Nick offered. "There's not much mischief she can get into, and you won't be long, will you?"

Eleanor checked her watch. "About half an hour. All right. You behave yourself, Teazle." She handed over the lead to Nick and told him, "Don't let her off till you're away from the road." She went round to the driver's seat and drove on.

The first farm she called at offered a couple of old wooden cart wheels with iron rims. The farmer's wife said her husband had found them at the back of the hayloft in the barn. She couldn't imagine why or when someone had lugged them up there. "I've seen such set up roundabout furriners' houses," she said, "so I thought you might be able to sell 'em. They're no earthly use to us."

"Lovely," said Eleanor. "People like to make garden fences with them. We get a good price once they're cleaned up and polished." Jocelyn, the vicar's wife who ran the shop, could be counted on to turn the battered, grimy wheels into decorative "antiques."

They wouldn't fit in the boot. The farmer had to be called to manoeuvre them into the backseat. As she hurried — insofar as the car was capable of hurrying — back towards Rocky Valley, Eleanor pictured Teazle sitting in among the spokes on the way home and she laughed.

She parked in the lay-by opposite the footpath, no more than a gravelled widening of the road. A moment later, a dark grey plainclothes police Mini stopped nose to nose with the Incorruptible.

16

"Nick decided not to come?" Did Megan sound disappointed?

"I dropped him off a little earlier, with Teazle. He wanted to catch the light. Or was it the tide? One or t'other, or perhaps both. Let's go and find them." Preparing to cross the road, Eleanor looked both ways.

"Aunt Nell, you haven't locked the car. You haven't even closed the windows!" Megan took the keys from her hand.

"At least I didn't leave them in the ignition. But can you honestly imagine anyone going to the trouble of stealing the Incorruptible, dear? And the only things in it are a couple of dirty old wooden wheels."

"Are those for the shop? If they're worth something to LonStar, they're worth something to a thief."

"Only if an inquisitive and dishonest antique dealer happened to pass. They're not worth the trouble anyway. If you'd seen the struggle the farmer had getting them in . . . I just hope we can get them out again."

By then, Megan had rolled up the windows, locked the doors, and returned the keys. They crossed to the drive leading down to the house that had been the old Trevillet watermill, built of irregular slabs of local slate mortared together.

17

On their right, amid trees and bushes still summer green, the Trevillet River rushed and tumbled over a series of low waterfalls, flinging droplets that sparkled in the sun. Then, clear as glass, it rippled down its stony bed, each pebble visible, from pale grey and yellowish through every shade of brown. A narrow, rickety wooden footbridge took them over the stream, almost hidden here in the lush growth of water-loving plants. Heedless of protruding tree roots, the rough path plunged into the cool dimness of greenery, winding along the chuckling brook. They came to the roofless ruins of Trethevy Mill.

The moss-draped walls were succumbing to the slow, inexorable assault of small trees, whose branches intruded brazenly through the empty rectangles of windows. In an odd sort of parody of spring blossom, ribbons bedecked the lower branches, pink, blue, red, white, purple, orange.

"What on earth . . . ?" exclaimed Megan.

At the sound of her voice, a small white ball of fur erupted from the interior. Teazle greeted Eleanor with delight and Megan with rapture, as she hadn't seen her for a couple of weeks.

Nick's tall, lean figure followed the dog, stooping beneath the low lintel of a still-standing doorway. He had his camera and Teazle's lead looped around his neck. "I thought I heard footsteps. Hello, Megan. How are the arrest statistics?"

"Fine." Megan's cheeks were tinged with pink, possibly from stooping to pet Teazle. "How's the artistic licence? Is this lot your doing?" She waved at the multitude of ribbons.

"Good Lord, no! Though I confess to having wondered whether to paint it. I decided it's really not my cup of tea."

"What on earth is it all in aid of?"

"I gather it's some sort of neopagan business. They find an esoteric significance in the labyrinth patterns in here." He led the way inside and gestured at a smoothed rock face, which appeared to have formed one wall of the mill. On it was inscribed a primitive mazelike pattern. "The experts say it was probably carved a couple of hundred years ago, not in the time of the Druids, as the nuts like to believe."

Megan was equally sceptical. "Surely it would have worn away, anyway. It's exposed to the elements — the lichen and that green stuff are evidence that the rock is usually damp. It would cover the designs if someone hadn't cleared them. Probably eat into them, too."

Nick grinned. "The detective at work. Some interesting mosses there, and that's navelwort or pennywort growing straight out of the rock."

"You dabble in botany as well?"

"I like to know what I'm painting. I've been photographing and sketching them, and the old mill wheel in the next room. Picturesque ruins always sell well. But I'm finished here and time's passing. Let's move on."

Bringing up the rear, Eleanor glanced into the room with the mill wheel. It lay flat on the ground, half buried under luxuriant stinging nettles and ferns. She found the sight rather depressing — something about the futility of human endeavour. A man had shaped that stone by the sweat of his brow. Others had carted it down from the moors, set it up, built a mill house over the stream, run the mill to produce . . . what? She had no idea what the mill's purpose had been. It had provided a living for who knew how many people, then its day had passed and now it was nothing but a tumbledown ruin, half-roofed with scarlet-berried honey-suckle.

Sighing, Eleanor followed the others.

They crossed another wooden bridge. The path now ran sometimes along the bank of the stream, sometimes rising high above it as it delved into narrow, invisible chasms between sheer walls of bare rock. Rocky outcrops broke through the grassy hillsides, bare of trees, where little else but bracken, gorse, and blackthorn thickets braved the thin soil.

In places the horizontal strata of slate were weathered so as to look like artificial walls. Down by the water, flat platforms and shelves invited sitting.

Nick stopped to snap a few photos, so Eleanor and Megan accepted the invitation. The rock felt deliciously warm. Megan closed her eyes and turned her face up to the sun. Teazle went paddling in a limpid pool where the stream bubbled down a series of steps. To her surprise and alarm, Nick joined her — involuntarily, in an attempt to leap to a good viewpoint.

"Damn! Lucky I'm wearing sandals."

Teazle scrambled out and shook herself vigorously.

"Damn!" Megan echoed, jumping up as dark patches of damp appeared on her Indian cotton wrap-around skirt and pale green sleeveless blouse. "Clumsy idiot," she muttered under her breath, casting an unfriendly glance at Nick. "And how can one small dog absorb so much water?"

21

"You'll dry off in no time." Eleanor, out of range of the shower, was unsympathetic. "And the water is about as clean as water can be. Nick, are you watching the time? You said something about the sun."

Nick glanced up at the sky. "Yes, it'll be at just the right angle. I need to get there before it dips below the headland. Let's go."

The stony path climbed the hillside. Here and there bedrock protruded, making natural steps, awkward however because of their odd sizes and shapes. Twice Eleanor stumbled and nearly fell, but her Aikido training helped her regain her balance.

Ahead, the valley widened, and soon the inlet came into view. The air was so still that there were no whitecaps, just an edging of creamy froth along the base of the cliff. The dark green swells rolled in with soothing regularity.

"*The Isle of the Dead,*" said Nick.

"What?" exclaimed Megan, startled.

"Rachmaninoff. The opening describes the sea's present motion perfectly, restless yet monotonous. But he was writing music about a painting, so I don't see quite how I can reverse the process . . ." He was momentarily silent, occupied with an inner vision. "Damn! I was hoping for waves crashing against the sheer headland over there in

22

sheets of spray. I should have checked the tide. Or maybe it's just that we haven't had much wind recently. Oh well, it'll have to do."

They walked on until the path petered out into terraces and steps of slate. The abrupt edge was two or three feet above the smooth tops of the swells that surged onward to meet the stream in swirls of foam. Clumps of thrift, the flowerheads brown now, clung in crevices here and there. A grey-and-white herring gull launched itself into the air and joined its fellows circling overhead, their raucous screams cutting through the constant yet ever-changing sounds of moving water. High above floated a buzzard.

"Gorgeous," said Megan.

"Good enough." Nick fiddled with his camera's settings, peered through, and fiddled some more.

Megan jumped down a slate step. Eleanor sat on it, the sun warm on her back.

"What's that?" Nick lowered the camera and pointed.

Eleanor peered, wishing she had brought binoculars. Something dark bobbed in the water. "A seal?"

"No." Megan's voice rang harsh. "It's a man. And if he's not already dead, he soon will be."

TWO

How the hell was she to get the poor bugger out? Megan took a rapid inventory of her resources.

"Hang on, we're coming!" Nick bellowed through cupped hands.

A good start. "Aunt Nell, go for help." As she spoke, she untied the bow of her skirt. "Doctor, ambulance, rope, rugs, hot drinks, anything else you can think of."

Her aunt hurried away up the path, white curls bobbing, Teazle at her heels. Megan turned to find that Nick had already stripped off his shirt.

"Good job I'm in long trousers." He knotted Teazle's lead together with one sleeve of the shirt.

Megan tossed her skirt to him. "On the diagonal."

As he tied the other sleeve of his shirt to one corner of the skirt, she slipped out of her shoes and ripped off her blouse, buttons flying, glad she was wearing a black bra and knickers. Just like a bikini, she assured herself.

"No need for that," Nick protested, tightening the knots. "I'm going in."

Megan shook her head firmly. "I'm a certified lifeguard. I'll need your weight and your reach to pull us out, if I manage to get him." Without further words, she leapt down the shelves of slate and, mindful of hidden rocks underwater, did a shallow racing dive towards the floating figure.

With a shock of cold, the sea enveloped her.

Surfacing in a trough, she swam to meet the next swell. From the crest she couldn't see the body. Had it been a seal after all? She glanced back at Nick, who waved and pointed.

Thank heaven he had his wits about him. She corrected her course slightly and ploughed on.

Down and up, and down and up . . . Was she actually moving forward, or was a current stalling her in one place while the swells passed beneath her, lifting, dropping, lifting? But the current was moving her target, too. Towards the rocks? She *must* be getting closer.

There he was! A brown-skinned man,

25

limp, floating on his back. Dead men float facedown after first sinking. The dark patch she had taken for hair was his face, unshaven, eyes closed. He was alive!

"I'm coming!"

Opening black eyes, he turned his head to look at her. As though the effort exhausted his last reserve of strength, he started to sink.

Megan would have said she was swimming as fast as she was able, but she put on a spurt. She caught him under the arms and raised his head above the surface. He neither struggled nor made any attempt to help. He hadn't choked on emerging. A bad sign?

She decided hopefully that his buoyancy meant his lungs must be full of air, not water. With one arm under his and across his chest, she swam backstroke, straining to hear Nick's shouted directions as single-armed swimming made her veer from her course.

"You're getting close!"

Megan changed tactics. One hand holding up the victim's chin, she twisted sideways and started a scissors kick. At the top of each swell she glanced backwards. As she neared the sheer rock face, she slowed, unsure what to do next.

Nick knelt down. "I'm throwing a loop of rope," he called. "Try to hook it under his arms."

Teazle's lead flew towards her. The weight of the leather and the metal clip carried the makeshift rope within reach, and the leather floated. Megan grabbed it with her free hand.

Hooking it under the arms of the flaccid body, while staying afloat and keeping his face out of the water, was easier said than done. She was growing tired by the time she accomplished it, but now Nick took the strain. He drew them slowly nearer. Megan was able to put out a hand to fend them off from the rock.

Unlike the smooth concrete edge of the swimming bath she'd trained in, this edge was sharp. The sea's action flaked the slate rather than smoothing it. Getting out — and especially getting the helpless man out — without nasty grazes was not going to be easy.

Nick was lying full length now, awkwardly, on the shelving rock, his shoulders and arms over the edge. "Can you lift him at all?"

"Don't think so. Can't feel anything to stand on."

"Never mind." He reached down. "I'll hold him. Can you get yourself up?"

"I'll manage." She moved over a couple of feet and waited for a swell to lift her, then grabbed the edge above her head. There were plenty of toe-holds. Somehow, with the loss of some skin, she hauled herself over. For a brief moment she let herself flop, all muscles relaxed.

"Let's get him out. Is he breathing? I don't like the look of him."

"Hypothermic." She pulled herself together and shuffled crabwise to Nick's side.

He had draped his shorts over the edge as some protection against scrapes. What a pair, she thought, her in sodden black bra and knickers, him in white Y-fronts and string vest!

Turning his head, he caught her eye and gave her a crooked grin. "Needs must when the devil drives. Come on, we can do it. On three."

She leant down. He shifted his grip and she hooked her hands beneath the brown man's armpit. As another swell raised him towards them, Nick counted, "One. Two —"

"Hey, hang on!"

Heavy footsteps hurried across the rock. Megan glanced back to see a young couple in hiking boots and shorts, shrugging off rucksacks as they came.

"We saw from the cliff path," the girl

explained breathlessly. "Sorry it took us so long to get here. We were way up at the top."

"I'll take over," the shaggy-haired youth said to Megan, kneeling down. "Super job, but you must be done in."

She was happy to relinquish her place. Her arms were beginning to feel like jelly.

As she sat up, Nick said, "Megan, be ready to support his head. All right, mate, at the top of the swell . . . One, two, heave!"

Megan managed to field his head before it struck the rock. She laid it down gently and brushed the straggling black hair from his face.

"A wog, eh?" said the stranger. "Indian, looks like. Stupid git, swimming in there. Starkers, too."

"Don't talk like that, Chaz," his companion remonstrated. "You don't know what happened. Is he breathing?"

Her hand on his chest, Megan put her ear to his mouth, which had fallen slightly open. "Can't feel any movement, but there's a faint wheeze. We'd better get him into rescue position so any water drains. Here, where it's flat. On his stomach — Careful, for heaven's sake! That's it. Head to one side. Arms stretched out and bent. Leg bent, like this."

A little water dribbled from his mouth.

Nick leant over him. "Still breathing."

"Unless it stops, I think the most urgent thing is to warm him up."

The girl tossed over a towel. She had already untied a sleeping bag from one of the packs and unrolled it. "Dry him off and get him in here. His arms and leg will have to be straightened out, though."

"He's so c-cold . . . B-body to body contact would be b-best . . ."

"You're shivering like mad yourself," the girl said matter-of-factly. "I knew we should have brought a thermos. Put this on. I'll do it." She tossed Megan a scarlet polo-neck shirt.

"Th-thanks."

Chaz muttered something irritable, but by the time Megan's head emerged from the shirt, which was a size too small, he and Nick were zipping up the sleeping bag with the Indian inside. Luckily he was very slight, not to say skinny. The girl was also slender. Stripped of her shirt and boots but retaining her short shorts — not much more than hot pants — she wriggled in beside him.

"Ugh! It's a bit like hugging a cold hot-water bottle! Don't look so uptight, Chaz. I can just barely feel him breathing. He's not about to try anything."

" 'Barely' is the word," said Nick with a grin.

He was trying to untie his shirt from the makeshift rope but the strain put on it had tightened the knot. Megan realised his shorts had slipped off the rock into the water and disappeared. He dug in his satchel and brought out an anorak. It wasn't quite long enough to cover him decently, but then she wasn't exactly decently dressed herself. Imagining what DI Scumble would say if he saw her made her hot all over — no bad thing, considering.

"Megan? Are you all right?"

"Yes. I think so." She sat down rather suddenly on the nearest step. "Sorry, just a bit woozy for a second. Did you say something?"

He regarded her with a worried frown. "I wondered whether we ought, Chaz and I, to try to carry Julia and the Indian bloke up to the road to meet the ambulance. But I'm not sure you're in a fit state to —"

"I'm perfectly all right. The sooner he can get to a hospital, the better. There's something about not jostling hypothermics, though. Better not, perhaps, if it's risky."

"We'll take 'em with Julia underneath," said Chaz, "so that if we drop them he's well cushioned."

"Hey!"

"No," Megan said decidedly. "We can't risk it. But someone should go to explain the situation to the ambulance men when they arrive and make sure they don't go astray on the way down. Aunt Nell may be there — she went for help — but I can't be sure. Chaz, it'll have to be you."

Chaz looked at his seminaked girlfriend snuggling in the sleeping bag with a completely naked male stranger. "Not me."

Megan drew herself up and stared him in the eye. "You're the only one who's decently dressed. I may not look like it right now, but I'm a police officer, and I'm requesting your cooperation."

"Police? Right!" he said sceptically.

Nick grinned. "Detective Sergeant Pencarrow of the Constabulary of the Royal Duchy of Cornwall," he confirmed.

Chaz's challenging gaze dropped. "Oh, all right. I don't know the way, though. We were heading for the youth hostel in Boscastle."

"Follow the stream. Thank you." Megan turned away, hearing the thud of his hiking boots recede across the rock. "Miss . . . ?"

"Julia. You don't need to come the copper over me."

"Julia, you will tell me at once if he stops

32

breathing, won't you."

"Of course. I'm not doing this for fun, though I must say it'll make a good story! He doesn't feel quite so cold. That may be because I'm getting colder, though."

"Seriously colder? Chilled?"

"Don't think so. I'm warm inside, if you know what I mean. But there's a bloody great rock sticking into my hip."

"I'll get the other sleeping bag," Nick offered. "We'll work it underneath you." He went over to the rucksacks and started unstrapping Chaz's sleeping bag. "How about you, Megan? I expect Julia has something else you can wear."

"Help yourself. I didn't bring a skirt, though, and I doubt you'll be able to get into my jeans. There's a long pully. You'd be halfway decent in that. And an anorak and a woolly hat, too."

"The victim had better have the hat," Megan decided.

Nick unrolled the second sleeping bag. Megan helped him ease it under the girl and the Indian. Julia assisted as best she could considering her swaddled condition and her inert companion.

"Thanks, that's better. But I hope your aunt brings help quickly."

"I just hope she hasn't broken her ankle

33

running along that path," said Nick. "It's rough going and she's not as young as she was."

"For heaven's sake," Megan snapped, "don't go envisaging extra disasters. Haven't we got trouble enough?"

THREE

Breathless, a stitch in her side, Eleanor hammered on the front door of Trevillet Mill House. No response. Only a blackbird's song disturbed the stillness.

She looked about. An open window caught her eye, and she contemplated burglary. What deterred her was not the thought of Megan's horror if she were caught but the apparent lack of a telephone line leading to the house.

Calves and thighs aching now, she tackled the last steep hill up to the road. Teazle scampered ahead, her short legs making light work of the slope.

A car swished past. Eleanor realised she had left the lead behind.

"Teazle, heel!"

At the top, she picked up the little dog, still sodden from the dip in the stream, and tucked her under one arm. Crossing to the car, she felt in her pocket for the keys. For a heart-stopping moment, she thought Megan hadn't handed them back. She'd have to try to hitch a lift to a phone, dog and all . . . No, here they were in the other pocket. Now, which way to the nearest phone?

She couldn't recall ever noticing a phone box in Bossiney or Trevalga, nor even outside the Old Post Office in Tintagel, but she was sure there was one in front of the Wellington Hotel in Boscastle. A few minutes later, she was knocking on the glass of the kiosk, mouthing "Emergency!" at a tall, broad-shouldered man in grey trousers, a reefer jacket over a white shirt and blue-striped tie, and a yachtsman's peaked cap.

He glared at her and turned his back. He must be much too hot in that jacket, enough to put anyone in a bad mood.

Eleanor stepped round to the front and opened the door. "Please let me use the phone. It's an emergency!"

Again the wide back turned to her.

Detaching a large man from a phone in a phone box was not a manoeuvre Eleanor had learnt from her sensei. She chose the better part of valour and made for the hotel. Surely it must have a public phone.

The lobby was deserted. Eleanor couldn't see a pay-phone in its dim depths, so she hurried over to the reception desk and pinged the brass bell.

No one came. Desperate by now, Eleanor leant over the counter. Behind the raised shelf in front lurked a telephone with an alarming number of buttons below the dial. It appeared to be labelled with instructions, though. With any luck at all, she'd be able to work out how to dial 999.

She started round the counter. A door behind it opened and a skinny, balding man in a bow tie appeared.

He looked her up and down, aghast. "Here, you can't —"

"It's an emergency," Eleanor said impatiently.

"A few scrapes and bruises. Unless you've booked a room —"

"What?" She glanced down at herself. Besides a large damp patch on her blouse from carrying Teazle and a smear of mud on her beige skirt, her hands, arms, knees, and shins were badly grazed, with a few trickles of blood drying on her skin. She had tripped and fallen on the path but in the urgency of her errand she hadn't realised the extent of the damage. Awareness made every scratch begin to smart. No time to deal with it now. She reached for the phone. "I must ring for an ambulance."

"I hardly think they'll appreciate being

37

called out for —"

"There's a man drowning! How do I get 999?"

"Here." He seized the receiver from her, pushed a button, and dialled. "You want a lifeboat."

"Ambulance," Eleanor insisted. A vision of that limp, floating body rose before her. A hearse might be more appropriate, she feared.

The man thrust the receiver at her. "You'd better explain." With one foot, he hooked a tall stool and pushed it behind her.

She sank onto it as a disembodied voice spoke in her ear: "Emergency. Which service do you require?"

Which service. Eleanor's mind went blank.

"Fire? Police? Ambulance?"

"Ambulance. Lifeboat? And, oh dear, I think you'd better send the police."

"Please explain, madam. What is the emergency?"

"A man — a person — drowning. Or drowned. I'm not sure . . ."

"Shouting or waving for help?"

"No. Just floating. In the sea."

"Are you certain this person isn't just enjoying a relaxing swim, madam?" the voice asked sceptically.

"Quite certain. Not there. No one would

choose to swim there."

"I see. Location, madam?"

"Rocky Valley. It's a narrow inlet, with no beach. Just sheer cliffs. North of Tintagel, between Bossiney and Tre . . . Tre . . ." The hamlet's name escaped her.

"Trevalga," prompted the hotel man, now engrossed.

"Trevalga."

"Mightn't you have seen a seal, madam? They're quite often mistaken for —"

"No! That's what I thought at first, but Nick and Megan . . . My eyesight's good but their eyes are much younger, and they both . . ." Eleanor found she was crying helplessly. "Megan — When I left to get help, she was preparing to dive in after him. What if she's in trouble, too? You *must* believe me. Send someone, quickly!"

"This . . . er . . . Megan, she has lifesaving skills?"

"I don't know! But she's a police officer. Detective Sergeant Pencarrow, of CaRaDoC — the Constabulary of the Royal Duchy of —"

"I know what CaRaDoC is, madam. Hold the line, please."

The man at her side handed her a box of Kleenex. She sniffed and dabbed her eyes.

"Sorry. It just suddenly struck me that

Megan — my niece — is in danger."

They both looked round as the front door opened. In came the man in the reefer, scowling. The scowl didn't appear to be directed at Eleanor, though. He seemed hardly to notice her as he strode over to the desk and demanded his key.

"Twelve, please."

"Here you are, Mr. Avery. Had a pleasant day, I hope? Beautiful weather. Will you be in for dinner?"

Eleanor missed the growled response as the phone said, "Hello? Hello? Could I have your name, please, madam, and where you're ringing from."

"Eleanor Trewynn. Mrs. I'm at the Wellington Hotel in Boscastle, inside the foyer as the public telephone outside was unavailable."

The large man gave her an irritated glance and went off towards the stairs.

"Mrs. Trewynn, the Launceston ambulance will be on its way shortly. The police have been notified, as well as the Coast Guard. Is vehicular access available?"

"Ve . . . Oh, you mean can the ambulance drive to the spot?"

"Yes, madam," said the voice patiently, "to the site of the occurrence. A farm track or —"

40

"No. There's a footpath, off the coast road. The B3 something. B3623?" She looked to the hotel man for help, but he had disappeared.

"B3263. I have it on the map."

"That's it. The path must be about a mile? I'm not sure . . ."

"Will someone be present to direct the ambulance men?"

"No. Yes. I'll drive back at once and wait for them."

"Thank you, madam. But first, I'll need your home address, please."

"Port Mabyn: 21a, Harbour Street. It's over the LonStar shop."

"Oh, *that* Mrs. Trewynn?" For the first time, the voice sounded interested. "Didn't I read about you in the paper?"

"Possibly." Eleanor very much wanted to forget that dreadful photograph, to which some of the more sensational newspapers had added a caption suggesting, in terms barely skirting libel, that she was about to be arrested for murder. "I must go. I don't want to be late for the ambulance. Thank you for your help. Good-bye."

She hung up, glancing at the clock on the wall behind the counter, not taking in what it said. There wasn't the least chance that the ambulance would reach Rocky Valley

41

before her. She had less than three miles to drive. The Incorruptible, in spite of age and decrepitude, could make it in ten minutes, fifteen at worst, even with a hill steep enough to require a hairpin bend.

Coming from Launceston, the ambulance would take at least half an hour, probably more. The driver had to choose between a roundabout route or cutting through lanes scarcely wide enough for his vehicle. Even if he didn't get lost, he might meet a tractor, or a herd of cows.

The road from Bodmin was more direct. "Why didn't they send the Bodmin ambulance?" Eleanor said aloud in her frustration. A few minutes could make the difference between life and death.

"Maybe it's out on a call already." The little man in the bow tie was back, and with him a stout woman in a navy overall, bearing a tin box with a red cross on the lid. "This is our housekeeper, Mrs. Jellicoe. If you'll step through to the office, she'll . . . um . . . patch you up a bit."

"It's very kind of you, Mrs. Jellicoe, but I'm in rather a hurry."

" 'Twon't take but a moment, Mrs. Trewynn." The housekeeper's soft voice proclaimed her a local. "You don't want it to get infected. Ivers! You've made quite a mess

42

of yourself!"

"Really, I must go. The ambulance —"

"If it's coming from Launceston," the man pointed out, "it won't arrive for ages. Leave my hotel looking like that and people will think you fell in here. They'll assume we're to blame for having dangerous stairs. People are always ready to believe the worst."

Eleanor gave in and let herself be ushered through the door behind the counter, into an obsessively tidy office. For some reason, it made her remember that she was expected for an early supper with Jocelyn and the Reverend Timothy. There was no guessing when she'd get away from this brouhaha.

"Oh, bother!" She turned to the man, who having showed her into his office was returning to the lobby. "I'm so sorry, I must make another call, I'm afraid. Just a quick one to warn a friend I may be late."

"Would you like me to ring for you?"

"That's very kind of you. It would save time." And she rather dreaded trying to explain to Joce. "Mrs. Stearns, at the vicarage in Port Mabyn." She gave the number.

"Right you are."

The housekeeper led her through another door, leading to a lavatory. She caught a glimpse of herself in the mirror, tear-stained face and white curls in wild disorder, before

43

she obeyed orders to sit on the loo seat while Mrs. Jellicoe filled the basin with warm water. Teazle had followed, of course. After a puzzled yip when the door closed behind them, she watched with interest. The housekeeper cleaned up cuts, grazes, scrapes, and scratches with gentle thoroughness, then applied sticking plaster to injuries small enough to be covered and smothered the rest of the damage with Germolene, which made the dog sneeze.

When Mrs. Jellicoe started taking gauze and bandages from the first aid box, Eleanor hastily demurred. "Oh, thank you, I'll be all right without those."

"Are you sartin?"

"Yes, honestly." She stood up and poked ineffectually at her hair. "You've been so very kind, I don't know how to thank you. And Mr. . . . I didn't gather his name."

"Mr. Wharton. A furriner, though he can't help that, poor soul. Some pernick, he is, but not a bad cappun, else. I'll just sponge your skirt, then. It'll dry in no time, het as it's been today."

"No, no, I can't wait. Just let me splash some water on my face."

This time, Eleanor managed to escape. In the foyer, Mr. Wharton was talking to a couple with a large number of suitcases, so she waved to him, mouthed "Thank you!" and hurried past.

When Eleanor reached the Rocky Valley lay-by, a stocky boy in shorts and hiking boots was half sitting, half leaning on the bank beside the drive leading down to Trevillet Mill and the footpath. He looked bored and sulky. He watched as Eleanor pulled in behind Megan's car. She set the brake, turned off the engine, then crossed her arms on the steering wheel and rested her head on them, eyes closed.

Teazle whined.

"Shush, girl. Patience."

She hoped the ambulance would come soon, for Megan's sake and the stranger's. On the other hand, if it was unavoidably dilatory, she could just sit here and . . .

"Wuff! Wuff!" Teazle's gruff little voice sounded an alert and a warning. She stood up on her back legs, her front paws braced on the cart wheel rim, ready to leap out.

"Hello? Are you all right?" The young man, one hand on the roof of the car, leant down to peer at Eleanor through the open passenger window. His public-school voice managed to combine tepid concern with an undertone of irritation.

"Yes." She blinked up at him. "Yes, thank you. Just a bit tired."

"You wouldn't by any chance be Megan's Aunt Nell?"

"I am. Is she safe?"

"Cold, and a bit bashed about, but otherwise fine. And, to answer your next question, she got him out. At least, she brought him in. That bloke and I lugged him out. Some kind of wog, or Paki, or something."

"I beg your pardon?" Eleanor said frostily.

"Sorry, a dark-skinned person whose ancestors probably originated on the Indian subcontinent."

Eleanor's thoughts flew to Dr. Prthnavi. She didn't know of any other Indians in the area. But Rajendra was kept much too busy by his GP practice to go in for sea-bathing. Furthermore, as a police surgeon, he had seen too many drowning victims to venture into the North Atlantic in September. No doubt it was a tourist, unaware of the dangerous currents and biting cold. "Is he all right?"

"He's alive, but it's touch-and-go, according to Megan. Is she really a police officer, or were they having me on?"

"Detective sergeant, with the Cornish police."

"Whew, who'd have thunk it? She's much too young and good-looking to be a copper, but she's got that way about her, all right.

46

She ordered me up here to direct the ambulance men, and I hopped to it pronto. They must teach them that tone of voice. I suppose there is an ambulance coming?"

"Yes, it shouldn't be long now. The emergency operator told me to wait here for them, to show them where to go."

"They won't need both of us. I could go back. My girlfriend's down there, you see, not to mention all our stuff. On the other hand, you look pretty beat up, if you don't mind my mentioning it, Aunt . . . Mrs. . . . I don't know your name, I'm afraid."

"Trewynn. But Aunt Nell will do. You're . . . ?"

"Chaz. You could buzz along home, or wherever you're staying, and put your feet up, and leave the ambulance men to me."

"Thank you, Chaz, it's tempting, but I think I'd better stay. I had the impression that the police would want to speak to me, because I was the one who called in."

"The police! Isn't one enough?" Something about his protest drew Eleanor's attention to a faintly herbal smell hanging about the boy, one she had come across in many parts of the world.

None of her business. "They called out the lifeboat as well," she said, "though, since Megan pulled the man out, it's not needed

47

after all. I expect the police will be able to get in touch and tell them not to bother. Radar . . . or do I mean radio?"

"Radio."

"Unless — oh dear! — he didn't say whether he went out alone?"

"He wasn't capable of speech. He was hardly breathing."

"That doesn't sound good. I hope the ambulance gets here soon. But what if he didn't go swimming on his own? What if there's someone else out there caught in a current and drowning?"

FOUR

The sound of a vehicle approaching from the south made Eleanor and Chaz glance back. As it appeared, Teazle started wagging her stump of a tail.

A black-and-white panda Mini drew up beside them. Chaz took a couple of steps backwards between the cars, as if he'd prefer to fade away.

"All right, Mrs. Trewynn?" PC Leacock called, leaning across his passenger seat to look through the open window.

"Yes, fine, thank you, Bob. Or rather, not so fine. We're waiting for an ambulance."

"You're hurt? Hold on a mo." Reversing, he parked beyond Megan's car and trudged back, his helmet now in place. "What's up? Anything I can do? This laddie bothering you?" He scrutinised Chaz.

"Hey, I'm trying to help!"

"He is," Eleanor affirmed, though she knew only what Chaz had told her. "He

49

helped Nick pull him out." As Bob Leacock scratched his head in a puzzled way, she explained, "After Megan — DS Pencarrow — rescued him. While I went to telephone for an ambulance, and they're sending a lifeboat as well. Police, too. More police, I mean."

"Oh? I didn't hear anything about it. Must have been in a valley, no radio reception. Well, in that case . . ." The local constable still looked confused. "If DS Pencarrow's on the job, I don't s'pose I'm needed. Unless there's something I can do for you, Mrs. Trewynn?"

"Mrs. Jellicoe cleaned me up thoroughly, thanks." She aimed a pink-plastered elbow out of the window at him. He blinked. "I'm just feeling a little shaken."

"Constable, have you by any chance got a thermos in your car?" Chaz demanded suddenly.

"A thermos? Fancy a spot of tea, do you, laddie? And that's 'Officer,' to you."

"As a matter of fact, I wasn't asking for myself."

Bob Leacock eyed him more kindly. "That's a thought. Let me get a cuppa for you, Mrs. Trewynn."

"I meant for the drowned chappie, actually. Megan — the DS or whatever she is —

said the most important thing is to warm him up. Though I don't know if he's in a fit state to drink. Or even still in the land of the living."

An irritable squawk came from the panda car.

"My radio! Hold on." Bob hurried back to the car, got in, and rolled up the windows. Eleanor could still hear the radio faintly squawking, but his responses were inaudible.

She and Chaz waited without speaking. With a resigned sigh, Teazle curled up in her cart wheel, nose resting on a spoke.

After a few minutes, Bob came back carrying a large thermos. "Here." He handed it to Chaz. "I only drank one cup. It's still hot. You'd better get it to the victim right away."

"Okay." Chaz was only too glad to get away. His hiking boots thudded on the tarmac as he loped across the road.

Bob took off his helmet again. "I've got orders to stick around, Mrs. Trewynn. To keep the traffic moving in case we get rubber-neckers, unless the ambulance men need help — though with *him* and Mr. Gresham, I reckon they'll manage all right."

"Don't let people go down the path. It's so narrow, it'd be chaos."

"I won't. The operator said DI Scumble's on his way, and he's not someone you want to get on the wrong side of."

"As I know from experience. Why is he coming? I wouldn't have thought a high-up detective was needed at this sort of thing."

"I dunno. I can't say I'm that clear about what's going on. Would you mind explaining again?"

"I'm not altogether clear myself. You'd have done better to ask Chaz."

"That young scoggan, wi' his la-di-da accent," Bob said scornfully.

"You can't call him a good-for-nothing if he helped Nick pull the Indian out."

"Indian! Where does this Indian come into it? I'd be obliged if you'd start from the beginning, Mrs. Trewynn."

"It doesn't really matter whether he came from India or the Islington." Eleanor told him about the discovery of the floating body and Megan's telling her to go for help. Leaving out her trials and tribulations on that errand, she added what little she had learned from Chaz about subsequent events.

If Mr. Scumble turned up, no doubt he'd extract every last detail, relevant or not. But why should he come? Detective inspectors didn't usually waste their time on an accident. A drowning or near drowning on the rugged North Cornish coast was, if not an everyday affair, unfortunately not abnormal.

Perhaps someone had told him Megan was involved. Eleanor remembered mentioning her niece's name and rank to the 999 operator, who didn't seem to want to believe her report of an emergency. Had she sounded hysterical and unreliable? Really, that dreadful man in the telephone box had been the last straw!

She hoped she hadn't got Megan into trouble. Even Scumble could hardly blame his sergeant for being on the spot when a rescue was needed, let alone for accomplishing the rescue, whatever the outcome.

"D'you hear an ambulance horn?" said Bob Leacock, perking up as the hee-haw blast approached. He put his helmet on again. "That was quick. Lucky there aren't too many emmets on the roads this time of year."

Eleanor agreed about the fortunate dearth of tourists, but hours seemed to her to have passed since she left Megan and Nick. Late afternoon was merging into early evening. The air was growing chilly.

"If only they've arrived in time!" she said, putting on her jacket and getting out of the car.

Bob grunted assent. "That'd be a pretty

dido, a furriner dying on my patch! Ambassadors and such nosing in, I daresay."

"High commissioner, if he's Indian. Stay, Teazle."

The dog, gathering herself for a leap from among the spokes, subsided with a whine of disgust.

As the ambulance, blue light flashing, came round the bend, Bob stepped forward to flag it down. He went round to speak to the driver, gesturing at the drive down to Trevillet Mill. "You can take it down there, mate. Hundred yards or so. Make it a bit easier. Mrs. Trewynn here'll show you the way from there."

Eleanor had just about decided to leave Teazle in the car, out of the way, but Teazle had other ideas. She sprang from the back to the front seat and was about to launch herself through the open window when Eleanor grabbed her.

"All right, you'd better come along. I haven't time to make sure you can't get out. We don't want to hold them up." The dog under one arm, she waved to Bob and trotted after the ambulance, which was taking the steep slope at a cautious pace.

It stopped at the mill house, engine still running.

The burly man beside the driver jumped

54

out. "No room to turn," he called to the driver.

Hands on hips, he surveyed the narrow wooden bridge crossing the Trevillet. At the near end, steps led up to it from the right. At the far end, another flight led down on the left. Two sharp corners to negotiate.

Eleanor arrived and set Teazle down. "Is the bridge going to be a problem?" she asked, following him back to the rear of the ambulance, where the driver was opening the door from inside.

"Nah, we negotiate much worse with some of the cottage staircases." He took a folding stretcher passed out by the man inside and leant it against the side of the vehicle. "You're Mrs. Trewynn? I'm Dave, and this here's Jim. What's the rest of the way like?"

"Oh dear, not very good, I'm afraid." She felt as guilty as if it were her fault. "It's very irregular and narrow, and overgrown in some spots. And then there's the ruins of Trethevy Mill. That might be awkward. And beyond, some quite steep slopes, with loose pebbles."

"We'll manage. The copper said there's a couple of young blokes down there to give us a hand with the stretcher coming back? That right?"

"Yes. Nick and Chaz."

"What about you? Looks as if you came a cropper. You all right?"

"Yes, thanks. I was in too much of a rush. Do be careful, won't you. But hurry!"

"More haste, less speed," observed Jim, who had handed out a first aid kit and a bright red blanket. "That's the lot. Let's get going." He jumped down.

They gathered up their impedimenta and started towards the muddy footpath leading to the bridge. "As we go, would you mind telling me all you know about our patient? But watch your footing, too. We don't want to have to carry two out."

Following behind, scurrying to keep up with their long strides, she explained again that she had no direct knowledge of the patient's condition, only what she had been told. She repeated what Chaz had said, which now seemed very muddled and incomplete.

Dave grunted. Stumbling over a root, he nearly dropped the stretcher in the stream but managed to save himself with a grab at a nearby branch. "Hell!" he swore. "Begging your pardon. It's going to be a bloody nightmare of a job getting him out."

"I'm sorry."

"I'm not blaming you, Mrs. Trewynn.

We've got to try. If we can save him, it'll be worth the trouble."

If they could save him . . . But he might be already dead, Eleanor thought sadly.

"Watch it," said Jim, in the lead. "There's an awkward spot here."

"Ha-ha. Show me a spot that isn't awkward. No room for four stretcher bearers here."

They tramped on to Trethevy Mill. The sun no longer sifted through leaves to brighten the multihued ribbons. They looked faded, pathetic now, not gay. Without comment, the men followed Eleanor's directions for the shortest way through the ruins.

After crossing the second bridge, Dave and Jim speeded up on the open, stony path.

"Do take care," Eleanor begged. "Just along here is where I fell."

"You take your time, Mrs. Trewynn," said Dave. "Straight on from here, is it?"

"A couple of paths go off up to the cliffs, one on each side. Keep straight on to the end. Though straight isn't quite the word . . ."

Eleanor toiled on in their wake, her legs feeling heavier with every step. When she came to the rough places, she had to force herself to pay attention, her mind on Megan and the Indian. She wasn't really needed any longer. She could have stopped to wait, or even gone back to the road, but she was too impatient to find out how they were doing. Besides, disgruntled as he was, Chaz might have taken his girlfriend and departed, in which case Eleanor might be needed after all, if only to carry Nick's camera equipment.

Though it was still broad daylight, the sun had sunk behind the western headland, casting its looming silhouette nearly to the crest of the opposite hillside. The rocky walls had metamorphosed from picturesque to threatening and the air was growing chilly.

" 'Yea, though I walk through the valley of the shadow of death,' " Eleanor murmured to herself. She didn't complete the quotation. She had seen too much evil in the world to put her faith in otherworldly protection.

No more than she trusted in god or gods did she believe that an Indian tourist had chosen to go for a swim in the cold Atlantic for plea sure. Something, or someone, had forced him to take the plunge that might yet prove fatal.

FIVE

Some distance to the rear, Eleanor paused by the stream to catch her breath. At this point, the path started upwards, away from the stream. She watched the ambulance men tramp up and safely pass the uneven natural step that had caused her tumble. They continued up the path, over the crest, and disappeared down the other side.

She plodded after them, using one hand to steady herself over the step.

On the way down, the scene of the drama — the shelving slate by the inlet — was hidden by a massive outcrop of rock with a crack wide and high enough to step into. It suggested to Eleanor a portal into a fairy world under the hillside, as described in ancient ballads and tales. If only she could pop in and come out with three wishes, or a magic healing potion . . . anything that might help.

The stretcher bearers would need all the

help they could get on these few yards of the narrow path. It hugged the outcrop, curling round, separated by a couple of feet of steep grassy slope from a sheer fall onto the rocks by the stream.

How on earth would they manage it? She decided not to watch when they came to that spot. It was all very well having seen the most dreadful sights in the poorest parts of the world; when she came home to Cornwall, she'd hoped for a peaceful retirement without the intrusion of any unnatural or unnecessary deaths.

So far, her record was not promising.

She trudged round the bend. Before her spread a scene of intense activity. Dave had already opened out the folding stretcher and, with Nick's assistance, was checking that it was securely put together. Nick was wearing his anorak over a Moody Blues T-shirt and a pair of jeans too wide in the hips and too short in the legs. Both must belong to Chaz, Eleanor assumed.

Beyond them, Chaz was helping an unknown girl extricate herself from a sleeping bag. "Be careful, you clumsy clot!" she snapped at him. "I didn't go through all this to have him die because you made me jostle him."

"Why don't we just unzip it?"

60

"It'd let the cold air in. Brrr, it's cold now the sun's set." She sat up, clad in nothing but a skimpy bra.

Next to her, motionless, a head protruded from the sleeping bag, half hidden by a scarlet woolly hat pulled well down over the dark forehead. The face was slack, mouth half open. From where Eleanor stood, she couldn't tell whether the man Megan had pulled from the sea was alive or dead.

Megan and Jim, the ambulance driver, knelt beside him. Megan seemed to be doing her best to hold him still as the girl pulled her legs out of the bag and stood up, revealing shorts almost as skimpy as her bra. Chaz wrapped a shirt about her.

Jim, a look of intent concentration on his face, had one hand inside the bag. "Got it! Pulse slow and feeble, breathing very shallow. Mouth-to-mouth, d'you think, Dave?"

"Yes, give him some air, but no chest compressions."

Jim bent down lower. Megan said anxiously, "I wasn't sure about the mouth-to-mouth, as he was breathing on his own. I knew it was important not to move him more than necessary, but we had to haul him out of the water . . ."

"Don't second-guess yourself," said Dave, with a glance at the rockbound inlet. "Give

yourself a break. You did a smashing job —
oops, bad choice of words! — a terrific job.
He survived, didn't he?"

"So far."

"Well, you did the most important thing,
trying to warm him up. Right, Jim, let's get
him out of here."

"Can't tell if there's any colour come into
his face," Jim grumbled, straightening. He
reached into the open first aid kit at his side
and took out something small. Eleanor
couldn't make out what it was. "You insert
the Guedel Airway, will you? You're the
expert."

"You need practice. I'll watch over your
shoulder."

Megan stood up and Dave took her place.
She caught sight of Eleanor and came over,
a spring in her step as she crossed the shelving slate. She appeared to have recovered
from her exertions in rescuing the Indian.
The same could not be said for her clothes.
Below a navy blue fisherman's jersey that
only just reached the top of her thighs, her
legs were bare, knees skinned, shins cut and
bruised; above the pullover, a scarlet polo-
neck poked out.

"Aunt Nell, you've been in the wars! What
happened?"

"I tripped on the path, dear. Very clumsy

of me, but I was in such a hurry, and worrying for you and the drowning man instead of paying attention. I'm all patched up and good as new. What happened to your clothes?"

"I tore most of the buttons off my blouse when I took it off, and Nick tied my skirt into such a tight knot with his shirt that we can't undo it, now it's wet. These are Julia's, of course, and Nick's wearing Chaz's shirt." She laughed. "Not exactly his kind of music!"

The Moody Blues must be a band, Eleanor deduced. Nick preferred classical music to pop. "It was kind of them to lend their stuff," she said. "Chaz seems . . . rather disaffected towards the police, I'm afraid. To tell the truth, I wasn't sure whether he would stay to help. That's why I came on, after showing the ambulance men the way."

"Julia definitely has the upper hand. But you should have gone home, Aunt Nell, and put your feet up."

"I couldn't possibly relax, not knowing what's going on." Eleanor wondered whether to warn Megan that her boss knew what was going on, or at least that something was going on. *Forewarned is forearmed,* or *Don't cross the bridge till you come to it?* The latter, she decided. With any luck,

63

Mr. Scumble would think better of coming all the way from Launceston. "I'll carry Nick's camera stuff," she said. "He and Chaz will have to help with the stretcher, and you and Julia can take the rucksacks."

While they talked, they watched the men pick up the lower sleeping bag by the four corners, stretching it tight, and lift the victim, still in the other sleeping bag, onto the stretcher. Jim and Dave fussed over him for a moment.

Megan watched, frowning. "I should have given him mouth-to-mouth. I had to make so many decisions without adequate knowledge."

"You did the best you could, dear, and you saved his life."

"So far, at least. I think I'd better take a first aid refresher course."

"What a good idea. I'll join you. I'm sure everything I learned is completely out-of-date."

"You've done first aid?" Megan asked in surprise. "I didn't think you were on the hands-on side of things, so to speak."

"That's how Peter and I started out. It wasn't till several years after the war that he became LonStar's troubleshooter and I . . . well, I was doing for conflict resolution what he did for practical problems. Even then, I was often hundreds of miles from a Western doctor, so knowing a bit of first aid was common sense. I've never heard of that airway thing they're using, though."

"The Guedel Airway? It's not something most people would carry around with them! Nor know how to use properly. It keeps the tongue from getting in the way of breathing, but it can do some nasty damage if it's not inserted right. I wish they had oxygen to administer. They do in the London ambulances."

"It looks as if they're ready to move."

Jim and Nick spread the red blanket over the stretcher and its burden and strapped it down. They took the front end. Jim would be on the outside of the curve when they passed the boulder, with Dave in the equivalent position at the back. Megan shook her head, stepping forward.

"No," she said in her police-officer voice. "I hope no one's going to fall, but if they do we don't want the first aid experts to be the ones to go over the edge. Parts of the path are pretty dodgy. You'd better swap places."

Dave looked annoyed but said grudgingly, "You're right. Switch round."

"Thanks a lot!" Chaz muttered sarcastically, just loud enough to be heard.

On a count of three, the four men lifted the poles.

"Now watch your step, for heaven's sake," said Dave. "If we go too fast for you, speak up. It's no good us coming all this way just to end up dumping the poor bugger in the stream. Right, let's go."

Eleanor didn't want to watch them round the outcrop, though she would have if watching and cheering them on — silently — could aid them in their peril.

Megan had already hoisted one of the rucksacks and slung it on her back. She picked up the first aid kit. "Sure you can manage Nick's stuff, Aunt Nell?"

"Yes. You go ahead."

With a wave, Megan followed the stretcher.

Eleanor crossed the slate to where Nick's satchel, camera, and tripod lay, well out of the way of the spray of any errant wave. The other rucksack was nearby, and bending over it, the girl, who had put on a sleeveless shirt.

"Hello. I'm Megan's aunt, Mrs. Trewynn. And you're Julia."

"That's right. I say, would you mind awfully if I took off these shorts and put on my jeans? Megan could have borrowed them if she could've got into them, but as

66

she couldn't . . . It's not as warm as it was."

"Of course not, dear. It's kind of you to lend your pullover to Megan. Have you brought another woollie?"

" 'Fraid not. But she's welcome to it. She was soooo cold when she came out of the sea. Isn't she fabulous? I've never known a police detective before. There, that's better." Fastening her jeans, she looked at Eleanor, who had Nick's satchel over one shoulder, the camera by its strap over the other, and the tripod clasped to her bosom. "Just let me get my rucksack settled and I'll take the camera and tripod, if you can manage the satchel."

About to respond with some indignation that she could perfectly well carry everything, Eleanor reminded herself of the wisdom of allowing people to follow their charitable impulses. Besides, she was tired, and she had already tripped once, and the camera was both heavy and valuable. Nick would not be happy if she were to damage it in another fall.

"Thank you, that would be a help."

By the time they had sorted themselves out, the stretcher party and Megan were out of sight, having rounded the curve without untoward incident. Eleanor and Julia set off after them, Teazle scurrying ahead.

67

"I hope Chaz wasn't too obnoxious," Julia said, falling behind as they reached the narrow path.

"My dear, even if he was, which he wasn't, I wouldn't dream of criticising your boyfriend when you're just behind me with a nasty drop to our left."

Julia laughed. "Oh, that's all right. He's not my boyfriend, though he sometimes behaves as if he thinks he is. We're both doing geology at Exeter, and as we live quite near each other, we sometimes do things together in the summer vac. The rocks on this stretch of coast are pretty interesting — but don't worry, I won't bore you with them!"

"Cliffs and coves and caves," Eleanor said vaguely. "And narrow inlets like this one. And there are mines of some sort, aren't there? I've seen warning signs about old mine shafts. I'm sure it must all be fascinating."

"To us. I'm glad Chaz wasn't too awful. He's racially prejudiced, you see, and he made the most awful remarks when the poor man turned out to be Indian. I had to shut him up."

"Yes, I heard a bit of that. To do him justice, though, he asked if I needed help when I —" She didn't want to go into her pathetic collapse over the steering wheel. "Well, never mind. You both live in this part of the world?"

"He's from Flushing. Across the river from Falmouth?"

"I know it. Where the Victorian ships' captains built their mansions."

"One of which is Chaz's family's. They're in shipping, I think, though his father's an architect. There's some sort of family connection with Boscastle, too."

"And you? Teazle, come! You've just dried off. Don't go swimming again."

Teazle, poised on the edge of the stream, hesitated a moment before obeying, scrambling up the steep slope to the path. They were well beyond the obtrusive boulder now, and safely past the spot where Eleanor had tripped earlier. The last glimpse Eleanor had caught of the stretcher party, they were on the bridge leading to the ruined mill.

"Good girl."

"She's a sweetie. Our dog, Merlin, is the result of an unintended encounter between a pedigree black Lab and a farm sheepdog, with all the best points of both. We live in Mabe Burnt house, not far from Falmouth. Chaz's dad gave us a lift to Tintagel, where we started this morning, and he's supposed to meet us in Boscastle tomorrow. He had to come over here on business. Hell, we're not going to be able to finish the hike before dark! Is it far by road to Boscastle?"

"Two or three miles. But don't worry about it, I'll take you in the . . . Oh, I forgot, I've got those dratted wooden cart wheels on the backseat!"

"Wooden cart wheels? I thought those went out with Queen Victoria!"

Eleanor explained her acquisition and the difficulty of extracting it from the Morris Minor. "But Nick and Chaz could get them out. Or, better, I can drive you down one by one and pick up Nick on the way home."

"That's very kind of you, but we can easily walk it."

"It's a narrow, winding road. I'd hate to think of you walking it in the dark. And I don't know what we're going to do about the clothes you lent Megan and Nick."

"They can't go home dressed — undressed — the way they were when Chaz and I first saw them! There's no hurry about returning the clothes."

"We'll sort it out tomorrow. Except — Heavens! — Megan can't drive a police car back to Launceston in nothing but a pullover and knickers. She'll have to come home with me."

"You wouldn't think rescuing a drowning man would lead to so many complications!"

They caught up with the others as the men were manoeuvring the stretcher across the upper bridge. To gct round the corners they had to lift it above the railings while two were climbing the steps and the other two walking backwards on the bridge. Then they reversed the process descending the other steps. It all looked very precarious to Eleanor, but they managed it without dropping the stretcher.

Megan stopped in the middle of the bridge, staring past the stretcher party, and said, "Oh, hell!"

Six

Detective Inspector Scumble stood at the top of the footpath, looking irritated, admittedly nothing out of the ordinary for him. Megan's boss was a large, solid man whose limited supply of patience was sorely tried by the vagaries of Eleanor's memory. He failed to understand why — though she always remembered people — she could be relied on to forget where she had put a vital clue, what time she had done what ever it was she had done, and whether she had locked her doors.

She regarded him now with quite as much apprehension as she saw on Megan's face. She couldn't see how he could blame either of them for what had happened, nor, indeed, what business it was of his. But she was quite sure he would find a reason.

Eyes narrowed, he glanced at the man on the stretcher as he stood aside to let it pass, exchanging a couple of words with Dave.

Then he stepped back to block the path.

"So you got him out alive, Sergeant."

"Yes, sir. Just."

"Good job. No sign of identification?"

"No, sir. He was naked."

"We need to find out who he is. You'll go with him in the ambulance and stay beside him till he speaks or till he croaks."

"Sir!" Megan protested. "I'm not properly dressed. I have to go home and change."

He surveyed her from head to toe. "You're decenter than half the totty-birds I see in the streets. If it bothers you, I expect they'll lend you a hospital gown."

"But if I'm on duty, I ought —"

"Are you complaining about night duty? You've had the afternoon off," Scumble said, most unfairly in Eleanor's opinion. He took a notebook from his pocket and handed it to her. "Here, I don't suppose you brought your own. You'd better get moving. Don't want them to go without you."

"I'll bring you clothes at the hospital, Megan," Eleanor called after her. "Teazle, come! We're not going with her."

Megan waved and hurried to climb into the ambulance, where Jim was already revving the engine. Slowly and noisily, it backed up the steep drive.

The inspector turned his gaze on Eleanor. "Well, well, well, I heard you'd taken a spill, Mrs. Trewynn. No serious damage, I trust?"

"No worse than Megan."

Nick broke in. "Yes, Megan was hurt, climbing onto the rocks. Not badly, but she ought to have her skinned knees seen to."

"She's going to the right place, then, isn't she," Scumble pointed out, with that exasperating patience that made one feel like an idiot. "Plus she gets an exciting ride in a helicopter."

"A helicopter?"

"That bloke doesn't like the look of his patient. He's going to radio for a Coast Guard helicopter to meet them somewhere there's room to land. I suppose you think I should give your niece a break before she goes back on duty, but she's the best person I've got available to make sense of anything the victim might say."

"Victim?" said Nick.

"Of an accident," the inspector said blandly. Producing a notebook and biro, he turned to Julia. "And who may this young lady be?"

"I'm Julia Merridew."

"Just where do you come into the picture, Miss Merridew?"

"I saw Megan — Detective Sergeant

74

Pencarrow — rescue the man. She was wonderful! And then I . . . um . . ."

"Lent the victim a bit of body warmth," Nick suggested.

"Exactly," said Julia with a grateful smile.

Unimpressed, Scumble asked, "Did you see the victim enter the water?"

"Gosh no. We were hiking, Chaz and I, up on the cliffs. We saw Megan dive in and we ran down to see if we could help. Chaz gave Nick a hand to pull the victim out."

"Chaz?" The inspector eyed the youth, who was hanging back from the group. Eleanor guessed he didn't want to come within smelling distance.

"Charles."

"Surname, sir?"

"Avery, if you really have to know."

"Thank you, sir. It's just a matter of routine, for my report."

Chaz didn't appear to be reassured. He muttered something inaudible.

"I can't think why a detective inspector should have to write a report about an accident," Eleanor said crossly, "but if you have any more questions, would you please postpone them. Miss Merridew is cold, as Megan is wearing all her warm clothes —"

"And not much else," Nick put in, grinning, as he stripped off his anorak and

75

presented it to Julia with a bow.

"— And I'm rather tired. You can come to Port Mabyn and ask me anything you please tomorrow. Not that I know anything. Right now I have to drive Julia and Chaz to Boscastle, one at a time because my car is full of stuff, then come back to pick up Nick —"

"You needn't worry about fitting people into your car, Mrs. Trewynn," Scumble interrupted. "Mrs. Stearns is waiting for you up there on the road. I'm sure she'll consider it her duty to ferry your Good Samaritans to Boscastle, being as how she's a vicar's wife."

Realising her mouth had fallen open, Eleanor closed it far enough to exclaim, "Jocelyn! What on earth is she doing here?"

"She said the vicar passed on a garbled message, from someone whose name he'd forgotten, saying that you were in difficulties in Rocky Valley."

That sounded like Timothy all right. Eleanor sighed. She had forgotten asking Mr. Wharton to warn Joce not to expect her for supper.

"I'll go up," Nick offered, "and tell her what's going on. Inspector, now that the ambulance has gone, I assume I'm allowed to drive down to save Mrs. Trewynn the slog

76

up the hill?"

"Be my guest."

"Oh, Nick, do you think the Incorruptible will make it back up this slope?"

"Good point. I'll ask Mrs. Stearns to come and get you."

"Thank you, Nick. Here are the keys . . ." She felt in her pocket. "Oh dear, I must have left them in the car. But that's all right: Bob Leacock is there. Why don't you just drive yourself home, Nick, and Jocelyn will bring Teazle and me."

As Nick trudged off, Scumble turned back to Julia and Chaz. "You two, you're planning to spend the night in Boscastle? Where can I find you if I need to?"

Chaz scowled.

"At the youth hostel," Julia said, "if you're early enough."

"And if I'm not?"

"We'll be hiking all day and going home in the evening. You'd better have our phone numbers." She gave her own.

"I can't see what you need it for," Chaz said truculently.

Scumble looked at him, nostrils flaring, nose wrinkling in a meaningful sniff. "Is there any particular reason you choose not to cooperate with the police, sir?"

"Of course not," he blustered. "I just think —"

"Your trouble is, you don't think." Julia reeled off another phone number.

Scumble nodded, wrote it down, and closed his notebook. "I know where to find you, Mrs. Trewynn." Though his tone was genial, Eleanor felt as much trepidation as if he'd threatened her. "Chances are I shan't have to bother any of you. Thank you for your help." With another nod, he set off up the drive after Nick.

Anxiously, Julia asked Eleanor, "Do you think your friend will mind giving us a lift?"

"Not at all."

And with luck, Joce wouldn't start scolding Eleanor for getting mixed up in police business again until she had dropped off the young people.

A few minutes later, Jocelyn's car nosed cautiously down the drive. As Eleanor hoped, she held her questions until they were leaving the youth hostel, an ancient building with a bowed roofline that used to be one of a row of fishermen's cottages.

As they drove back across the old stone bridge, Jocelyn demanded, "Well?"

"We were just going for a walk." Eleanor was annoyed to hear the defensive note in her voice. She told her part of the story, glad to have missed seeing the harrowing rescue, so she didn't have to describe it.

"Hmm. I suppose as he's apparently an Indian, he wouldn't care for a pastoral visit. But Timothy and I will pray for him, of course. As soon as we get home, I'm going to take a look at those grazes of yours, to make sure your Mrs. Jellicoe cleaned them thoroughly. Very kind of her. I shall remember her in my prayers, too."

"Please do." It couldn't hurt, Eleanor thought, though a thank-you letter and perhaps a box of Black Magic would probably be better appreciated. "But, Joce, I can't stay to be doctored. I must take Megan some decent clothes. She'll be feeling pretty silly wrapped in a hospital gown."

"I can't believe That Man sent her off improperly dressed!"

"I can. It doesn't surprise me in the least. I wonder what I have in the way of skirts that would fit her."

"Nothing, I imagine. She's at least three inches taller —"

"Length doesn't seem to matter these days."

"— And commensurately larger in the waist and hips. I'm sure I can find something suitable in the shop. Not mini, as she's on duty. There's a nice tweed, come to think of it, that would fit perfectly, though it's rather a bright plaid."

If Jocelyn Stearns said the skirt would fit perfectly, then it would. She had an inerrant eye for clothes, far more inerrant than her husband's somewhat vague theology. She was always discreetly but smartly turned out, though she bought almost all her clothes from the LonStar shop.

"I'll buy it for her. I hope Nick will go with me to Launceston. I don't like driving at night."

"I'd take you myself except that there's a parish meeting tonight that will collapse in chaos if I'm not there to hold the reins. But I'm sure Nicholas will drive you. I'll say this for him, he's generally obliging, in spite of his casual dress and manners. You'd better take my car. It's more reliable than yours."

"The Incorruptible hasn't broken down in ages!"

"Therefore it's the more likely to break down now. I don't like to think of you stuck on the moor at night."

"Well, thank you, we'll certainly get there quicker in yours, especially with the weight of the cart wheels in the back of mine. Iron rims instead of tyres! I can't think how the poor horses pulled them."

"You found some cart wheels? Wonderful!

We always get a good price for those once they've been cleaned up. We'll take the Incorruptible up to the vicarage tomorrow and Timothy can help unload them."

Eleanor tried to envision the tall, thin, wispy vicar struggling to extricate the wheels from the backseat. "I think you'd better ask Mr. Irvin from the newsagent's to help you."

"Good idea. Now, Eleanor, promise me you'll have a nurse look at your injuries when you get to the hospital."

"It's not necessary, honestly. Mrs. Jellicoe slathered Germolene on everything. Can't you smell it?"

Jocelyn sniffed. "Now you mention it . . . I didn't notice before because that boy smelled of an illegal substance." Her second sniff expressed her disapproval.

"It's not likely to do him much harm, unless he's arrested. The Indians and Chinese use it in all sorts of medical preparations. Speaking of medical, I do hope Mr. Scumble will talk to Rajendra — Dr. Prthnavi — about the man Megan saved. He, if anyone, is likely to know something about him."

"There aren't many Indians hereabouts," Joce agreed. "The restaurant in Camelford, of course. I don't know of any others, though of course they're not likely to turn up in church. Oh, Timothy mentioned a new canon at Truro Cathedral who's Indian. What I can't see is why a detective inspector has any interest at all in the unfortunate man, except that it was Megan who got him out of the water."

"Only because his identity is a mystery, I suppose. Naturally that would appeal to a detective. But, you know, it's all very well Megan sitting by his bedside waiting for him to speak, only what if he doesn't speak English? It would be much more useful for Rajendra to be there. Except, of course, that India has so many languages . . . Oh well, in case Scumble doesn't ask for Rajendra's help, I'll talk to him myself."

"Eleanor! You had much better stay out of it. You know what That Man thinks of your meddling in his crimes."

"But he's been at pains to tell us there is no crime."

"True. Very well, if you insist on going to see Dr. Prthnavi tomorrow, I shall come with you."

Eleanor would have much preferred to go alone. However, she knew better than to try to dissuade Jocelyn from doing what she chose to perceive as her Christian duty.

"All right," she said, holding back a sigh.

"I'll ring him up and see when a visit would be convenient."

SEVEN

Eleanor rang up Rajendra Prthnavi from home while Jocelyn retrieved the chosen skirt from the shop. He was out on a call, but his wife, Lois, a cheerful Birmingham girl who had never lost her Midland accent, assured Eleanor he'd be happy to talk to her that evening.

"And you'll stay to supper, of course."

"That's sweet of you, but a friend will be with me —"

"Any friend of yours is welcome, too."

That evening, Jocelyn's duty to her parishioners trumped her duty to accompany Eleanor to see the doctor, but she was rather annoyed. "You should have asked to see him tomorrow," she said severely.

"Nick and I are going over to Launceston anyway . . . And for all we know, it may be urgent."

"Oh, very well. But you must tell me all about it in the morning."

In comparison to the Incorruptible, Jocelyn's car was so comfortable that Eleanor dozed as Nick drove over the moors to Launceston. The journey took about half as long as in the aged Morris Minor, though, and she was still very weary when they reached the hospital.

"No need for you to go in. I'll take it," Nick offered, reaching for the bag on the backseat that contained the tweed skirt Joce had picked out for Megan.

"Thank you, dear. Ask how he's doing, will you?"

"Of course."

Eleanor waited anxiously for news. At last Nick returned, shaking his head when he saw her watching.

"Not visiting hours. The porter wouldn't let me go in to find someone to ask, as I'm not a relative. I told him the poor chap has no known relatives and that I helped rescue him, but nothing doing. I left the skirt with him. I hope it gets to Megan."

"I suppose he's just doing his job, but how maddening."

"If nothing else, the doctor should be able to find out his condition."

"True. I do hope he's come round by now."

They drove north through the town and

across the ancient bridge over the River Kinsey. From there, Nick followed Eleanor's directions — though she frequently lost her keys, she rarely lost her way. Near Good- mansleigh, they pulled up in front of a west- facing thatched cottage converted from two farm labourers' tiny dwellings. In front, enclosed by a white picket fence, was a small garden crammed with dahlias of every conceivable colour and shape. They glowed in the afterglow of the sunset.

"Damn, I wish I'd brought my camera! Too twee for words, but the tourists would eat it up."

"I expect Lois has photos, or would let you borrow their camera."

Nick instantly metamorphosed from a solicitous friend into an artist with a mis- sion. "Come on then, quick, before the light changes." He herded Eleanor up the short path and reached past her to knock on the door.

Lois Prthnavi opened the door wearing an apron and wielding a wooden spoon. A nurse when she married Rajendra, she had given up work when they had children. Now that the boys were away at school, she took on part-time supply jobs during term time, but she loved cooking, so the doctor had no cause for complaint. Mouthwatering smells

86

of Indian spices and frying onions wafted past her. "Eleanor, lovely to see you. You didn't bring the little dog?"

"No, I left her at home this evening."

"Come in, bab, come in, I've got stuff on the range that needs stirring. And you're Mr. Gresham —"

"Nick, please. How do you do, Mrs. Prthnavi. Your garden is magnificent."

"Nick's absolutely dying to take some photos in this evening light, but he didn't bring his camera."

"You must use ours. Here, Raj always keeps it on the hall table. He says it's no use if you can't lay your hands on it when you want it. It's not fancy, but there should be plenty of film."

"Thanks!" Nick strode back down the path.

"He'll apologise once he's caught the light." Eleanor closed the door behind her against the chilly air and followed Lois into the small slate-floored kitchen, dominated and warmed by a modern oil-fired Aga.

"Not to worry. We've got one of his pictures of the coast, and Raj would buy one of his musical abstracts like a shot if we had anywhere big enough to hang it. Eleanor, you're not ill, are you? No, of course not. You'd go to the surgery."

"Do I look as if I'm on my last legs? I'm just tired and a bit banged up. I tripped on a rough footpath, nothing serious."

"Raj should be home any moment. He rang when he left the patient's house."

"No, really, that's not what I want to talk to him about. Though it's sort of connected. I wouldn't have troubled him till morning except that we had to come over to Launceston to take a skirt to the hospital for Megan."

"Megan — your niece? She's in hospital? I'm sure Raj will go and examine her if you're not happy with her care, only there's etiquette to be observed with second opinions. He'll explain —"

"Megan's there as a police officer, not a patient. Sorry, I'm muddling you."

"Never mind. You can explain it all to Raj after dinner."

"Perhaps I'd better leave the explanation to Nick!"

"He's mixed up in what ever it is, too? No, don't answer, it can wait. Let Raj relax over supper before you tell us." Lois took an earthenware casserole from the slow oven, emptied into it the fragrant contents of one of her pans, and returned it to the oven. "Or is it private?"

"Not exactly. I expect Megan's inspector

would just as soon the story didn't get about, but too many people know what happened to keep it secret."

"You're really whetting my appetite!"

"Not as much, I'm sure, as the smell of what you're cooking is whetting mine!"

"And mine! I hope you don't mind, Mrs. Prthnavi, I let myself in. I've finished your film, I'm afraid. Would you rather I had it processed and sent you the prints and negatives of your pictures, or the other way round? I'd pay for mine, of course."

"You do it, would you? Otherwise you might wait weeks before I remember to take it in." She tested a grain of rice. "This is ready. I need to drain it and I don't want to scald anyone. Do go through to the other room and help yourselves to sherry. You might pour one for me, too. Or there's beer if you prefer, Nick."

The whole of the rest of the ground floor was one room. Where the wall between the cottages had once stood, a beamed arch divided sitting and dining areas, the latter denoted by a gate-legged table in the window overlooking the dahlias.

Once when visiting the Prthnavis, Eleanor had gone upstairs to the loo and, through an open bedroom door, had caught sight of a picture of Krishna and his lover, the milkmaid Radha. In the downstairs room, however, the furnishings were thoroughly English, chintzes in lavender blue and lavender green, and polished oak. Above the fireplace hung a painting of Kynance Cove.

While Nick poured sherry for the ladies and a beer for himself, Eleanor told him what Lois had said about his paintings.

He grinned. "I expect I could do something that would fit in here." He took Lois her drink. On his return he went over to the record player and started looking through the records. "Mozart Clarinet Quintet, Benny Goodman. Britten's *Four Sea Interludes.* It might help to listen to different sea music . . ." His gaze became abstracted. Humming a tune unfamiliar to Eleanor, he took an LP out of its sleeve and put it on the turntable.

The sound of the front door opening and closing distracted him before Eleanor had time to suggest he should ask their hostess's permission before playing the record. The doctor was home.

Eleanor was instantly certain that she'd be wasting his time. If he knew of someone missing, he'd have rung the police. If he was needed to communicate with the rescued man, DI Scumble could hardly fail to think of him.

They heard him talking to Lois in the kitchen. Then he came to greet them.

"Namaste, Eleanor. Namaste, Mr. Gresham."

"Namaste, Rajendra."

Self-consciously, Nick said, "Namaste, Doctor."

"I am happy to welcome you to my house. You will excuse me if I go and change before dinner."

"Would you mind if I put on a record?"

"Please, help yourself." With a little bow, he went out.

"He's not going to put on a dinner jacket, is he?" Nick asked in a voice full of misgivings.

"Good lord no. Even if he usually did, he wouldn't because you and I aren't in evening dress. He wouldn't want to make us uncomfortable. I'm sure he's just changing into something more comfortable than the suit he wears for work."

"He does dress rather formally. Not the tweedy country doctor sort."

"With patients already wary because of the colour of his skin, he can't afford to give them anything else to cavil at."

"Surely there isn't much of that sort of attitude here in Cornwall. Enoch Powell does his rabble-rousing in the big cities."

91

"That's where his audience is," Eleanor pointed out, "where most Indian immigrants settle. People here don't in general feel threatened by the influx."

"And then there are always mindless idiots like Chaz. He really embarrassed Julia. She's a nice girl."

How times changed, Eleanor reflected, and not always for the worse. In her young days, a "nice" girl might well have let the victim die rather than strip and climb into a sleeping bag with him, naked as he was. That part of the story was better kept from Jocelyn. It would pose her a moral dilemma bound to upset her no end.

"She said Chaz isn't her boyfriend," Nick said ruminatively. "I wonder whether she has a steady."

Eleanor didn't like this trend in his thoughts. She still nourished hopes of a closer rapport between Nick and Megan. But she had nothing against Julia, not to mention that it was none of her business.

"She's a bit young to settle down, isn't she? She has her degree to think about."

Nick laughed. "These days, having a steady boyfriend is a temporary state of affairs, not necessarily a precursor to settling down. *O tempora! O mores!*" With that he turned on the record player and set the needle on the disc. As peaceful, contemplative music filled the room, his eyes took on a dreamy, faraway look.

Eleanor didn't understand how music became transformed into pictures in his mind. To be honest, she didn't understand the pictures once he put them on canvas. But she was delighted that, since her art dealer friend had taken him up, he had been doing very well with his musical abstracts — his "real" art as opposed to his "tourist" art.

Lois came in to set the gate-legged table. Jerked from his dream, Nick got up to help and then went with her to the kitchen to carry dishes through. Rajendra came down in grey slacks and a handknitted maroon pullover. They all sat down to eat.

Eleanor discovered she was very hungry. Since lunch, she'd had nothing but the sherry, not even a cup of tea from Bob Leacock's thermos.

As Lois had requested, Nick and Eleanor didn't broach the reason for their visit while they were eating. Nick and Rajendra talked about music and art, with Lois contributing a word now and then. Eleanor, her mind a little fuzzy from the effect of alcohol on an empty stomach, concentrated on the food. The meal tasted as good as it smelled.

Her travelling life had allowed Eleanor little opportunity for cooking — or art and music, for that matter — so she always greatly appreciated other people's culinary skills. Nevertheless, she was glad when everyone finished eating and they moved to the other side of the room.

At least, she and Rajendra did. Nick, ever obliging, helped Lois clear the table.

Rajendra stooped to turn on the Calor gas log. "The evenings are getting chilly. What is it you wanted to talk to me about, Eleanor?"

"It's complicated. And, come to think of it, I don't actually know the whole story." She had missed the rescue, and the odds and ends she'd heard from the others did not make a coherent whole. On the other hand, did the doctor really need all the details? Lois would want to hear the story, though. Feeling muddled, Eleanor hesitated, unable to decide. "I'm too tired to think straight. Perhaps Nick had better tell you."

"He's in on this . . . whatever it is? I thought he was just acting as your chauffeur. This is all very mysterious."

Lois returned with an electric percolator, followed by Nick with a tray of cups and saucers, sugar bowl, and milk jug. At the doctor's request, Nick embarked on the tale.

Eleanor was eager to hear the bits she had missed. Despite her best intentions, however, she drowsed off, as she discovered when the ring of the telephone roused her.

"Oh dear . . ."

"I've just got to DI Scumble's unexpected arrival," Nick informed her. "You've deflated my high opinion of myself as a raconteur."

Rajendra answered the phone. After giving the number, he listened for a moment, then said, "Speak of the devil! We've been taking your name in vain, Inspector . . . My wife, myself, Mrs. Trewynn, and Mr. Gresham . . ." An explosive noise came from the receiver. "You'd better ask them yourself . . . Ten minutes? Right you are."

"He's coming here?" Lois asked. Eleanor saw she was upset by the plight of the victim and the hazards Megan had run to save him. "I'd better put on another pot of coffee."

Nick sighed. "No doubt he'll be posing the questions I was leading up to, so I won't bother. We really came in case he didn't."

Lois turned at the door. "But you will finish the story? You're an excellent raconteur. You can't stop now. I shan't be a minute."

"All right. There's not much more, but I'll stop when Scumble arrives, finished or not.

95

He's not too keen on me."

"A competent officer," said the doctor, "but his manner is not ingratiating."

"You're telling me!" said Eleanor.

Lois came back and Nick resumed the story, telling how the inspector had sent Megan off half dressed in the ambulance. "It was a sort of compliment, in his backhanded way. He said — after she'd gone — that she was the only available officer he could rely on to make sense, if humanly possible, of anything the chap might say. That's assuming he'd speak in English, possibly garbled to some extent."

"And if he doesn't speak English?" Rajendra said dryly. "I take it that's where I come in."

When the doorbell rang, Rajendra went to open the door. He could be heard exchanging polite greetings, in English, with DI Scumble, then he ushered him into the room.

Scumble's greeting to Lois was punctilious. "Good evening, Mrs. Prthnavi." Then he turned to Eleanor and Nick. "All right, so what are the pair of you doing here?"

"The Prthnavis are good friends of mine," Eleanor protested. "Am I not allowed to visit them? And bring a friend?"

"In the circumstances, something tells me

there's more to it than that. Gresham?"

"And good evening to you too, Inspector. We were afraid you might not find time to consult Dr. Prthnavi about the man DS Pencarrow rescued." Nick glanced provocatively at his wristwatch.

"I hoped," said Scumble through gritted teeth, "to avoid disturbing a busy GP. However, enquiries elsewhere have got us nowhere so far. Doctor, I take it you've heard all, or most, of the story by now."

"Yes indeed. Mrs. Trewynn's niece appears to have played a heroic part."

"All in the day's work for a police officer." Noting Eleanor's outrage, he relented slightly. "She did well. I walked down to the inlet, and it's a hairy spot. Not where you'd choose to bathe."

"But he's going to be all right," Lois said in a tremulous voice. "The boy she saved."

"That remains to be seen, Mrs. Prthnavi. I rang the hospital just before I spoke to you. All they told me was that his condition is unchanged, which is worrisome."

Rajendra frowned. "Do you want me to examine him? It's not for me to interfere at the hospital with someone who is not my patient. If the house men are out of their depth, they must call in a consultant."

"But you are the local police surgeon,

97

Doctor. There's something fishy about him being found in the water there — pun unintentional. Whether it was accident or a suicide attempt, which may yet prove successful, the police are obliged to investigate. I'd like you to take a look at him. If you prefer, I'll ask Superintendent Bentinck to authorise —"

"That won't be necessary, Inspector. Can it wait till morning?"

"I'd rather you saw him to night, sir. I'm sorry, I know you've had a long day." As Rajendra started to stand, Scumble went on, "Just a couple of things I'd like to clear up first, if you don't mind. I'm assuming, since you haven't mentioned it, that you haven't heard from anyone trying to locate a young man of . . . Indian appearance?"

"No. There aren't many of us in this part of the world."

"That's why I'm asking you. And Mrs. Prthnavi would have told you, of course, if someone had tried to contact you?"

"No one did." Lois was close to tears. "That poor boy!"

"Then one last question, sir. If . . . when . . . the young man comes round, supposing he doesn't know English, do you speak any Indian languages? I gather there are several."

"Hundreds, Inspector," Rajendra said dryly. "I speak Gujarati fluently — my parents' language. My Hindi and Urdu are passable. Otherwise, a few words here and there."

Scumble sighed. "Then as well as your forensic medical expertise, Doctor, we may have to call in your services as an interpreter."

EIGHT

Megan wasn't worried about whether the patient spoke English or not. She was more concerned about whether she was going to fall asleep and slither ignominiously off her chair at his bedside. After working late last night and starting early this morning, followed by fresh air and strenuous exercise, she could barely keep her eyes open.

The ride in the Coast Guard helicopter had been mercifully brief. The noise alone was horrendous, and though they'd done their best to keep the patient warm, Megan had been bitterly cold.

On arrival at the Launceston hospital, she had been lent a pair of surgical-green drawstring trousers rather than a flimsy gown. Once she'd thawed in the well-heated ward, Julia's pullover was rather too warm. She'd taken it off, but the scarlet polo-neck underneath seemed inappropriate, so she'd asked for a top to match the trousers. Not that anyone but the nurses could see her, as they were curtained off from the rest of the men's ward.

The cubicle was in a corner. It included part of an outside window, the blind now drawn as night had fallen, and a slice of the interior window of the nurses' room, so that the nurses could keep an eye on both the A&E patient and the ward as a whole. The cottage hospital didn't run to a casualty ward.

From the patients beyond the curtains came the sound of muted chatter. Someone laughed; someone coughed. A rumble and squeak suggested the arrival of a trolley. A youthful female voice offered a choice of Ovaltine or Bovril. Their mingled odours seeped in, battling the prevailing smell of disinfectant.

Either drink would send Megan straight to sleep. She needed strong coffee.

She tried to concentrate on the man in the bed at her side. A mask covered his nose and mouth, connected by a tube to a machine on the other side of the bed that produced a soft, regular hiss. The sister had explained that it was to assist his breathing, which was still wheezy. If he roused and tried to take it off, Megan had to ring the bell for a nurse.

101

If he roused. The young houseman had found a contusion on the back of the patient's head, which the ambulance men had missed. In spite of this, he was not actually unconscious, or comatose, just suffering from extreme lethargy caused by exhaustion and hypothermia. Megan couldn't tell the difference.

Besides the breathing mask, he had an IV needle in his arm, leading to a bottle on a high stand. She hadn't asked what was in the liquid, sure she would be none the wiser for knowing. She had asked what were the man's chances of survival. The houseman refused to commit himself. A consultant would see the patient tomorrow; no doubt he'd provide a prognosis.

Megan sincerely hoped she would be relieved before then.

Between the curtains appeared a round face with flyaway blond hair escaping from a nurse probationer's cap. "Hello," she whispered. "Would you like something to drink, miss . . . officer . . ." She blinked at the green cotton trousers and smock. "They said you're police?"

"I am. Detective Sergeant, but *Miss* will do. I don't suppose you have coffee? I have to stay awake."

"I'll make you some. We don't give it to

the patients at bedtime. Just Nescaff, okay?"

"Fine. Black, please, no sugar."

The face disappeared and the curtains closed. The trolley rumbled and squeaked away. Megan returned to her contemplation of the dark face on the snowy pillow.

The part she could see was smooth, no age lines, not even sun creases at the corners of his eyes. Early twenties, she guessed. Young and strong, or he'd not have survived his ordeal. Surely not even the stupidest, most ignorant of daring young men would choose to bathe in that narrow, rockbound arm of the sea, even on the calmest of days. There had been no sign of friends he might have been showing off to, no clothes cast off on the slate shelves bordering the water.

So where had he come from? What errant current had carried him to the perilous chasm carved by the waves and the Trevillet stream?

Megan tried to picture a map of the north coast. The overall shape of Cornwall was easy, sticking out into the ocean between the Bristol and English Channels, like a pointed, high-arched foot. But it was a much-battered foot, its margins indented, etched, hollowed out by the ceaseless assault of the stormy North Atlantic. It zigged and zagged unpredictably, like a choppy, whitecapped sea in a stiff breeze.

She knew her way about the district covered by CaRaDoC's Launceston HQ, knew how to get from here to there, though she didn't pretend to match her aunt's intimate knowledge of the back lanes. If the coast zigzagged, the lanes twisted and turned like a coil of serpents, sea serpents, entangling her limbs, dragging her down, down —

"Miss!"

Startled, Megan opened her eyes and jerked upright. "I wasn't asleep." How trite! "Nearly," she acknowledged.

"Your coffee. I made it good and strong."

"Thanks. I really need it."

"I can tell. I brought a couple of Rich Tea bics, too. I'll come back now and then, if you like, and make sure you're awake."

"Super. My boss isn't likely to pop in, but if he did and found me nodding off . . ."

The young nurse-in-training giggled. "Don't I know it. Sister would kill me. Oh, and the night porter said a young man delivered a skirt for you."

"A young man! Not my aunt?"

"A young man, he said." She giggled again. "You must have a secret admirer! Do you want to change now?"

"No, thanks, when I leave. I'm better in

104

these while I'm here."

"Okay." She whisked off, closing the curtains neatly behind her.

Nick, Megan thought, but how had he got hold of one of her skirts? The one she had been wearing, the one he'd used for the rope, was past resuscitation. Aunt Nell must have lent him the Incorruptible and the key to Megan's flat. She didn't like the thought of him rooting through her wardrobe, though it was something her job required her to do to other people's personal belongings. It was kind of him, she supposed, even if probably done at Aunt Nell's instigation.

The coffee was hot and bitter. It hit her stomach with a jolt. Gobbling down the biscuits, not usually one of her favourites, she realised she had had nothing to eat since lunch, and she was ravenous. Horlicks for "night starvation," said the advert. She should have asked for some, or a cup of Bovril.

Did the small hospital have a canteen? It must have a kitchen, to feed the patients.

She dragged her mind away from food to check her own personal patient. He seemed unchanged. She couldn't tell whether the faint wheeze was from his lungs or the machinery. Surely someone somewhere was worrying about him, wondering where he'd got to. Someone would report him missing. His identity would soon be discovered without her sitting here all night, starving and trying desperately not to fall asleep.

The girl — her name was Mitzi: "Mary, really, but everyone calls me Mitzi, except Sister" — came to fetch the cup and saucer. She was perfectly willing to ask Sister's permission to go in search of a sandwich for Megan. While she was gone, the night sister herself came in to take the patient's pulse and temperature, and to check the IV and respirator.

"How is he doing?" Megan ventured to enquire.

Sister looked at her consideringly. "I suppose it's all right to discuss his condition with you, Sergeant. His pulse is much stronger. Temperature nearly normal. Breathing still not good. I can't tell whether he has any colour in his cheeks."

"He looks to me a bit less sallow than when we pulled him out. But I don't know what his normal complexion is."

"That's the trouble with all these dark-skinned people coming into the country. Though I suppose in the big cities, where there are more of them, they learn to judge."

"In London, there are quite a few Indian doctors, and West Indian girls often go into nursing."

"So I've heard. If he's not obviously better in the morning, I might suggest calling in Dr. Prthnavi."

"What a good idea," said Megan admiringly, having been angling for just that result. Aunt Megan's friend Rajendra Prthnavi was her own GP.

"Only if the consultant's in a good mood, mind."

"Of course."

"I've brought your — Oops, sorry, Sister!"

"That's all right, Mary. I'm finished here."

The sight of a sandwich, however limp and curled at the edges, and a packet of crisps brought Megan's thought processes back to life. "Thanks, Mitzi. Sister, if you're not in a hurry, I'd like to clarify something . . ."

"No hurry. What is it? You may go, Mary. I'm sure you can find something useful to do." She turned back to Megan with an expectant look.

"It's this business of 'lethargy.' I'm not clear on how it differs from a coma. He looks comatose to me."

"Oh dear, I don't think I can really explain. Coma is usually caused by head trauma, and this patient doesn't appear to have any major injury, just a bit of a bruise.

107

Poisoning can be another cause. Lethargy has many causes, but what it amounts to is exhaustion. He's just too tired to make any physical effort, even opening his eyes. We can't be sure without X-rays and maybe an EEG, which we don't have here, but the doctor thinks he's sleeping naturally and with luck will wake up naturally, having slept off the worst. If not, he'll be taken by ambulance to Plymouth. They have the specialists and equipment to make a proper diagnosis."

"I see. I think. Thank you, Sister."

Sister nodded graciously. "Is there anything else? Don't hesitate to ring the bell if you notice the slightest change in his condition. There's always a nurse next door, but we haven't got as good a view as you do, and I have the women's ward to keep an eye on, too."

She departed. Megan ate her sandwich with more relish than it deserved. Digging the twist of dark blue paper out of the crisp packet, she sprinkled salt and crunched happily. Of course, that made her thirsty. She cast a longing look at the glass and jug of water on the bedside table but decided any germs she might be carrying had better not be transmitted to the patient if he wanted a drink when he woke up.

Assuming he did awake normally. Once again, she studied what she could see of him.

Did those enviably long, dark eyelashes flicker?

Had she imagined it? Should she ring the bell or knock on the nurses' room window? Should she say something reassuring?

She stood up and leant over him. His eyes opened, vague and unfocussed, lids drooping. One hand lifted a fraction of an inch from the sheet, then flopped back.

Megan reached towards the bell, then hesitated. He looked no different now from when Sister left. The change in his condition was so brief it was probably meaningless. Glancing back at him now, she wondered if it had been wishful thinking. He looked exactly as he had before.

Suddenly his eyes opened again. There was something odd about them, Megan thought, but she was more interested in their expression: bright with consciousness, wide with fear. He made a noise in his throat, halfway between a cough and a gargle. The fear turned to panic and he started to raise the arm with the IV. It must have hurt, because he let it drop, reaching with his other hand towards the mask on his face.

"You're all right. You're in hospital." Megan remembered that he might not speak English, even as she pressed the bell with one hand and held his arm down with the other, to prevent his dislodging the mask. "Okay. You're okay." "Okay" was international, wasn't it?

For a moment he resisted her grip. Then he stopped fighting, though she felt tension in his thin wrist, the tendons taut beneath her fingertips. She could feel his pulse, much stronger now.

His eyes slewed towards her, as if he didn't dare turn his head. He still looked frightened, but questioning, too.

"You're okay. A nurse is coming. Do you understand English? Blink twice if you understand."

He blinked — once, twice. Megan breathed a sigh of relief.

A staff nurse bustled in. "Ah, waking up, are we?" she asked with professional cheerfulness. "That's a good sign."

The sight of the nurse seemed to reassure the patient. His wrist relaxed, but Megan kept her hand on it, lightly, to make sure he didn't try to grab the breathing apparatus. She was sure that if she woke up with a thing like that on her face, her first reaction would be to get rid of it instantly.

110

"I need to talk to him," she said. "Apparently he understands English. Can he do without the respirator, at least for a little while?"

"Please step aside — Sergeant, is it? — and let me take his pulse. You really ought to leave. It's most improper —"

"I've been ordered to stay with him." Megan had felt his arm twitch at the word "Sergeant." It made her the more determined to follow DI Scumble's instructions, even if she didn't understand his reasons. She wished he'd had time to explain.

"Is he under arrest?"

"Good lord no. We just need some information from him. Urgently."

The nurse pursed her lips. Megan watched her face as she took the patient's pulse. Though she didn't comment, she gave a satisfied nod. She wrote the result on the chart hung on the rail at the foot of the bed, then read what was written on it.

Turning back, she caught the man raising his hand to his face again. "Don't!" she said sharply. "I'll deal with it. Doctor says we can try taking it off you for a few minutes, but you're not to talk until you've breathed without it for a while. Sergeant, I must insist that you step outside the curtains until I'm sure the patient is not going to react badly."

Megan meekly obeyed. The ward was in near darkness, lit only by the light from street lamps filtering through the curtains and a well-shaded lamp glowing through the window of the nurses' room.

Mindful of bedpans and such indignities, she didn't watch what was going on in the cubicle, but she listened. The ward was noisier than she expected: snores, moans, the sounds of restless movement and laboured breathing. They masked and merged with the sounds from the cubicle, until the nurse exclaimed, "Oh dear! Now, you mustn't worry, but I'm going to ask Sister to ask our house physician to come and take a look at you."

Footsteps, then a croak of a voice: "Please!"

"You must lie still. What ever you do, don't move your head. I'll be back shortly." She burst through the curtains. "You can't possibly talk to him," she snapped at Megan. "You'll have to go. I'm fetching a doctor. He has concussion. Possibly bleeding or swelling in the brain." She hurried off.

Megan immediately slipped through the curtains, taking the notebook the DI had lent her from the pocket of the smock. The breathing mask was off, so the patient's whole face was able to express his renewed terror. His eyes — unequal pupils, Megan thought. She should have noticed. And again they were glazed, not focussing properly.

"Don't move your head. Just a couple of quick questions before she comes back. What's your name?"

"Kalith Chudasama," he whispered.

She guessed at the spelling. "And where — ?"

"The cave. My family . . ." He clutched his forehead as if he had a splitting headache. As he probably did.

"Where's the cave?"

"High cliff. Rocks. Bad currents."

"Yes, but north or south of where we found you?"

"Sunset . . . I can't think . . . They didn't come. Must swim . . ."

"Who didn't come?"

"Don't know." His voice slurred. "My mother . . . dying."

NINE

The houseman arrived at a run, followed by a straggle of nurses. Megan was firmly ejected from the curtained cubicle, just managing to grab Julia's woolly as she fled. Urgent voices tossed about words like "haemorrage," "haematoma," "intracranial pressure."

Patients were beginning to rouse, some just enough to turn over and go back to sleep; others — less accustomed, perhaps, to spending a night in hospital — muttered to their neighbours.

"We can't cope with this here," snapped the houseman. "We're not set up for it. Sister, please ring the ambulance people and tell them we need emergency transport to Truro."

The dignified night sister burst forth and dashed round the corner to the nurses' room. Megan saw her lift the telephone receiver, dial, and speak urgently into it.

"Plymouth's closer, Doctor," said someone, "and better equipped."

"True. I'd better ring Plymouth General myself and make arrangements for the transfer."

Megan was dismayed. If they moved Chudasama, was she supposed to follow? How? They wouldn't let her travel in the ambulance again. Besides, Plymouth was out of CaRaDoC's jurisdiction. She had to talk to her boss, or to whoever was in charge at HQ tonight.

They must have a public telephone in the lobby. Not that that would do her much good. She hadn't got a penny on her — nor her warrant card, come to think of it. Everything was locked in the police car she'd been driving, which, for all she knew, was still parked in the lay-by on the B3263. Its key had been in the pocket of her skirt. Very likely it was now at the bottom of the Atlantic.

What had become of the skirt Nick had brought? Presumably the porter still had it. Changing would have to wait till after she had phoned in.

She could dial 999 free, of course, like any member of the public. The night operator at HQ served the emergency lines as well as the station's internal lines.

At any rate, she wasn't doing much good standing here. She hurried out to the lobby. Glancing round, she couldn't see a phone, so she asked the porter. Without looking up from his football pools, he pointed.

She didn't bother to try to borrow pennies for the call. He obviously wasn't the cooperative sort, possibly a bit bolshie and not likely to be impressed that she was a police officer, even if she had proof.

She went in the direction indicated, round a corner, found the wall telephone, and dialled.

"Emergency services. Fire? Pol—"

"Nancy, this is Megan Pencarrow. I'm at a public phone, at the hospital, on the job. Is Mr. Scumble in?"

"He went to see Dr. Prithnavvy," the switchboard girl told her, "or however you say it. Listen, I have to keep this line free. I'll call you back. What's the number?"

Megan read it to her, hung up, and waited till the phone rang.

"Nancy?"

"Yeah. Want me to see if I can raise the car?"

"Yes, please. Who's driving?" Scumble hated being driven, but he wasn't much keener on driving himself, especially at night, other than from home to the nick and back.

"Dawson. Hold on, I'll be right back."

PC Dawson — a demon driver, one not calculated to soothe the boss's nerves. Dawson must have been the only man who could be spared from the sparse night shift. Megan was relieved that Scumble hadn't taken a detective with him, who might supplant her in the case.

Because, if what a semidrowned, concussed man said was to be taken seriously, an investigation was surely warranted.

The prospect reinvigorated her. Impatient now, she waited for Nancy's voice.

"Megan, you still there?"

"Yes, of course."

"They're at the doctor's house. Dawson's going to give the inspector your number so he can ring you back direct."

"Okay, thanks. Bye." She hung up and waited.

At last the phone rang. "Pencarrow?" came Scumble's abrasive voice. "What's up? Is he dead?"

"No, sir. Or not when I came out to phone, about five minutes ago."

"Then what are you doing away from his bedside? Or did he come round and talk?"

"Sort of."

117

"Sort of? What the devil's that supposed to mean?"

"He woke up, but it turns out he has concussion."

"Concussion! The ambulance men —"

"You can't really blame them for missing it, sir. The doctor said the contusion was hard to see, and he may not have had any symptoms at that point. If I understood correctly, they were talking about bleeding and swelling of the brain."

"Intracranial haemorrage? You'd better brush up on your medical terminology, Pencarrow. So you didn't get a chance to ask any questions."

"Just a couple. His name is" — she consulted the notebook — "Kalith Chudasama. I'm not sure about the spelling. I'm not sure whether he understood my questions, or whether he really knew what he was saying, but he did understand and speak English."

"That's a help, at least," Scumble growled.

"But he was pretty incoherent. I asked his name, as I said, and where he came from. He talked about cliffs and caves and rocks. I have his exact words —"

"Later. Just give me the gist. Caves, huh?"

"A cave. *The* cave, he said. It sounded as if his family was stranded in a cave."

"His family!"

"I can't be sure exactly," Megan protested defensively. "He wasn't speaking in whole sentences. But he said something about his mother dying, and 'They didn't come.' Only he couldn't tell me *who* didn't come. I told you, sir, he wasn't coherent. For all I know, he'd had a nightmare."

"Is that it? Nothing else?"

"No, sir. The doctor came and I was thrown out. He looked bad. I don't think I'd have got any more out of him if I'd been able to stay."

"Coherent or not, we have to assume he was in his right mind and telling the truth. His family stranded in a cave, his mother dying, he swims for it. What we've got to find out is where the cave is and who didn't come. As he speaks English, you needn't stay. I'll have someone relieve you."

"Sir, he won't be here. They're sending him to either Truro or Plymouth."

"Plymouth!" Scumble exploded. "They can't take him out of CaRaDoC territory! He may be a vital witness."

"It's a matter of life or death. He urgently needs care they can't provide here. He'll be off as soon as the ambulance — In fact, I can hear them coming in the front door now. I suppose they'll go to whichever hospital the driver thinks they can get to quickest, or send a helicopter again, maybe."

"Bloody hell! Pardon my French, ladies." Ladies? Who was there with him besides the doctor? The doctor's wife, Megan assumed, and . . . Surely not Aunt Nell? No, it couldn't be. "Pencarrow, find out where they're taking him. Then get back to the station. I'll meet you there."

"Yes, sir," Megan said absently as she heard the receiver clunk down.

Aunt Nell? Nick had dropped off a skirt for her — which she was going to have to wrest from the unfriendly porter. What could be more likely than that he had driven Aunt Nell over to talk to Dr. Prthnavi about the drowning Indian?

If so, the inspector must have been seething even before Megan's report. He had probably wanted to observe the doctor's initial reaction to the news, just in case he was somehow involved. Aunt Nell, whom Scumble considered a vague and forgetful old woman, had beaten him to the punch.

TEN

Shivering in a chilly breeze, Megan slogged up the hill from the hospital to the town centre. The skirt and Julia's pullover were warm, but her legs were bare and would have to remain so for the foreseeable future. She wondered how long she was going to be kept hanging about the station waiting for Scumble, and what his plans were once he arrived.

"I hear you're a heroine," the desk sergeant greeted her.

"You can break out the champagne tomorrow. All I want now is coffee."

"There's a reasonably fresh pot going."

"Good. Do you know if someone fetched my car — the car I was using — from Rocky Valley? I left my jacket and bag locked in the boot."

"The Super had Orton and the kid drive over to get it. Orton treated himself to a bit of a carry-on about women drivers who lose their keys. He said you'd have to go and sign for your stuff."

"Bugger Orton," Megan said tiredly. The mechanic in charge of the police cars was a constant thorn in her flesh. "Is there someone you can send to pick them up? I'd like a chance to comb my hair before the DI comes in."

He grinned. "You do look a bit as if you'd been blown through a bramble bush backwards."

"Thanks a lot!" The skirt was long enough to hide her bashed-up knees. The men — most of them — had stopped ogling her legs after her first few weeks on the job, so she hoped the sticking plasters hiding the gashes on her shins would go unobserved.

"Not to worry. I'll find someone to get your things."

"Thanks."

She took her mug of coffee up to the room she shared with Scumble and DS Eliot. Her notes on the hospital wouldn't take long to write up. However, doubtless the inspector, and probably Superintendent Bentinck also, would want a proper report on the rescue of Chudasama.

What was his first name? She sat down at her desk and opened the notebook. Kalith . . . Kalith Chudasama. How close her scribble was to the proper spelling was anyone's guess, but she headed the page with his name.

She kept her description of the rescue brief, trying to explain the unlikelihood of anyone choosing to bathe there without glorifying her own decision to jump into the hazardous waters to pull him out. As for relating how Chaz and Julia had helped, she was hampered by her inability to remember their surnames, if she had ever heard them. She hoped Scumble had taken them down.

A very young constable delivered her shoulder bag and jacket. She went to the ladies' to try to do something with her salt-encrusted hair. In the end, she dunked her head in a basin of lukewarmish water and dried it on the roller towel as best she could. Naturally, Scumble arrived during her absence. He had rolled her unfinished report out of the typewriter, thus messing up her carbons so she'd have to retype the page.

He greeted her impatiently. "Where did they take him?"

"Plymouth, sir."

"Damn! Get me the central station, whoever's in charge at this time of night. Urgent. If Chudasama comes round again and no one's listening —"

Megan passed on the order to Nancy, glancing at the wall clock as she spoke. It was not yet eleven. The way she felt was more like three in the morning.

Plymouth, being a large and lively port city, had a superintendent on night duty. Megan listened as the inspector made his case for sending someone immediately to Chudasama's bedside to take notes of anything he might say.

"Yes, sir, I realise the bloke may be an ordinary, everyday bather in trouble. The thing is . . . Yes, sir, lovely weather for the time of year, but . . . Yes, sir, but I've talked to the only locals of Indian extraction . . . Family restaurant in Camelford, sir, and our local police surgeon. They don't . . . Sir, my superintendent agrees that we just can't risk . . . Superintendent Bentinck, sir. I can give you his home telephone number . . . Thank you, sir. And you'll have him let me know . . . Thank you, sir." He put down the receiver, making sure it was firmly in place before letting out an explosive breath. "Bloody nitpicking bastard."

"Is that why you didn't ask him to have a police doctor look at the head injury?"

"That would make it a possible cross-jurisdiction criminal case, instead of just an unidentified accident victim. He's the pernickety sort to insist on going through our respective chief constables. Who knows, maybe even call in the Yard. You want the Boy Wonder buzzing around again?"

"No, sir!" The Boy Wonder, also known as DS Kenneth Faraday of the Metropolitan Police, had been Megan's boyfriend when she worked in London. He still pursued her in a desultory way when her existence happened to be drawn to his attention, though long-legged blondes were more his style.

"It'll be a different matter if the bloke dies. They'll call in the pathologist as a matter of course."

"Yes. But the Plymouth super's posting a man in the hospital?"

"Yes. He knows our super. Bentinck would back me to the hilt, even if he didn't know what the hell I was talking about. I've stuck out my neck on this one, Pencarrow, so don't go changing your mind about what Chudasama said!"

"I wrote it down immediately, sir, and transcribed it word for word in my report. Sorry I didn't quite finish. I couldn't swear to the spelling of his name."

"Both names are Indian and not uncommon, according to Dr. Prthnavi. He says he doesn't know of anyone missing, of that name or any other, and in my opinion he's telling the truth."

"Why shouldn't he, sir?"

"Because it's conceivable that he might be mixed up in this racket. But I've known him for a good few years and I'm ninety-nine percent certain he wouldn't touch it with a ten-foot pole."

"Racket?"

"Use your head!"

Megan felt as if she had treacle circulating in her brain. "I'm sorry, sir, I can't see it."

"All right, let's assume for argument's sake that Chudasama was in his right mind. His family is stranded in a cave, somewhere not too far from Rocky Valley. There are plenty to choose from on that bit of coast. How did they get stuck there?"

"Exploring, and the tide came in?"

"That's reasonable," Scumble conceded grudgingly. "In fact, it would have been my first thought if I hadn't already pretty much ruled it out in the case of Chudasama. I talked to the lifeboat people and the Coast Guard. They agree that even seasoned climbers think twice about tackling the cliffs in that area. They're too unstable. Bossiney Cove is the only place you can safely scramble down to, and it *is* a scramble. When you get to the bottom it's all rocks, with sand exposed only at low tide."

"I didn't know that." Megan tried to keep the accusatory tone from her voice. It was entirely unfair of him not to give her the facts before asking her to speculate, but protesting was pointless. "I grew up at the other end of the county. By the sound of it, even if Kalith might have gone there, his mother, a middle-aged Indian woman —"

"We mustn't make assumptions based on age, race, or sex," the inspector said sanctimoniously. "You're right, though, it's a dead cert she wouldn't go near the place by choice. So how did they end up in a cave?"

"By sea? In a boat, that is. It must be possible; smugglers used to use those caves, didn't they? I read a book about smuggling in Cornwall and they were very active roundabout Boscastle. But why . . . ? You think they were being smuggled into the country!"

"Makes sense of everything, doesn't it?"

"Ye-es. I know the Commonweath Immigrants law has left lots of people holding British passports but not allowed to live here. There was a lot of talk about it on the Beeb."

"No right of residency. And who's it hit hardest? In fact, who was it aimed at in the first place? Indians, the ones living in East Africa. Now the Africans are independent,

127

they don't want 'em. Some of the poor buggers are being shipped round from country to country and not allowed ashore anywhere."

"So someone was bound to get the idea of smuggling them in. But why here? There are so few coloured people they couldn't go unnoticed."

"Just because it's unlikely," Scumble suggested. "The immigration people can't keep an eye on all the little fishing ports. By the time they heard about it, the refugees'd be in Birmingham or wherever they could disappear into a bunch of their own people."

"Not without help."

"Which didn't arrive."

Megan was horrified. "You mean someone took their money and abandoned them?"

"Looks like it, doesn't it?"

"But that's murder!"

"We'll let the lawyers quibble about charges. Our business is to find these people before they die. I'm glad your interpretation is the same as mine, because I'm laying my credibility on the line over this. I just hope Chuda-whatsit was in his right mind."

"I think so." But she couldn't be certain. She'd been neatly steered into agreeing with his guess at the implications of Chudasama's words. Not that it really mattered.

They had to act as if it was true. "So what do we do now, sir?"

"I interrupt Mr. Bentinck's nightcap and get things moving."

"With the RNLI and Coast Guard?"

"Lifeboats certainly. I imagine the Coast Guard will want to be involved as it's a matter of smuggling and illegal entry. Or should I say, that's what it may turn out to be. They won't be able to do much till daylight, though."

"Sunrise at six, sir."

"So, first light about five, unless the clouds roll in. Go and snatch a few hours' sleep."

"Thank you, sir."

"And be back here at half four."

Another short night, but at least she'd spend it in her own bed. Scumble might not make it home to Tregadillet, the village where he lived. If he got any sleep at all, it would be scrunched in a chair with his head on the desk. He had said Megan looked peaky before the rescue and the bedside vigil. She probably looked like death warmed up by now. She decided not to look at herself in a mirror until she got home, and then to take a long hot bath, even though it would rob her of half an hour's sleep.

She was about to step over the threshold

on her way out when Scumble attacked: "Can you explain your aunt and Gresham being at Dr. Prthnavi's when I arrived?"

Surprised, though not as surprised as she tried to appear, she swung round. "Aunt Nell?"

"She's the only aunt of yours I'm acquainted with, thank heaven."

"My other aunts are far less . . . enterprising. I've no idea why she was there, but I'm sure Nick Gresham was just chauffeuring her. They brought me this skirt, at the hospital."

He scrutinised her. "Hmm. Very fetching."

"It's not mine. I don't know where . . . Oh, probably from the shop."

"Mrs. Stearns's car was parked outside the doctor's house. She wasn't present, though. I hope it means she has the sense not to stick her nose into police business again."

"She must have lent it to them. The Incorruptible is getting a bit creaky and I know Mrs. Stearns worries about Aunt Nell driving any distance at night."

"If a breakdown stops Mrs. Trewynn interfering," growled Scumble, "then I, for one, hope the damn car —"

"I'll be back at four thirty, sir," Megan interrupted, and she stalked out.

Walking home through the quiet moonlit streets, she contemplated her irascible boss. His fulmination against Aunt Nell was nothing new, and not unreasonable, though rude and excessive. What had surprised her was his knowledge of the effects of the Commonwealth Immigration Act, especially his sympathetic tone towards its victims. She'd always assumed his only interests were the job and his garden.

His interest in the stranded refugees started with their presumed status as victims of a crime, of course. But he seemed to care genuinely about their plight and to be willing to battle the brass to save them.

"My family," Chudasama had said. Not "my parents." His dying mother. His father? Grandparents? Brothers and sisters? Aunts and uncles? *Children?*

ELEVEN

Eleanor and Nick didn't stay long at the Prthnavis' after Scumble left. Lois was still deeply distressed by the whole affair, though relieved that the patient's removal from Launceston meant that her husband would not be called upon to go out again that night to examine him.

Rajendra was grave. Showing them out, he said, "Confusion is a common symptom of concussion. We must hope the young man spoke of a dream, a nightmare, or something he had read. A film or television, perhaps. However, I'm glad the inspector is taking it seriously."

"Mr. Scumble can be extremely irritating," said Eleanor, "but he's a good detective, for all that."

They repeated good nights and she and Nick went on out to Jocelyn's car.

Nick drove in thoughtful silence as Eleanor navigated back to the main road. Once he knew where he was and where he was going, he said, "Given that Scumble is a good copper, don't you think it's odd that he repeated aloud all — or most — of what Megan told him? Almost as if he wanted the rest of us to know."

"You're right, it was odd. And I don't believe that man ever does anything without a reason. Could he have been hinting that he wants us to do a bit of investigating?"

"Come off it, Eleanor! After all the times he's warned us off? You won't catch me giving him an excuse to arrest me again."

"You weren't actually under arrest."

"It felt like it. Anyway, if you ask me, he was aiming at Dr. Prthnavi."

"Rajendra? Why?" Eleanor asked in surprise.

"Because he thinks — or thought — he might be involved somehow, that the people in the cave, if they exist outside the chap's imagination, could be relatives of the doctor trying to get into the country. Didn't you notice how closely he was watching him? Of course doctors have to perfect the poker face, so he didn't have much luck. Though I suppose detectives must get good at reading poker faces."

"Really, Nick, as if Rajendra would abandon relatives to die, in a cave or anywhere else! Or any*one* else, come to that. You're letting your imagination run away with you."

"I'm not suggesting he would. Not even that Scumble believes him capable of it. Just that, Indians being thin on the ground in these parts, it crossed Scumble's mind that there might be some connection. The doctor might have known of such a plan without having any part in it, or any knowledge of when it would take place. So he wouldn't be worried about their not appearing, but when he heard . . ."

"I suppose so. It sounds much too complicated. Besides, having been born here, couldn't he bring relatives in legally?"

"Don't ask me. I'm sure you're much better up in immigration law than I am."

"That's even more complicated. I doubt anyone really understands the implications of every detail, even those who wrote the new law. But that's beside the point. If people are in danger and I can do anything at all to help them, I don't give two hoots what Scumble has to say."

Nick sighed. "No, you're right. Though I can't see what we can do that he can't do a thousand times better and faster. He has the resources."

"But we, between us, may have local information he doesn't. You've taken thou-

134

sands of photos of the coast —"

"Dozens. Hundreds, perhaps."

"Lots. Didn't you once go out in a fishing boat to take pictures from the sea?"

"More than once," Nick admitted. "Including Bossiney Cove. I had to pay for that trip. Neither fishermen nor lobstermen like it. Tricky rocks and currents."

"Bossiney Cove — is that where Rocky Valley comes out? I'll have to look at my map. I know how to get from hither to yon, but picturing the lie of the land is another matter."

"When you see it, you'll agree that — What was the bloke's name?"

"Kalith Chudasama, the inspector said."

"Chudasama almost certainly started his swim from somewhere in the cove. If he'd been swept round Lye Rock from the east or the Saddle Rocks and Darvis Point from the north, he wouldn't have had a chance in a thousand of surviving."

"Did you see many caves there?"

"Plenty. A lot of them, you'd have to have an inflatable dinghy to reach them. Only when high tide covers the rocks, at that. Some you could get to in a wooden rowboat, if you knew what you were doing, where the submerged rocks are and where the currents are dangerous."

"Only local fishermen would know."

"And not many of them. As I said, they don't like going there."

"That must be why no one saw the young man or his family. They must have waved and shouted for help from the mouth of the cave, surely."

"The mouths of some of the caves are underwater, though they're dry farther back. I went into a couple to see if there were any interesting rock formations, but nothing worth photographing."

Eleanor shuddered. "Horrible!"

"At least Scumble seems to be taking it seriously. The police will get the lifeboat out tomorrow. They have inflatables. They'll soon find . . . Hell!"

They had reached the highest point on the road over Bodmin Moor. Below and ahead of them, bright moonlight shone on a flat white sea of fog, stretching towards the coast as far as Eleanor could see.

"Oh, Nick, the lifeboat won't go out in that!"

"It could be clear at sea level. Down there it may be just low cloud, or not half as solid as it looks from above."

"I do hope so. Or it might clear by tomorrow," she said doubtfully.

Nick zipped downhill, slowing as they

reached the fringes of the fog. At first it was wispy. As they penetrated, it became denser, until they had to crawl along. The full beam of the headlights reflected back blindingly, so Nick dipped them. Eleanor stuck her head out of the window from time to time to warn him if the car was about to go off the road. Not that she could see much.

"What I'd really like," said Nick, leaning forward over the steering wheel, peering into nothingness, "is someone else's tail-lights to follow."

They nearly missed the turn off the main road, but once in the lanes, driving was easier, if no faster, because of the vague, looming presence of hedge-banks closing in on each side. They met no other vehicles, no stray cows or sheep, not even a rabbit or a pheasant.

Though the drive seemed to go on forever, at last the crowding hedges ended as they reached what Eleanor thought of as the bungalow zone, where meadows were rapidly disappearing beneath the onslaught of summer visitors and retired people. The lights of the small self-service grocery appeared, fuzzily haloed. The fog was no less dense down here. It smelled of the sea.

Just where the slope steepened, entering the old village, Nick pulled over to the side of the road. "Whew, made it."

"What . . . Oh, the Vicarage. Joce's car. I forgot. I wonder whether they're still up?"

"It looks as if they've left the lamp on over the front door."

"We'd better pop in. Poor Teazle will be in despair, but another few minutes won't make any difference."

"Hold on a mo. I'll go and see whether there's a light in any of the windows. If not, I'll just lock up the car and put the keys through the letterbox."

Eleanor heard him tapping on glass. A moment later, a curtain was drawn back and she saw his silhouette against the light within. She rolled up the window, and as she got out of the car, she heard Jocelyn's voice.

"Nicholas! I'm so glad you've made it back safely. Where is — Oh, there you are, Eleanor. Come in, do. What a foul night." She swung the casement to and closed the curtain. A moment later the front door opened. "Come in," she urged again. "Tell me everything."

Nick followed Eleanor in, but he said, "Not tonight, if you don't mind, Mrs. Stearns. Eleanor's had a long, hard day, and I've been gripping the steering wheel with all my might and main for what seems like hours."

"You both look frozen, and your hair's wet. Come in by the fire, and I'll make hot chocolate. The instant kind, it won't take a jiffy."

Eleanor realised her hair had collected moisture from the fog and was dripping down her neck. She had been too chilled to notice it. The sitting room, furnished with slightly worn prize pieces from the LonStar shop, was warm and welcoming. She and Nick exchanged a look and sank into chairs by the flickering driftwood fire.

Nick rubbed his eyes. "I don't believe I've blinked once since we hit the fog." He stretched.

"I'm very glad you were driving."

Jocelyn reappeared. "Have you eaten?"

"Yes, thanks, Joce. Very well, with the Prthnavis."

"Only, there's soup. Plenty of it, as Timothy's not coming home."

"What?" Nick exclaimed. "Don't tell me the vicar's stuck out in this fog somewhere on his scooter!"

"No, no. He was called out before it rolled in and they rang to say he'd stay the night."

"Good. I can't say I fancied having to go and look for him."

The kettle whistled and Jocelyn disappeared again.

"Cocoa, and then home," Eleanor said firmly. "I'm not staying up half the night talking."

"Scumble warned us not to talk."

Joce was back, with a tray. "Did I hear That Man's name?" She handed out mugs of hot chocolate.

Gratefully warming her hands on the mug, Eleanor said, "The inspector told us we mustn't tell anyone about what's happened."

"In the first place, I am not 'anyone.' In the second place, I already know most of it. If I'm left in ignorance of the rest, how can I help?"

Nick grinned, shaking his head. "I rather think Scumble would be much happier without our help, Mrs. Stearns."

"I daresay. However, it is our duty to aid our fellow man, even if he's a Hindu or a detective inspector."

Once Jocelyn had rationalised her desire to interfere as her duty, nothing could stop her, and Eleanor wasn't about to try.

Besides, she had the glimmerings of an idea of how she and Jocelyn might be able to help. The police search for the cave could not start until the fog lifted, but once they got going, it would be speeded up if the area they had to search was narrowed down. The sort of people who . . . The sort of people . . . The thought slipped away.

"Eleanor!" Nick rescued the tipping mug from her hand. "You're half asleep. Come on, let's head for home. We're going to have to take it really carefully."

"Eleanor, you'd better spend the night."

"I'd love to, but I left Teazle at home."

"Nicholas will let her out, won't you, Nicholas." It was a command, not a question, let alone a request.

"Of course," Nick said meekly. "I'll give her a Bonio and she can spend the night with me."

"We'll talk in the morning," promised — or threatened — Jocelyn.

Eleanor was awoken early by daylight filtering through the blue-striped cotton curtains of the Stearnses' spare room. The room faced west so the morning sun didn't shine in, but the light was not the grey gloom of a foggy day. A flood of relief swept over her. She would not have to embark upon the awkward embassy she had envisioned undertaking in the slim hope of speeding the search for the cave.

She stretched, a necessary precursor these

141

days to getting out of bed, especially a bed other than her own. Stiffly, she clambered out, stretched again, and padded barefoot to the window.

The rising sun gleamed on the windows of the houses opposite and the lantern of the Crookmoyle light house at the top of the slope beyond them. But when Eleanor looked down the hill to her left, the bridge and the harbour were invisible beneath a white blanket of cotton wool.

The fog had abandoned the high ground; over the water it still clung. It might be local and short-lived. Or it might hang along the entire North Coast for days, keeping frustrated fishermen in port and foiling the rescue of a desperate family.

TWELVE

Megan arrived back at the nick just as the first faint hint of dawn lightened the eastern sky. The duty sergeant had warned her that her boss was still in, had been there all night, so she took up two mugs of coffee. It was from the bottom of the urn, barely hotter than lukewarm, but better than nothing.

She found Scumble at his desk, on the telephone, eyes red and bleary. He took his mug from her and gulped greedily, listening as he drank.

"All right, if you say so, who am I to argue?" he said at last, in the tone of heavy patience that failed to disguise his impatience. "You'll let me know at once? Yes, of course." He slammed down the receiver.

"What's up, sir?"

"The bloody watch officer of HM sodding Coast Guard says it's too f . . . frigging foggy to search." He had long ago given up an initial attempt not to swear in Megan's

143

presence, but he still drew the line at certain words. "Hell, it's foggy on the coast more often than not! What use is the Coast Guard if a bit of fog stumps them?"

"It must be a really bad one."

"Isn't that what they have radar and sonar for? Bloody useless gits."

"They probably can't take radar and sonar equipment in a small boat."

"Whose side are you on?" the inspector snarled. "He says he won't risk the lives of his men, but what about the lives of the stranded family? It's the RNLI who have to do the dirty work, anyway. The Coast Guard 'coordinates operations' and sends in a copter if needed."

"Maybe he's taking into account that we aren't absolutely sure —"

"As far as I'm concerned, they're British citizens out there and in danger, unless I get definite evidence to the contrary."

"Yes, sir."

The phone rang and Megan answered: "DS Pencarrow."

"It's the skipper of the Port Isaac lifeboat, Sergeant."

"Put him through." Megan relayed the information. Rubbing his eyes, Scumble picked up his receiver, then gestured to her to take the call.

"This is Pete Larkin, Sergeant," said a sober voice. "Bad news, I'm afraid. The fog's so thick we can't even get down to the lifeboat house. I rang Bude, and it's the same up there. Boscastle, too — I talked to a chap I know there, hoping we might be able to get a fishing boat on the job. The Padstow all-weather boat went out earlier, to look for other survivors — or bodies. It's on station beyond the fog line, a couple of miles out, but the inshore boats won't be able to get going till it thins. Sorry."

"Okay. Thanks for letting us know. Any idea when it might clear?"

"That's anyone's guess. The Met Office says there's a front coming in, but they won't say when it's due to arrive. That'll blow it away, if it hasn't already lifted. You never can tell."

"How far inland does it reach, in your area?"

"Oh, no distance. It's sitting on the water like a goose on its nest. From a hundred yards up the hill, you can see Lobber Point. The harbour's invisible, though. Don't worry, I'll call in the crew as soon as there's any hope of launching."

"Thank you, Captain Larkin." Megan looked at Scumble. He shook his head: no further questions. "We'll get back to you if

145

there's any news at this end."

Scumble hung up. "News? There isn't going to be any news till those buggers get moving."

"It does sound hopeless to attempt a search at present, sir. I was thinking of news from the hospital. Or did you talk to them before I got here?"

"They're supposed to ring here if Chudasama's condition changes."

"You know how hospitals are. The last thing on their minds is letting anyone know what's going on."

"You're right." Sighing, he rubbed his eyes again. "Jesus, I'm tired. Give them a buzz."

It took ages to get through to someone who knew something and was willing to tell. The night shift were just going off, unwilling to be delayed, and the day shift had to bring themselves up to date with what was going on. At last, Megan spoke to the sister of the surgical ward.

"Chudasama, Kalith? Yes, I have his chart here. It looks as if he came out of the theatre in good shape. Intracranial bleeding — the surgeon thinks he's stopped that, and with a bit of luck the swelling will go down now. This sort of case, it takes a bit of luck," she added with professional cheerfulness. "He's young. That's in his favour. And it seems he's fundamentally healthy, though recently he's not been getting enough to eat."

"Can he talk?"

"Talk? I should say not! Even if he was physically capable, which he isn't at present, I'm sure Doctor won't want him trying for at least a couple of days. I really must run, Miss . . ."

"Sergeant. Cornish police, Launceston station. You will keep us informed?"

"Yes, certainly, I'll make a note. Bye now."

Click.

"Fat chance!" Megan snorted.

"Fat chance of what?"

"Of them keeping us informed. She 'made a note.' He was basically healthy but recently he hasn't been getting enough to eat. So presumably his family's running out of what ever rations the smugglers left them, if any."

"The bastards! When will he be able to talk?"

"She reckons he won't be allowed for a couple of days. At least. Even if he's able."

"If he starts babbling, the Plymouth force should let us know. But let's hope we're talking to the family long before two days have passed." He yawned. "Right, I'm glad you asked about fog inland. Good thinking. You can drop me off at home for a couple of hours kip, and run on down to Camelford to see the Indian restaurant people. Last night, I just had someone ring and ask if they knew of anyone missing." He checked his watch, heaving himself out of his chair. "They should be up and about by the time you get there."

So much for breakfast, Megan thought. But if she was nice to the restaurant people, or if they had guilty consciences and wanted to placate her, perhaps she'd discover what Indians had for breakfast.

Jocelyn gave the last of the breakfast dishes a final vehement swipe with the tea towel and put it away. "Family in a cave! It sounds like sheer nonsense to me. His mind must have been wandering."

Eleanor pulled off the rubber gloves Joce made her wear for washing up — she never bothered at home. It was still early. After trying for half an hour to go back to sleep, she had tiptoed down to the kitchen to make herself a cup of tea. In spite of her care, Jocelyn had heard her and come down. They had decided they might as well dress and eat.

"It's possible he was muddled," Eleanor said now. "I haven't spoken to Megan, so I don't know what sort of state he was in at the time, just the inspector's end of the

148

conversation. But as long as it might be true, we have to act as if it's true. At least, I do, and the police do. Mr. Scumble certainly seemed to be taking it seriously. There's no reason you need be involved, of course."

With a martyred sigh, Jocelyn sat down at the kitchen table. "I can't see what you hope to do. The weather forecast said the coast is fogged in all the way from Hartland Point to Kelsey Head. Even if it was clear, you couldn't compete with the lifeboat people in searching for this mystery cave."

"Not *searching,* exactly."

"And supposing it exists, how on earth did they come to be stuck in it?"

"That's what gave me the idea."

"What idea? What *do* you mean, Eleanor?"

"Of course, it's the difficult situation in Kenya and Uganda that makes it particularly likely just now."

"You told me the young man Megan saved was Indian! Now you're saying he's African?"

"No, no. Well, sort of. Indians have been trading with East Africa for centuries, and naturally some settled there. Then the British brought in Indian labourers to build the railways, and lots of them stayed after the work was finished. Now the Africans are

getting their independence from the Empire
—"

"I do listen to the news, you know. They don't want the Indians staying any more than they want the British. Unfortunate, but understandable."

"Unfortunate" was not the word Eleanor would have used. She found it heartbreaking that those who had suffered from racialist discrimination should be so quick to discriminate against others.

As Jocelyn claimed to be in the picture already, Eleanor decided to skip long explanations. "My guess is that they're trying to get into the country without the proper papers. Someone brought them as far as the cave, but the arrangements to pick them up went wrong. The cave couldn't be one of those easily visible from offshore, one that lots of people know about, or they'd have been spotted. It must be one of the old smugglers' caves, where they hid cargoes until it was safe to bring the goods ashore."

" 'Five and twenty ponies, trotting through the dark,' " Jocelyn warbled unexpectedly. " 'Brandy for the parson, 'baccy for the clerk.' "

"Exactly. All the little harbours along this bit of coast were havens for smugglers, especially Boscastle. I imagine most of the population knew what was going on, though only a very few would know how to find the secret caves. I bet the secret was passed down from father to son."

"Someone must still know, or those people wouldn't be there."

"It makes sense, doesn't it?"

"Yes. Not that making sense necessarily means it's true," Joce pointed out. "All the same, you'd better mention it to Megan, in case That Man hasn't thought of it. If they find out where to look, they can go straight there as soon as the fog clears."

"The trouble is, smugglers might refuse to give information to the police."

"You mean they're still smuggling? I thought we were talking about a couple of centuries ago."

"The duty on brandy and tobacco is still high," Eleanor reminded her. "And there's always drugs, I'm afraid. Not to mention people."

"People! Yes, of course, someone local must be involved." The vicar's wife was appalled. "What a dreadful thought!"

"Or at least someone with local knowledge. Someone who used to live here perhaps," Eleanor said comfortingly, "or who knew enough to ask the right questions about the location of the caves. Local fishermen couldn't possibly set up an international scheme of this scope. It's on a different level from slipping across to Brittany one dark night for a few crates of bottles."

"They do that? The Boscastle fishermen?"

"So someone let slip once, though he didn't admit to doing it! But, you see, I do know people there, and they do talk to me."

"You meet them when you're collecting for the shop, I suppose. Eleanor, asking awkward questions is a very different matter from asking for donations. It could be dangerous. And you don't need to remind me that you've been in dangerous situations in dangerous countries —"

"Life is dangerous. It invariably leads to death. But there's a tendency to try to put the end off as long as possible." She was tempted to add, *even among those who expect to go to heaven.* "It's just possible I may be able to save an entire family from premature departure from the earth. Perhaps they'd be rescued in time without my help. Perhaps they don't even exist. But how can I not try?"

Jocelyn shook her head in foreboding. "Well, when you put it like that . . . I have a lot to do this morning, but I suppose I can put it all off to go with you. Not before Timothy gets home, though."

"Never mind. I do think I should go right away, because if the fog dissipates, the people I want to talk to may go out fishing. I'm sure Nick will go with me if I ask him."

Eleanor had no intention of asking Nick to accompany her, and she was glad Joce wasn't coming. People would be much more likely to talk to her if she was on her own. She was quite confident of being able to defend herself, should the unlikely necessity arrive. When she had started working in some of the more dangerous parts of the world, Peter had insisted that she learn Aikido.

She continued the practice, though those days were behind her. It was good exercise and helped her achieve mental tranquillity. She had kept it secret, sure that people would scoff at a white-haired old lady involved in the martial arts.

The moment she stepped out of the door, she heard the foghorn wailing up at the light house. She realised she'd been distantly aware of its sound, muffled by walls, since she woke up.

She walked down the hill. The LonStar shop, with her flat above, had wisps of mist curling about it, and a haze enveloped Nick's gallery next door. The bridge was still invisible. She remembered with relief

153

that the Incorruptible was in the car park at the top of the hill, beyond the vicarage, though she couldn't remember why they had decided to leave it there rather than in its shed on the far side of the bridge.

Both the LonStar shop and Nick's still had their CLOSED signs displayed. Eleanor, finding her keys in the pocket of her jacket for once, unlocked the side door beside the shop. She went past the stairs, out through the back door, and down the footpath that ran behind the row. Looking in at Nick's wide back window, she saw him hard at work in his studio, as expected. At this time of year, he didn't waste the shortening hours of natural light.

Teazle lay beneath his three-legged easel, her nose on her paws. When Eleanor tapped on the glass, the little dog sprang up and rushed at the window, barking. Her bark changed to a whine as she recognised Eleanor; her stubby tail wagged her entire rear half.

Nick looked round. Having waved his palette at her, he placed two more careful dashes of paint on the canvas, put down brush and palette, and came over to open the window.

"Morning, Eleanor. You've come for Teazle." He handed her out and she enthusiastically licked Eleanor's face. "She's been good company. I might have to get a dog for myself. Any news?"

"Only that the fog's thick right up and down the coast, so they won't be able to start searching yet. I don't know about Kalith Chudasama's condition. Jocelyn's going to ring the hospital later, hoping they'll be willing to give information to her in her semi-official capacity."

"She should have the vicar ring in his official capacity. With her standing at his elbow to remind him what he's asking about. Sorry, I've got to get back to the paint before it starts to dry out. Took me an age to get exactly the right shade."

"I'll see you later. Thanks for having Teazle."

"She's welcome, anytime. By the way, don't let her kid you: She's had breakfast already."

Eleanor laughed. "Thanks. We're off to Boscastle. I know some fishermen there who must know about caves."

She put Teazle down. Usually she'd go snuffling in the blackthorn and gorse beside the path, but now she anxiously stuck to Eleanor's heels. They went upstairs. Eleanor changed into slacks, then they walked up to the car.

The cart wheels — of course! Luckily, someone had got them out of the backseat.

Today, on the drive to Boscastle there were no glimpses of blue sea. As she came down the hill into the village, the bridge and the long low buildings along the stream were invisible. Once fishermen's cottages and net sheds, they now housed gift shops and cafés, as well as the youth hostel. Eleanor hoped Julia and Chaz were all right. Once they were up on the cliffs they'd have a beautiful day for hiking, but the first part of the path would be hard to find.

Luckily, Eleanor didn't have to cross the bridge, as the main part of the village was on the south hillside of the valley. She turned off the main road and found a spot to park, tucked well to the side on a narrow street.

She wanted to talk to one particular person. Now that all she had to do to reach his house was to walk round a couple of corners, she found Jocelyn's warning lingering in her mind. Though she honestly didn't believe she was in any danger, it might be just as well to call first on a few other people who had given her things for LonStar in the past. It would be a sort of camouflage for her real purpose, she hoped.

THIRTEEN

The India Palace was a modest shop-front
restaurant in Camelford's High Street, just
a couple of doors down from the tiny police
house. Megan parked her unmarked car,
not difficult so early in the morning, and
went to pay a courtesy call on the local
constable. A notice on the door announced
that he was already out on patrol. Anyone
in need of assistance was advised to dial
999 in case of emergency; for other information, the Launceston police station number
was provided.

Glad not to have to explain her errand,
Megan walked along to the India Palace. A
CLOSED sign hung crooked between the
spotless glass of the door and the white
blind hiding the interior, with a smaller sign
giving hours of opening. The main window,
to one side, was also covered by a blind.
Gold lettering on window, door, and fascia
announced the name of the business. It was

unlicensed, so the name of the owner did not appear.

A faint smell of exotic spices lingered in the doorway. Megan's mouth watered. Though their menu couldn't compare to the Indian restaurants of London, she had had excellent takeaway from the India Palace. She wasn't sure how her stomach would react to curry for breakfast.

Listening, she heard footsteps inside, and the sound of furniture being moved.

She couldn't see a bell, so she knocked on the glass.

Sudden silence inside, followed by a woman's voice speaking rapidly in a strange language, a shrill reply, and a scurry of feet. Then a large lorry rumbled by behind her — the High Street was also the A39. When it had passed, she was about to knock again when she heard a heavier tread within. The edge of the blind was pulled back and a man's round, brown face stared at her.

She didn't want to announce her identity in tones loud enough to reach him through the glass. A greengrocer was busy setting out his wares on the pavement just across the street, and next door but one, a butcher had come out to gaze in admiringly at his neat display in the window. If they heard that plainclothes police were visiting the

Indians, rumours would fly.

Megan took out her warrant card and pressed it against the glass.

The man read it. He looked alarmed, but that was the normal reaction of any perfectly law-abiding citizen.

He nodded, then fiddled with a chain and the latch. The door opened a few inches. "Yes, officer? What is it?"

"Are you the owner, sir? Or the head of the family?"

Again he nodded. "I am both." These places were all family businesses. "I have the health certificate. We have papers." His English was heavily accented, not like Chudasama's, let alone Dr. Prthnavi's.

"I'm not here about those, sir. I need to talk to you. Routine enquiries."

As always, the formula soothed. He closed the door briefly, took off the chain — pretty pointless with all that glass — and opened the door, moving backwards. The room was a forest of chair legs sticking up from the tabletops; more of a copse, really, as it was a very small restaurant. They must do well with takeaway meals.

"Come in, please. My name Mr. Khan. Is allowed to offer a cup of tea?"

"I'd love one, thank you, Mr. Khan. I haven't had breakfast yet."

Turning, he fired a stream of incomprehensible words at a youth in school uniform who leant against the wall at the back of the room, by the swinging door that presumably led to the kitchen. The boy went out.

"My son." Mr. Khan bustled over to a table for two, lifted one of the upended chairs, and set it down on the floor. He wore a heavy gold ring, with a raised pattern of leaves on the head. "Please, sit."

As Megan stepped across, he took down the other chair, then went to fetch a white tablecloth, which he flipped onto the table with a practised gesture.

"You don't need to put on a cloth for me," Megan protested.

The boy stuck his head back into the room. "Mum says, chai or English?"

"Miss?"

"That's Sergeant. What is chai?" She addressed the question to the son. "I've seen it on menus but never tried it."

"It's tea with milk and spices, Sergeant. Not spicy hot."

"I'd like to try it." In the interests of community relations and a friendly interview, and hoping it wouldn't upset her empty stomach.

He called something back into the kitchen, then said, "Dad, I've got to run or I'll miss

160

the bus."

"All right, Achmed, run, run." Adding something in his own language, Mr. Khan flapped his hands at his son. "In sixth form," he said proudly to Megan, "take A levels. He very good at numbers. Mathematicals, physics. And speak English good, too."

"So do I speak good English, Daddy." A girl of nine or ten came through from the kitchen, carefully carrying a cup and saucer. She set it down in front of Megan, the gold bangles on her slim brown arm jingling. "Here you are, Miss Sergeant. My brother said you're a policeman, but you don't look like one."

Mr. Khan spoke sharply to her. Megan held up her hand to stop him.

"I'm a detective. We mostly don't wear uniforms. Sergeant is my rank, not my name. I'm Detective Sergeant Pencarrow. What's your name?"

"Lily. It's an English name *and* Indian."

"A pretty name. Lily, I need to talk privately to your father. Perhaps you could bring him a cup of . . . chai?" She waved Khan to the other chair.

He nodded at his daughter and sat down gingerly on the edge of the seat. In the short time before Lily came back, Megan tried to

161

frame her first question. Scumble hadn't told her what to ask, a mark of confidence that left her floundering. Usually, before they started an interview, they had more to connect someone to a crime than their race. And this time they weren't even sure a crime — or what crime — had been committed.

Lily returned with a cup for her father and a plate of fried potato chunks, which she set before Megan. "Achmed said you didn't have breakfast, Detective Sergeant Pencarrow, so Mummy made this for you."

"That's very kind of her, but I can't accept —"

"This is not a bribe," Khan said, agitated. "We do nothing bad. No reason for bribe. Potatoes! You can accept potatoes, Miss Detective. Is not business, is what we have for breakfast. Eat, eat!"

Embarrassed, Megan apologised. Lily, hovering anxiously, laid a knife and fork and napkin by the plate. She gave Megan a tentative smile, then scurried out at a word from her father.

Megan took a bite. Tears sprang to her eyes and she felt her face turn scarlet. Mrs. Khan had not made allowances for Western taste buds, reinforcing her husband's statement that this was what the family had for breakfast.

Somehow Megan managed to swallow the mouthful and followed it with a cautious sip of chai — milky and sweet, not spicy hot, as Achmed had promised. It soothed her fiery tongue enough to enable her to speak.

Her prepared words had gone up in metaphorical flames. "Do you know many other Indians in this area?" she blurted out.

He shook his head. "Not many. Hard for wife — she speak only few words of English. Is one family, in Bodmin, in restaurant business, like us. Always busy, like us."

"You don't have any employees?"

"Without, we manage. In middle of Achmed, Lily, I have boy, girl. For dinnertime, they help. *After* homework," he added firmly. "In summertime holidays, wife's nephew come from London to work here."

"You have family in London? How about relatives abroad who'd like to come to work in Britain?"

"They not like to leave India. Achmed call them stay-in-the-mud." He giggled, then looked dismayed. "Is not bad word?"

"*Stick*-in-the-mud. No, not at all. It must be difficult bringing up children in a strange language and culture."

"Culture. Please?"

Megan did her best to explain the word. "You like living here in Cornwall better than London?" she asked. She had the information she'd come for: She was pretty sure he knew nothing of a family being smuggled in — if they existed. But two pieces of potato remained on her plate. By interspersing questions and sips of chai, she had managed to down the rest; she didn't want to insult him by leaving the remainder.

"For us, Cornwall is best. My wife's nephew said, here we are curiosity to wonder at. In London are many people from India, Pakistan. English people think we are too many." He shrugged. "Not so good for business here, maybe. Better for children."

"I expect you're right." She washed down the last of the potato with a final gulp of chai. She pushed back her chair. "Thank you for answering my questions, sir, and for the breakfast. Please give your wife my thanks."

Standing, he bowed. "You are welcome. I hope I help you. Please to come again when not on police business."

"I will," Megan promised. It hadn't been so bad, really. By the last mouthful she'd almost got used to the fiery spuds. All the same, next time she'd make sure to order medium.

She sat in her car and wrote up a report of the interview. She hadn't wanted to alarm Khan by taking notes, but just about every word was still clear in her memory. Then she wondered what to do next.

She hadn't known about the Indian restaurant in Bodmin. It must be in a backstreet. Scumble would certainly have sent her there as well, if he'd been aware of it.

Should she just go there, or ring to ask first? Scumble would probably still be at home and asleep, which would mean talking to the super. She didn't want to do that; for one thing, she wasn't sure how up-to-date he was on the case. However, Bodmin was HQ of its own district, and Scumble had had to take over a case from the incompetent local DI, Pearce, not so long ago. The respective superintendents had not been happy about it.

Best not to trespass on Superintendent Egerton's turf without specific permission from Superintendent Bentinck, she decided.

The situation was too complicated to explain on the car radio, and she didn't want to use all her change on a public phone. The simplest answer led to exactly what she wanted to do anyway: go and see Aunt Nell and make sure she was all right after the travails of the previous day. Her aunt wouldn't mind her using her telephone.

She was already quite close to Port Mabyn. Starting the car, she turned down a side street and was soon winding her way along a narrow lane.

Fog! she remembered suddenly. Aunt Nell's cottage might well be within its perimeter. The vicarage was more likely to be above it. Mrs. Stearns would probably let her ring from there. What was more, the fog gave Megan another excuse for going out of her way. She'd find out just how dense it was so she'd be able to tell the boss whether the infuriating delay was really justified by the conditions.

At the top of the hill, she stopped. From here, the fog looked almost solid enough to walk on.

Leaving the car in the car park, occupied only by a van, a middle-aged Vauxhall, and a newish Jaguar, Megan walked down into the village. She passed the local police station, a cottage where the constable lived — PC Bob Leacock, a friend of her aunt. He was married, she was pretty sure, so even if he was out patrolling, she ought to be able to ring Launceston from there. But first to check on Aunt Nell.

From the vicarage, she could see the

lighted window of the LonStar shop, wreathed in curling mist. Today's volunteers were doubtless doing something useful in the stockroom at the back, in the absence of customers.

The sight reminded her of the skirt that had mysteriously turned up at the hospital last night. She would have to ask Aunt Nell whether it came from the shop and ought to be returned. If so, she would have to get it dry-cleaned, she supposed, another bill to pay. She had to replace the clothes lost in her lifesaving stunt — she hadn't been on duty so she couldn't put them on expenses. And somehow she had to return Julia's polo-neck and pullover.

Apart from the moaning roar of the fog-horn from the lighthouse, the single street was eerily quiet. On the other side, a man in a nautical jacket and yachting cap came out of the newsagent's carrying half a dozen newspapers, and farther down, opposite LonStar, a dowdy woman with a string bag went into the bakery. The people living on the far side of the harbour, unless they were willing to feel their way over the narrow stone bridge, would have to put off their shopping until the fog lifted. In fact, three shops displayed CLOSED signs, the shop keepers no doubt stuck over there, unable to open their premises.

Megan crossed the street. She tried the handle of the side door beside the LonStar shop and wasn't at all surprised when it opened. She would have been more surprised if Aunt Nell had remembered to lock it.

A murmur of voices came from the stockroom at the far end of the passage. Megan went up the stairs and knocked on the door at the top.

No response. She frowned. Even if Aunt Nell was up on the second floor, in the bedroom or bathroom, Teazle should have heard, come running, and barked her head off at the door.

Of course, they might have just popped out to do some shopping. But what if Aunt Nell had been hurt worse yesterday than she thought? Suppose she had managed to get home and now was stuck in bed with a wrenched back, a slipped disc or something of the sort, unable to get downstairs to the telephone to ring for help?

Megan tried the door handle. Amazingly, it was locked. She knocked again, then dug in her shoulder bag for the key Aunt Nell had given her and went in.

The flat had an unoccupied feel, but she called up the stairs. That should have brought at least a yip from Teazle. Megan went to the kitchen window and looked out into the street. A few more people had appeared, but her aunt was not among them.

Aunt Nell must be all right, mustn't she? since she had gone out.

Megan reminded herself that she was on duty. If she rang from here instead of PC Leacock's, perhaps Aunt Nell and Teazle would return before she had to leave.

She dialled the operator and asked for a reverse-charge person-to-person call to Superintendent Bentinck. The duty sergeant said the super was on another line, adding gratuitously that Mr. Bentinck was speaking to the chief constable. That was a conversation not to be interrupted. Before the operator cut them off, Megan managed to squeak in that she'd try again in a few minutes.

If Mrs. Stearns was in charge of the shop today, she would probably know where Aunt Nell had gone. Megan went downstairs and round to the front of the shop. The bell above the door jangled as she entered. A woman she didn't recognise darted through the open door at the back, from the stockroom.

"Can I help you?" she asked. She wore a drab shirtwaister and a cardigan, rather old-fashioned, though she didn't look much older than Megan.

"Is Mrs. Stearns here?"

"No," the woman said sharply, obviously offended. "It's *my* day today."

She must be Mrs. Davies, the Methodist minister's wife, who alternated with Jocelyn Stearns, though Mrs. Stearns was overall manager. Aunt Nell, the most charitable of people, had been known to mutter uncharitable things about Mrs. Davies's propensity for inserting her religion into her work for the strictly secular LonStar. Aunt Nell certainly wouldn't have told her where she was going.

"Sorry to disturb you."

Nick Gresham was a more likely source of information. Megan went next door.

Those few steps down the hill brought her into a heavy mist, and she could barely see the building beyond the gallery. No wonder the Lifeboat people hadn't been able to start a search of the cliffs and coves.

No one was in the gallery itself. Megan would have liked to browse among the pictures, enjoying the local scenes and trying to understand the abstracts without interruption, but she couldn't spare the time. She knocked on the door to the studio behind the shop.

"Just a minute!"

"It's me, Megan. Don't stop whatever you're doing."

"Oh, all right, you'd better come in." Paintbrush in hand, he was scowling ferociously — at the canvas on the easel between them, not at her.

"Wow!" The windowed wall behind him showed impenetrable fog. It filled the room with a pale, diffused light, its eeriness enhanced by the orchestral music coming from Nick's record player.

It came to an end. Nick said, "Would you mind putting it on again at the beginning?" He remained intent on his painting.

Megan went over to the stereo, lifted the arm, and set it gently back at the beginning. Even to her uneducated ear, the music evoked the sea, the smooth swell and ebb of endlessly rolling waves. Though she loved the sea, it was definitely spooky. It sent shivers down her spine. Though that could have been because the room was decidedly chilly.

Turning away, she caught a glimpse of his picture in progress, which was equally eerie. "What is it?"

"*The Isle of the Dead.* Rachmaninoff."

"Oh yes, I remember you talking about it."

"I've got to catch this light. The fog's suddenly crept up and it may go away any

171

minute. Don't distract me. I hope you haven't come to bug me with official questions?"

"No, to thank you for pulling me out yesterday. And wondering if you know where Aunt Nell is."

"She said something about going to Boscastle to ask fishermen about caves."

"What? Why didn't you stop her?"

"She's an adult, Megan. I couldn't stop her if I wanted to."

"She's a little old lady! And she could be running into danger!"

"I doubt it, but why don't you go after her, if you're worried. Boscastle's not very big, and everyone in the village probably knows her. Someone will tell you which house she's visiting."

"When did she leave?"

He shrugged. "I've no idea. Half an hour? An hour? Hour and a half maybe."

"You're hopeless! You could at least have gone with her."

"I've got work to do." Nick turned back to his canvas.

"Bloody irresponsible!" Megan stormed out.

FOURTEEN

What Eleanor hadn't reckoned on was that news of the rescue of a drowning man had spread. She should have expected it. Mr. Wharton, the manager of the Wellington Hotel, and the housekeeper, Mrs. Jellicoe, had no reason not to talk about the unusual events of the previous day. Eleanor's dramatic entrance into the foyer, her still more dramatic call to emergency services, and the patching up of her minor injuries were inevitable fodder for gossip.

In cottage after cottage, she was invited into the kitchen for a cup of tea, with a bowl of water provided for Teazle. As she'd hoped, the husbands and sons who were fishermen were home, unable to go to sea, hanging about waiting for opening time. If the vicar's wife had been with her, the visitors would have been ushered into the rarely used front parlour and the men would have made themselves scarce.

Polite queries as to Eleanor's general health and well-being led to hopes that she had recovered from yesterday's shock and thence to wondering about what exactly had happened.

After the second house, she declined the tea, but she repeated such details as she was able. Her listeners were disappointed that she couldn't give an eyewitness account of her niece's dramatic plunge into the billowing wave, not having been present. She had a feeling they would have liked her to make it up.

No one was aware that the man Megan had rescued was an Indian. Scumble had apparently succeeded in suppressing the fact. Eleanor didn't know why he wanted it kept quiet, but it suited her. When she was asked about his identity, she just said he had been unconscious and unable to talk.

"Must 'a' bin a furriner," was the unanimous opinion, but by "foreigner" they meant not a Cornishman.

Only foreigners went sea bathing for pleasure and none but a great "gaupus" would choose Rocky Valley for a swim. Not that any of them had ever been there — hardworking people did not walk for pleasure, either, and taking a fishing boat into so narrow an inlet would be begging for trouble.

"It's dangerous all along the cliffs round Bossiney Cove, isn't it?" Eleanor asked ingenuously.

Sage heads nodded, but not until she reached the Hawkers' house did her hint lead any further.

"Them cliffs, thet wurr where the Old Squire did his bit o' wrecking," quavered an ancient mariner seated in a rocking chair in the corner. His eyes were filmy with age, his hands knobbed with rheumatics.

"Now, Father," said the lady of the house, a foreigner herself to judge from her speech, "the Old Squire died afore you was born."

"Yas." The wobbly head nodded. "An' didn't me granfer work for un? The stories un told we! It warn't just the wrecking. Seems like there warn't a business he didn't own. Mining, quarrying, shipbuilding, buying and selling — farm stuff and ship stuff, and stuff that hadn't paid no duty. An' the women! Never married but that fond o' women un were."

"Father! That's enough. Your granfer hadn't ought to've talked like that to children."

Assuming she was objecting to the women rather than the avoidance of duty, Eleanor pressed on with the subject that interested her. "He was in league with the smugglers,

175

was he?" she asked. "The squire, I mean."

The old man cackled. "Waren't nothing going on hereabouts wi'out his say-so."

"The caves must have been useful for hiding contraband till it was safe to bring it ashore. From the cliff walks, you can see quite a few caves."

"Yas, but 'tain't the ones you can see as they used. Stands to reason, if you can see 'em, so can the revenuers. There's a couple or three you'd never find wi'out summun showed you. Granfer used to take us seal hunting —"

"Seal hunting!"

"Waren't much in the way o' smuggling b'then. O' course, smuggling or hunting, you wouldn't want to take a boat to them caves lessn it were dead calm and slack o' the tide, but Granfer reckoned it were worth the risk. Sealskins and oil brought in a fair bit in them days. The seals sleep in the caves, see. You go in with a bright light and take 'em by surprise." He rambled on about the bloody details, his voice sinking to a mumble as his daughter-in-law scolded him.

Eleanor realised she wasn't going to get precise information from him about the location of the hidden caves. She turned to his son, who was sitting warming his hands on his mug of tea, one eye on the clock.

"Did he ever take you, Mr. Hawker?"

He shook his head. "Not much call for seal oil these days! Nor much in the way of smuggling neither, and what there is, it's drugs, which is what I don't hold with."

"I should hope not!" said Mrs. Hawker. "Funny you should ask, though, Mrs. Trewynn. Didn't you say, Jack, there was a bloke yesterday, poking about down the harbour, asking about smuggling?"

"That's right. He were hanging about when we come in wi' the catch. Odd sort of bloke."

"Odd?" Eleanor queried. "In what way?"

"I dunno." He scratched his chin thoughtfully. "It's usually emmets wanting to know about the old days, or summun writing a book, or a copper's nark — you can tell them a mile off. But this bloke, he was tearing along, too hurrysome to wait for answers."

Trying to rush a Cornish fisherman was a mug's game, Eleanor knew. He needed time to consider what he was going to say, whether the subject was smuggling or merely the weather.

The weather — "How long do you think the fog will last?"

"Might stay put a day or two or three. Might come creeping ashore later. Might

177

disappear with the ebb o' the tide. What we need is a nice sou'westerly to blow it away. I got lobster pots out there need tending." He pushed back his chair and stood up. "You'll excuse me, Mrs. Trewynn, I'm meeting me buddies at the Napoleon for a game o' darts."

"I must be going, too." Eleanor got up. She turned to thank old Mr. Hawker for his stories, only to find him fast asleep, still rocking gently.

Mrs. Hawker found a little something for the LonStar shop — salt and pepper shakers in the form of monkeys dressed as clowns. "A present from my sister-in-law. Fair turns my stomach those two sitting on the table staring at me. But summun'll like 'em, I don't doubt. I'll just wrap 'em in a bit o' newspaper for you."

The garish clowns were added to the bits and bobs in Eleanor's basket. She hurried round the corner to the house that was her main target, hoping she wouldn't find Abel Tregeddle already departed for the Napoleon Inn. She hadn't wasted her time, though. She knew now that there were indeed concealed caves in Bossiney Cove. With that information she might be able to pry the location from Abel.

He had told her a certain amount of

smuggling still went on in Boscastle. He was a chatty man and had probably said more than he intended. The cagey way he had then shut up on the subject had suggested to her that he was involved. He must surely be familiar with the caves. Whether he'd be willing to tell her was another matter.

He'd certainly be curious about her reason for asking.

Eleanor tried to work out how little of the story she'd need to tell him. Not everything, she decided, but enough to upset Mr. Scumble. Too bad. She was quite willing to risk his wrath to do anything that might help the lifeboat men find those poor people quicker.

The Tregeddles' cottage opened directly onto the narrow street. A large grey cat was asleep in the sun on the slate window-sill, its tail hanging down. The tip twitched. Teazle was usually very good with cats, but this was too much for her.

Barking, she reared up against the wall, dancing on her back legs. The cat whisked its tail away just in time and stood up, back arched, hissing and spitting. Naturally this incited Teazle to further frenzy.

As Eleanor pulled her away, the front door swung open.

"What the . . . !?" The small, wiry, weatherbeaten man recognised Eleanor. "Oh, it's you, Mrs. Trewynn. Sounded like there was an Alsatian going for our Smoky. Quite a voice your little un's got, hasn't she?" He bent down and scratched under Teazle's chin. By now the Westie's rear end was wagging madly, while the cat was already apparently asleep, his tail carefully tucked up under his chin.

"I'm sorry. It was very naughty of her."

"No harm done. Out collecting, are you?" He peered into her basket. "Looks like you're doing nicely. Come in, come in. The wife was saying just now she has summat or other for your shop and she hoped you'd drop in soon."

Eleanor hesitated. He had his cap in his hand, apparently on the point of going out, and he was the one she really wanted to talk to. But as he waved her in, Teazle accepted the invitation, dragging on the lead. Taken by surprise, Eleanor followed. Abel Tregeddle shut the front door and came after them.

Naturally, Teazle headed straight to the kitchen. The door was open and she trotted in, Eleanor in tow. Mrs. Tregeddle, a stout woman busy at the kitchen table, looked round at the click of toenails on the lino.

"Mrs. Trewynn, how nice to see you. Set

180

yourself down, do." She tossed a scrap of the meat she was chopping to Teazle. "We bin dying to hear what happened yest'day."

"I told Mrs. Trewynn as you got summat for her shop," Abel chided.

"I 'spect I can find something. You'll have a cuppa, Mrs. Trewynn." She filled the kettle at the sink and set it on the gas.

Eleanor was still sloshing about inside from the tea she'd already drunk, but Abel was more likely to stay and chat with a cup in his hand, she thought, so she accepted. Too late, she realised that having invented a donation to inveigle her in, he wasn't likely to leave before hearing about the rescue. Resigning herself to further liquid intake, she recounted the story again, her own minor part and what the others had told her.

All the talking was giving her a dry throat. When the tea was made, she sipped it gladly.

As before, she omitted the young man's race. She stressed the drama of Megan risking her life to save a stranger. "It's a beautiful spot, but dangerous. Do you know it, Mr. Tregeddle?"

"Yas," Abel admitted. "Took a boat in once, when I were a young duffer. But it's risky even at high tide in a calm sea. No use setting pots if you can't be sure when you'll be able to check 'em."

"A funny place to go for a swim," said his wife, "but these young lads'll do anything for a bit of a thrill. In a bad way, was he?"

"He was still unconscious when the ambulance took him away. But I heard later that he came round, just briefly, and he said something rather odd."

As one, the Tregeddles leant forward eagerly. "What'd he say, then?" asked Abel.

"He said his family were stranded in a cave. What no one can work out is how they reached the cave in the first place, and if they could get in, why can't they get out?"

"That's easy. Went in by boat, climbed out to explore, didn't tie it up secure. Landlubbers in a hired boat, could be. First thing a seaman learns is to be sure of his knots."

"Oh, yes, that might explain it. The awful thing is that the lifeboat won't be able to go looking for them because of the fog."

"Whereabout is this cave supposed to be?" he asked warily.

"The boy couldn't explain. It must be somewhere in Bossiney Cove, don't you think? He couldn't have survived a swim from farther away."

"Likely not."

"There are lots of caves. If they have to search all of them, I hate to think what condition the family will be in by the time they're found — if they're found. I've been told there are hidden caves, used by smugglers. I remember you saying, Mr. Tregeddle, there's still some smuggling going on."

"That's as may be."

"Suppose they chanced to come across one of the smugglers' caves, and that's where they're stuck? That could be why no one has seen or heard them. They might never be found."

Mrs. Tregeddle was aghast. "Oh, Abel, the whole family dead!"

Abel's lips set in a thin line.

Eleanor played what she hoped was her ace in the hole. "The boy said his mother is dying. Even if he was exaggerating, even if they find them in the end, any unnecessary delay —"

"Abel, his mam! You can't . . ." She faltered as her husband glowered at her.

"My niece risked her life." Eleanor spoke quietly. He met her eyes, and she held his gaze. "What would you risk? Information given to me in confidence would be passed to the authorities without any mention of where it came from." She paused. He looked down sulkily at the table, his weathered cheeks flushing. "What would you have to

lose? A couple of convenient hiding places.
Against several lives."

FIFTEEN

Megan was late picking up DI Scumble.

"Where the hell you been, Pencarrow?"

For once the question was justified. Megan, having learnt from experience to turn the car in the narrow lane outside his house before announcing her arrival, had no excuse to delay answering.

"In Bodmin, sir."

"Bodmin! Am I going to have to explain to Mr. Bentinck why he's getting a complaint about trespassing from Egerton?"

"I hope not, sir," Megan said cautiously.

"You got permission? From DI Pearce?" "Scepticism" was too mild a term for his tone.

"Well, not exactly. I didn't think he'd be likely to give it. And I was in a hurry, because of picking you up, sir."

He sighed heavily. "All right, explain."

"I went to Camelford first, of course. I'm convinced the people at the restaurant there

185

don't know anything."

"A good detective is never convinced without incontrovertible evidence."

Megan bit her lip. "I'm pretty sure."

"That'll do to be going on with. I'll withhold judgment till I read your report."

"I asked whether they knew any other Indians locally. I think — I hope — I managed to make it sound like casual chitchat."

"Hmm."

"Mr. Khan mentioned a family running an Indian restaurant in Bodmin. I had no idea there was one. I tried ringing the super — Superintendent Bentinck, that is, not Egerton — but he was busy. It seemed to me important to get to them right away, so I went."

"As you're not too worried about repercussions, I take it you're convinced they know nothing that requires further investigation."

"I'm pretty sure, sir."

"You were lucky. If we'd had to pull them in for further questioning, you'd have been knee-deep in the sh . . . soup. Not but what we still may be," he added gloomily, "if you're wrong about them. Anything else I need to know about?"

"Well . . . From Camelford, as I was so close to the coast, I went over there to look at the fog. It really is incredibly thick, sir. From the LonStar shop, you could hardly see the gallery next door, let alone the bridge and the harbour."

From the corner of her eye she could see the scowl he aimed at her. She concentrated on slipping the car in front of an ancient lorry chugging round the roundabout towards them. As a distraction, it didn't work for long.

"Port Mabyn," he said in a long-suffering voice.

"It's the closest point on the coast to Camelford, sir."

"I daresay. So, how is Auntie doing today?"

"I don't know, sir. At least, I suppose she must have recovered okay, because she apparently went to Boscastle looking for smugglers."

"She *what*?" Scumble exploded.

"That's what I was told."

"Who by?"

"Gresham."

"Oh, him. Did you check with Mrs. Stearns?"

"No, sir." She'd nearly gone straight after Aunt Nell, until she realised what the time was. Aunt Nell couldn't really come to any harm. Everyone knew her . . . "I was in a hurry to get to Bodmin and back to pick you up."

"Late," he grumbled, coming full circle.

Megan dropped him off in front of the nick, in the Market Square (actually a triangle), and parked the car in the police lot behind St. Mary Magdalene.

"How many dents? Scratches?" asked Sergeant Orton, the mechanic in charge. "Does it need petrol?"

"None; and I didn't look at the gauge."

"Women drivers!"

"But it shouldn't, if it was full when I took it out." As all cars were supposed to be, because of the size of the rural district. So he had to fill it what ever the gauge said. Megan wasn't sure who had won that round.

She no longer took his jibes personally, but it was still a running battle every time she encountered him.

Walking round the church, she marvelled, as always, at the intricate carving that covered almost the entire exterior. People had been admiring it for half a millennium, and there was something very soothing about the fact. Cops and criminals came and went, but Cornish granite endured.

Unfortunately, the coast near Rocky Valley was not granite. Megan wasn't exactly sure what it was; doubtless Julia or Chaz could tell her. Slate, probably, like the valley itself — comparatively soft, holed and hollowed and split by pounding waves, always changing as arches collapsed, huge boulders tumbled before the force of winter storms, windblown rain ate away at sheer cliff faces. Did anyone really know where all the caves were?

They were hunting for only one particular cave, though, and someone knew where it was, or the family could not have been taken there. Perhaps Aunt Nell had the right idea, searching out someone familiar with the secret caves used by smugglers, past or present.

When Megan entered the station, the desk sergeant told her DI Scumble had been called in to see Superintendent Bentinck. She went up to the office and started typing up her report of the interviews in Camelford and Bodmin. Though she wasn't an expert typist by any means, at least she'd learnt to touch-type, unlike the poor sods who used two-fingered hunt-and-peck for their reports. She had finished one and started on the second by the time the inspector came in.

He was not happy, that much was obvious at a glance. Megan, having already been

189

bawled out for going to Bodmin, expected to be bawled out for getting caught going to Bodmin. She wondered who on earth had seen and recognised her.

But Scumble stalked across to his desk without a word and slumped exhaustedly into his chair.

"What's up, sir?"

"While I was gone, the super reported to the chief constable, who talked to London — damned if I know which department! The Home Office or Immigration, I suppose. He says the powers that be think it's all a load of codswallop. They won't act on the vague word of a half-conscious concussion patient."

"Chudasama wasn't half conscious," Megan said indignantly, thumping the desk. "Not when he spoke."

"But he was vague, incoherent, and you were the only witness."

"I'm a police officer!"

"I don't think they're doubting your word, Pencarrow, just your interpretation. Anyway, if there's any policing aspect to this business, it's in our lap."

"What about the Coast Guard? Don't they have immigration responsibilities?"

"Not really, these days. Pretty much search and rescue. I told you their watch officer in Falmouth notified the RNLI. They can send out a helicopter if necessary, but there's not another bloody thing they can do until those people are found."

"The fog might not lift for hours. Or days. The Padstow boat can't stay out there indefinitely."

"As long as there are lives in danger . . . If only we had any sort of proof that lives are in danger! The lifeboats are manned by volunteers, remember. They have livings to earn."

"But the old woman's dying! The whole family will die!"

"Kalith Chudasama's mother is not necessarily an old woman," Scumble pointed out harshly. "He's not much more than a boy, you said. She could be in her thirties. There may well be young children in that cave." Megan was startled by his vehemence. "So use your brains, Pencarrow! We can't just sit and wait."

"Don't you think it might be worth following up my aunt's idea?" she said hesitantly.

"Chasing smugglers!" he scoffed. "Needle in a haystack in this part of the world."

"Well, *someone* must know, and if we could suggest to the lifeboat people the best places to start looking —" The phone rang, and Scumble gestured to her to pick it up.

"Pencarrow."

"Mrs. Trewynn's here," announced the duty sergeant, "to see DI Scumble." She could hear the grin in his voice. Everyone knew about Aunt Nell, and Megan came in for a certain amount of teasing, but at least her aunt had never before invaded her workplace. "And the little dog."

"You're having me on."

"What is it?" Scumble asked impatiently.

Megan covered the receiver. "He says my aunt's here, sir, asking for you."

"What the devil . . . ?"

"I'm sorry, I can only suppose she —"

"Send her up. Maybe she's found her smuggler."

"Sir, I —"

"I'm not going to bite her head off."

"No, sir. Send her up, please," she said into the phone.

On the way from Boscastle to Launceston police headquarters, Eleanor had carefully marshalled her arguments for having to see Mr. Scumble at once, busy as he must be with a complicated case. Determined to pass on her news directly to him, she announced her name and errand with uncharacteristic belligerence.

192

"Mrs. Trewynn from Port Mabyn?" The stout, avuncular desk sergeant beamed at her. "Half a tick, madam." He pressed a couple of buttons on his telephone and spoke into it. After listening for a moment, he said, "Right away, Sergeant," and hung up. "The inspector says to go right up, madam."

He seemed surprised that she didn't know the way to Scumble's room. Obviously, she was notorious for her previous forays into the DI's investigations, and he assumed she had been here before.

However, their clashes had always taken place elsewhere, on neutral ground or on her own territory. Now Scumble was in his own element. He ought to be glad to receive her information, but Eleanor considered it inevitable that he'd dig up a reason to be irritated with her.

The sergeant called a constable to escort her. He looked very young without his helmet. "Can you manage the stairs, madam?" he asked solicitously.

Eleanor, still feeling slightly belligerent, almost gave him a frosty look. She caught herself in time. It wasn't his fault she always came to blows with Scumble. "Yes, thank you," she said, and just to show him she practically ran up, Teazle bouncing up a step behind.

He ushered her into a dingy room. Two desks faced each other across the scratched beige lino. Behind one, Scumble was rising to his feet. From the second, Megan came towards her.

"Good morning, Inspector. Unless it's afternoon. I must have left my watch at Jocelyn's." She remembered just in time not to greet Megan with a hug when she was on duty, though she couldn't resist a peck on the cheek. "Hello, dear. I've brought you some useful information, I hope."

Reaching into her bag, she went over to Scumble's desk and placed on it her 2 1/2-inch Ordnance Survey map (the secret of her ability to find secluded farm houses and cottages).

"Well, well, well, what have we here?" He unfolded it and turned it so that he had the southern edge.

Eleanor leant across the desk, her finger hovering indecisively as she tried to decipher the map upside down. "Here. That's Lye Rock, so this is Bossiney Cove, and here's Rocky Valley. My informant told me how to find three hidden caves once used for smuggling."

"Three! Who's your informant?"

She shook her head. "I can't tell you that. I promised."

"Come on, he's probably leading us on a wild-goose chase. I'll have to judge for myself how reliable hc is before I go making a fool of myself sending a lifeboat to investigate nonexistent caves."

"I'm not going to break my promise, Mr. Scumble. I believe he was telling the truth. He wasn't keen to, but his wife and I, between us, persuaded him. You'll just have to trust my judgment."

"Sir." Megan came to join thcm after having a word with the constable at the door. "Twitchell says the weather forecast reports breezy conditions on the way as a front moves in. The fog's expected to begin breaking up."

"When?"

"This afternoon. They're never more precise than that."

"True. All right, Mrs. Trewynn, for the moment I haven't got time to run over to Boscastle to interview your smuggler. Where are these caves?"

"And how are they hidden?" Megan asked. "I mean —"

"Good question, Pencarrow. What exactly does 'hidden' mean?"

"They're all different. You see where I've

drawn arrows on the map? This one, in the . . ." She paused to work out the upside-down map. "At the north end of the cove. These offshore rocks, the Saddle Rocks, make the water between them and the cliff turbulent, so no one goes there. There's a channel, though, deep enough for a row-boat, which can be found with sounding poles, but it's feasible only at slack tide."

"Slack tide?" Scumble said blankly.

"It's a period on either side of high or low tide, sir. Currents are less dangerous, or even die away altogether, I think."

"Dammit, I forgot the tide might be a factor. Do we know what it's doing?"

"Yesterday afternoon," said Megan, "mid afternoon, when we were in Rocky Valley, it was low tide. So today it'll be about three quarters of an hour later."

"That's good news, isn't it? If the fog dissipates in time. Go on, Mrs. Trewynn."

"Once you're in close, behind the Saddle Rocks, you can see that they have another member, so to speak. From a distance it looks like part of the cliff, but there's water between, and tucked in behind it is a cave."

"So it's invisible from offshore," said Scumble. "No revenuers spotting the cave and looking for loot. And no standing in the

196

cave mouth, waving at passing fishing boats."

"Then this one . . ." She pointed to the middle arrow.

"I'll believe it's similar. Don't waste time explaining it to me. You need to talk to the RNLI skippers. Pencarrow, you've got their phone numbers?"

"Yes, sir." Megan returned to her desk.

"But it isn't really similar. I don't think I can describe the location well enough over the phone," Eleanor protested. "Not this one, especially. I need to show exactly where it is on the map."

Scumble stared at the map for a moment. "All right, I can see that. We'll have to send you and your map to Port Isaac. Give me those phone numbers, Pencarrow. I'll ring and explain, and tell them you're on your way. Take a panda and use the siren if you need to. Enough time's been wasted already. You and Auntie get going!"

SIXTEEN

Reluctantly, Eleanor left the Incorruptible in Launceston. With great aplomb, Teazle hopped into the backseat of a police car. Eleanor sat in the front beside Megan.

She didn't speak until they were clear of the town traffic. Then she said, "I was sure he'd pooh-pooh my caves. He seemed angry, but not with me."

"No, not with you, Aunt Nell. With the situation. In taking Chudasama's words seriously, he's put his credibility on the line, and he's furious with the top brass who don't see the urgency as he does."

"Which top brass? Your superintendent?"

"Higher than that, sounds like. He didn't tell me exactly what Mr. Bentinck said to him, but he — the super — had been on the phone with the CC —"

"CC?"

"Chief Constable. CaRaDoC's top copper. I don't think he was the difficulty. The

198

CC talked to London — someone in the government, don't ask me exactly who — but they just don't really believe what Kalith Chudasama told me."

"The RNLI is nothing to do with the government, though."

"No, thank God. They're all volunteers, supported by donations, though they do work with the Coast Guard. The thing is, if the situation is the way we've worked it out, whoever left these people committed more than one crime, first in smuggling them into the country and then in abandoning them. The second part may amount to murder."

"If Kalith or his mother dies . . ."

"Well, murder's our business, but the immigration stuff isn't really. I think, with all the ramifications, the boss would like to have a bit of support from officialdom."

"Considering how keen the Home Office is to keep Britain white," Eleanor said bitterly, "I'd have thought they'd be eager to find out what's going on."

"You'd think so. Who knows what the politicians are up to? I suppose it's within reason that they won't act on a few words from a half-conscious man. If only there weren't lives at stake! What's really upsetting Scumble, though, is the idea that there are very likely children in danger."

"Children! I didn't know he had any particular interest in children."

"Nor did I. In fact I assumed he didn't, because he doesn't have any. Aunt Nell, are you sorry you never had kids?"

Eleanor thought carefully before answering. Megan was thirty — or thirty-one, she never could keep track — and unmarried, with no regular boyfriend. The question was fraught with implications. Her response had to be honest yet noncommittal.

"I won't pretend I've never had regrets. I certainly didn't set out in life intending not to have children. As you know, Peter and I were constantly on the move, often in different directions."

"I've still got every postcard you ever sent me."

"Have you really? You see, starting a family would have meant choosing between settling down, leaving important work we were good at, or abandoning them to nannies and boarding schools. Or, to be honest, giving up the job myself and hardly ever seeing Peter. I suppose, in fact, we were always too busy to actually make that decision, always looking ahead to the next disaster."

"There's always a disaster going on somewhere, isn't there."

"So it seems, both natural and man-made.

As it is, there are children all over the world who might perhaps not have survived if we'd not been there to help."

"Have you been happy? Apart from what happened to Uncle Peter, I mean."

Peter had been killed in Indonesia, not long before they would have been able to retire together. "Of course I've had sad times. No life always runs smoothly. But I've come to the conclusion that happiness is more a matter of attitude than anything else. I've known people in mansions who were miserable and people in huts who were happy. It's certainly not a matter of whether you have children or not. Children bring both joy and sorrow."

Unexpectedly, Megan laughed. "Too true. According to Mum, I'm ruining her life, both by being a copper and by not marrying and having kids. So far. But if her child's making her miserable, why is she so desperate for me to follow her bad example? I wish you'd talk to her, Aunt Nell."

"I would if I thought it might help, dear, but love and logic don't mix. If the subject arises, I'll do what I can."

"Oh well." After a moment's silence, she reverted to their present task. "Well, here we are running to salvage a corner of another man-made disaster. The Africans throw the Indians out. The English refuse to let them in. People with attitudes like Chaz make me sick."

"He's repeating what he's been told. Unfortunately, prejudice and logic don't mix well, either. At least the lifeboat people are willing to rush to the rescue regardless."

"I don't know whether anyone's actually told them they're looking for Indians, but I don't think it'd make any difference. They turn out for shipwrecks, and quite a few British cargo ships have dark-skinned seamen. I remember seeing them coming ashore in Falmouth when I was a child."

"Lascars. True."

"So the idea of rescuing Indians won't come as a shock. And we have a much better chance of finding the Chudasamas in time with your map."

"I hope so. I do hope they really are in Bossiney Cove."

"The boss seems to think so, and he's the one who talked to the Coast Guard and the RNLI. The lifeboat crewmen would have the best knowledge of currents within the cove, wouldn't they? Them and your smuggler friend. Aunt Nell, he didn't have anything to do with stranding them, did he? Because if so, you *can't* go on protecting him!"

"Of course not, dear. I'm sure all he's involved in is an occasional foray across the Channel to Brittany to bring back duty-free cigarettes and brandy. He may well have relatives there. There's a long history, after all."

"Yes, I read about it. Wrecking, too."

"Another of the men I talked to went on about the 'Old Squire,' who sounds like a dreadful character."

"In Boscastle? A century or so ago? That's what the villagers called the villain I read about. Did he own a prosperous shop, general merchandise, where he sold the proceeds of the smuggling and wrecking? Something like that."

"So I was told. One of the men I talked to said his grandfather — or great-grandfather — worked for the Old Squire as a carpenter. He was a shipbuilder, too."

"A dangerous man to cross, and he scattered bastards all over the countryside."

"That was mentioned, or at least that he was a ladies' man."

Megan frowned. "I wish I could remember his name. I have a feeling . . . No, I've lost it. Did your chap say anything else useful?"

"I don't know about useful, but he and a couple of the other fishermen I talked to mentioned a stranger hanging about the harbour yesterday asking questions about smuggling. A foreigner, but you know how they use that word."

"Not from this part of Cornwall," Megan said with a grin. "May come from as far away as Bodmin, or even Truro. I'd have thought tourists often ask about smuggling."

"Yes, but about the old days. Apparently yesterday's man wanted to know about present-day smuggling, though I don't think he came out and asked directly."

"I expect they misunderstood him."

"Could be. They didn't think he was a copper's nark, which I presume covers Customs and Excise men, as well. One said he was oddly dressed, but when I asked how, he could only say he looked like a businessman trying to disguise himself as a seaman! Come to think of it, he could have been the man in the suit and reefer jacket who so rudely refused to let me use the phone box, even when I told him it was an emergency."

"What? I haven't heard about that, Aunt Nell."

"He was the reason I had to go into the hotel, the Wellington, all dirty and dripping with blood. The manager was horrified, poor little man. Not at all what he was used to in his guests. But when he understood the situation, he came round nicely." Eleanor told Megan about the kindly housekeeper. "You looked quite a mess, too," she went on, "when Mr. Scumble just about shoved you into the ambulance. They took care of you at the hospital?"

"The ambulance men cleaned me up and plastered me, and lent me a blanket so I was semidecent to walk into the hospital. Which reminds me, I've got to return Julia's clothes."

"I'm sure she won't mind waiting till it's convenient. A nice girl. Oh dear, the fog looks as thick as ever!"

They had reached the top of the hill down into Port Isaac. Here, too, the haunting wail of a foghorn could be heard.

The village was very similar to Port Mabyn and Boscastle, somewhat larger than either. However, the harbour faced north, rather than west into the teeth of prevailing gales, and the harbour entrance was comparatively wide and straight. These advantages explained why it had an RNLI station and the other two did not.

By the time they were halfway down the hill, Eleanor could see that the fog was in fact thinning. Dense patches loomed like ghostly monsters, yet here and there the sun shone through to glisten on the damp roadway. When Megan stopped the panda on the hard by the lifeboat house and slipway, the salty, seaweedy air wafted in through the open windows, stirred by its own motion, not the motion of the vehicle. The promised breeze was arriving, taking its own sweet time.

A number of small boats moored in the harbour were tilting sideways as the ebbing tide abandoned them. The orange-and-black inflatable lifeboat, wreathed in swirls of mist, had already been dragged down on its trolley over the muddy sand to the edge of the water. A man in overalls and high rubber boots was examining the outboard engine. Another similarly clad stood near him, chatting. A third man, dressed in a yellow oilskin jacket, orange lifejacket, and what looked like black tights disappearing into yellow wellies, came out of the lifeboat house and walked towards the police car.

"Stay there, Aunt Nell, while I find out what's going on."

"Yes, Sergeant."

"Sorry." Megan smiled. "Please!"

"I'll stay."

The approaching man held out his hand. "DS Pencarrow?"

Megan shook it. "You're the captain?"

"Technically, the coxswain, but yes, I'm in

charge on board. 'Skipper' is what most call me. I'm a bank manager in everyday life. Larkin is the name. Pete."

"Oh yes, I had a word with you on the phone earlier. DI Scumble has explained matters to you . . . Skipper?" After a slight hesitation, Megan settled on the informal rank.

"Yes. You've brought the map?"

"My aunt has it." Megan, slightly flushed, gestured at the car.

Eleanor decided it was time to make her appearance. She rather wished she wasn't wearing slacks. In view of her age, they detracted from her dignity, she felt. As she stepped out of the car, map in hand, Teazle bounded between the front seats and jumped out after her. Eleanor grabbed for the lead and her last shred of dignity vanished.

She could only hope the lack wouldn't prejudice the coxswain against the information she had obtained in such an unorthodox manner.

Megan introduced Eleanor and Teazle. Larkin stooped to scratch between the dog's ears. She wagged madly.

"I've got a Newfoundland. This little girl's about the size of his head. Come on in, Mrs. Trewynn, Sergeant, and let's spread that map of yours on the chart table."

Eleanor had her Ordnance Survey map folded to display the correct section. She found it difficult to reconcile it with the much-larger-scale nautical chart. The chart confused her with its multiplicity of lines and numbers indicating the depth of the sea, hazards to navigation, currents, high-water mark, and low-water mark where hers was plain blue; and nothing but the odd landmark where hers showed towns, villages, farms, roads, and footpaths, in varying shades of green and brown.

Even the margin between land and sea was much more complicated on the chart. Once Larkin had pointed out Lye Rock and the Saddle Rocks on both, she began to orientate herself.

"Oh, I see. That's Bossiney Haven, and that must be — Yes, there's Rocky Valley, where we found him."

"That's right. I hear you pulled him out, Sergeant?"

"With help. And the sea was calm."

"All the same, a nasty spot, that inlet. Well done." He turned back to the chart table, picked up Eleanor's map, and peered at the pencilled arrows. "Right, Mrs. Trewynn, what's going on here? DI Scumble said you're going to suggest where we should start looking."

"Yes. You see —"

"Don't bother with explanations for now. I'll ask if I need to know. Just tell me what these signify." He placed a fingertip on each arrow in turn.

"They're all hidden caves. I'm sure Mr. Scumble told you that. The top one — the northernmost one — can't be seen until you're really close." She repeated the description she had given Scumble. "The middle one is half full of water even at the lowest tides. But if you take a boat right to the very back, it turns a corner and slopes upwards. Mr. . . . He said it opens out into quite a big, dry cavern."

"Mr. Anonymous, huh?" Larkin glanced at Megan. "Well, it's none of my business, as long as he's given you a straight tip. And the southern one?"

"It's in the crevasse between Lye Rock and the main headland. The gap is quite narrow — a 'gut,' he called it — and the cave is on the southwest side, facing north-east, so its mouth is almost always in shadow. The gut is sometimes dry, some-times underwater, but there's no reason for anyone ever to go there."

"Except smugglers?" He grinned. "Don't worry, I won't tell tales, not that I know anything to tell. That's the lot, those three?" He pencilled in matching arrows on the chart.

"I got the impression there may be others, but not in Bossiney Cove."

"As I told the inspector, there's general agreement that your chappy is most unlikely to have survived if he entered the water anywhere outside Bossiney Cove. He'd have had to swim or be swept by currents right round Lye Rock, through the dangerous passage between it and the Sisters — these offshore islets here. But he'd be equally unlikely to survive coming into the cove from the north. You got him out at low tide, didn't you?"

"Thereabouts."

"Hmm. The main current flows up the coast with an incoming tide and back down, to the southwest, with the ebb, but there's a couple of hours when it's not sure what it's doing. Sounds as if he went in at the beginning of the slack — sensible, if he was aware of it."

"He must have started out in the cove, then," said Megan, grasping the point though somewhat confused by the currents.

"I'd say so. In any case, what ever the main current's direction, water swirls into the cove and splits up in all directions, dependent on the topography. Which is re-arranged by big storms. The rocks and currents within the cove are so changeable they've never been charted. Boaters are advised to stay clear."

"But you've been there? The lifeboat has, I mean."

"Oh yes! Bossiney Haven has a nice beach at low tide that disappears at high tide. Benoath, too. People explore and don't pay attention. We've had to go in to bring them out. A couple of times, I've seen a lobster-man setting or checking pots there, in calm weather, when I've sailed up that way. I reckon the know-how is passed down from father to son, though I've come by it the hard way."

A man and a young woman hurried in, staring at Eleanor and Megan.

"What's the gen, Skipper?" the man asked.

"Cave rescue. We've got a family, number and condition unknown, reported stuck in a cave, probably in Bossiney Cove."

"Bossiney Cove! A million caves!"

"A family?" said the woman. "Not too many to fit in the *Belinda,* I hope. Nowhere nearby to land them, not where they can be got out easily."

"The Bude inshore is coming and the *Daisy D.* is already there, waiting to pick them up if necessary." The coxswain eyed the woman. A sturdy figure, wearing dungarees and emanating a faint smell of cows, she looked confident and fit for anything.

"I've been heaving bales of hay," she said belligerently, "while Walter's been lounging behind his counter."

Walter opened his mouth to retort.

"Don't say it," the coxswain warned. "All right, Maggie, you've made your point. Get suited up, the two of you."

They collected their kit from a bank of lockers. Maggie disappeared through a door on the far side, the man behind a curtain in one corner. From behind it, he grumbled, "Complicates things having a woman on the crew."

"She pulls her weight, Walter."

"I know, I know."

A couple more men came in.

"What's up, Skipper?" one asked.

"Cave rescue. I've got a crew, Walter and Maggie. You can help with the launch. What's the fog doing?"

"Breaking up fast. The foghorn shut off its bloody racket a couple of minutes ago."

"Good. Get on the radio and tell Falmouth we're on our way, would you, Jerry? Des, see if you can find — Oh, Maggie, that was quick."

"Have to prove I can change as quickly as a bloke, don't I!"

"Good. Now find an outfit to fit Sergeant Pencarrow, here. She can't go in a skirt."

"What!" Megan exclaimed. "I'm not —"

"Didn't your boss warn you?" asked Larkin. "He wants you along with us. Something to do with evidence at the scene of the crime and questioning witnesses? I didn't follow all that."

"The bastard! Sorry, Aunt Nell. No, he did not warn me."

"Perhaps he thought of it after we left," Eleanor said soothingly.

"He could have radioed the car."

"Very inconsiderate of him. Perhaps we were out of range? But of course you'll go, dear. Just leave me the kcys of the car —"

"Aunt Nell, he'd kill me if I let you drive a police car. Ring someone to fetch you."

"Here you go, Sergeant." Maggie handed over a bundle — of what, Eleanor couldn't make out — together with a bright yellow oilskin jacket emblazoned RNLI and a pair of yellow wellingtons. "They shouldn't be too bad a fit. Ever put on a dry suit before? No? I'd better give you a hand. Change in the loo." She pointed at the door she had used. "There's not much room, so you can put the lifejacket on out here. Stick your head out when you've got the woolly bears on and —"

"Woolly bears?"

"Thermal undies. These here. Don't decide you can do without the woolly bears underneath."

"You may think it's a warm day, but it'll be bloody freezing once you get out there," Jerry agreed, hanging up the radio mike.

"Once you've got 'em on, I'll give you a hand with the dry suit."

"Make it nippy, Sergeant! We're ready to launch." The skipper strode out, carrying a helmet, his chart, and Eleanor's map. Walter followed. Megan disappeared into the loo.

"You take care of her, Maggie," said a small, bright-eyed old man in ordinary clothes. He'd kept well out of the way before and Eleanor hadn't noticed him. "I don't hold with taking civilians out."

"She's a copper," Maggie pointed out. "You want to tell the police what they can't do? Ready, Sergeant?" She joined Megan in the loo.

"I'm shore helper," the old man told Eleanor, "ground crew, as you might say. I take care of things here while they're out. On the boats for twenty-five years, I was. Nice little dog." He made encouraging noises at

Teazle, who went to be petted.

In a remarkably short time, Maggie reappeared. Megan followed a moment later, putting on the yellow jacket and walking awkwardly. "Borrowed clothes again," she moaned.

"You'll have to leave your bag, miss. I'll lock it up, never you worry."

"All right, but I must have my notebook." She took it out and handed over the shoulder bag. "It'll fit in this pocket; I hope it's waterproof."

"More or less." He helped her don the lifejacket. "There you go."

"Thanks. And thank heaven it's calm. But just as well I didn't get any lunch, I suppose. Wish me luck, Aunt Nell." Putting on the helmet, she hurried after the others.

"I do, dear," Eleanor called after her. She took her leave of the old man and went out.

With a group of tourists and locals, she and Teazle watched the shore crew haul the *Belinda* into water deep enough to float her shallow draught. She chugged between the quays and out of the harbour. The fog had vanished. In the sunshine, the water glittered like the silvery scales of a giant fish.

Fish. Lunch. She was starving. She decided to ring Jocelyn and see if she was free to pick them up. If not, she'd try Nick. And then she'd go in search of fish and chips, or a pasty, she didn't mind which.

The plight of the stranded family might well include hunger, she thought. She should have suggested that the skipper take supplies. But probably the larger Padstow boat would have food aboard. Boat or ship? She had no idea how big the *Daisy D.* was, not that she had any idea how big a vessel had to be to count as a ship. It was, she gathered, big enough to take more people on board than the *Belinda.* That was all that mattered.

She wished there was something she could do to help, but even if she'd managed to persuade them to take her, she and Teazle would only have been in the way.

She went to find a phone box. This time her call was not urgent, so naturally no one was occupying the box. Picking up Teazle, who always refused to enter the small, enclosed space on her own feet, she opened the door.

As it swung closed behind her, she found herself muttering, "Ship. Ships."

Teazle licked her cheek. "Chips" was one of her favourite words. Putting the dog down, wiping her face, saying, "All right, fish and chips for lunch," Eleanor lost the tenuous thread of thought that had resulted in her mutter.

She was sure it had been important.

SEVENTEEN

"Jocelyn, it's —"

"Eleanor! I've been so worried about you. I thought Nicholas was going with you, but he didn't know where you'd got to. He was quite rude when I rang him. He said Megan had been round to pester him —"

"It's all right, I've seen Megan. And Inspector Scumble. I haven't got enough change to explain just now. I'm in a phone box in Port Isaac, and —"

"Port Isaac! What on earth — ? No, tell me later. Eleanor, I've had an idea. Something Timothy said . . . Are you coming home now?"

"No car. Could you possibly come and pick us up? No rush."

"I'll be there in twenty minutes."

"Thanks, Joce. We'll find somewhere to sit near the harbour."

"I'll find you. I'm on my way." Jocelyn rang off before Eleanor could ask her whether she had phoned the Plymouth hospital for news of Kalith Chudasama's condition.

With a newspaper-wrapped bundle of cod and chips, Eleanor found a seat on a bench overlooking the harbour. Teazle sat directly in front of her, a mesmeric gaze fixed on the paper and its contents.

The only other occupant of the bench was a wrinkled, weathered ancient. He looked as old as the elder Mr. Hawker, but he had all his marbles. He exchanged a nod of greeting with Eleanor when she arrived, bright blue eyes assessing her, then he returned his attention to the harbour. Most of the small boats now lay on their sides in the sandy mud, only those nearest the quays still afloat.

Eleanor, with help from Teazle, ate quickly. Jocelyn didn't approve of eating in the street. Though Eleanor had been brought up with the same taboo, after all her travels she considered it ridiculous. Still, Joce was doing her a favour coming to fetch her, so she wanted to dispose of the evidence.

As soon as she fed the last scrap of batter to Teazle and balled up the greasy newspaper and supposedly grease-proof paper, her neighbour on the bench addressed her. "I were pulled out o' the sea by yon, I were.

219

Back when she were a proper boat, not a bitty canvas thing. I allis comes down to watch when she goes out. I don't hold wi' young maidies on the boats."

"Grace Darling," said Eleanor.

He gave her a toothless grin. "Oh, aye, I were forgettin' her that went out in a rowboat and saved the shipwrecked sailors, hundred years sin' and more. Eighteen hundred and thirty-eight, that were. You've the right of it, there, missus. Saw you gettin' out o' that there polis car, I did, and talking wi' the coxswain." He paused invitingly.

"My niece is a police officer." Eleanor evaded the implicit question. No doubt he'd find out soon enough what the lifeboat's mission was today. It wasn't for her to enlighten him.

"Ah." He shook his head. "I don't hold wi' young maidies in the polis. What'll they think of next?"

Unable to answer the question, she said lamely that the police seemed to grow younger every year.

"Ah, well, I don't have much to do wi' they. I be a law-abiding man."

Eleanor had been wondering whether it would be worth asking him if he knew anything about local smuggling. His firm claim of rectitude decided her against. They chatted for a little longer about the fog, and then Jocelyn arrived and Eleanor excused herself.

Teazle recognised the car and pulled her towards it. She and Jocelyn were not particular friends, but Jocelyn was associated with the vicar, who almost always carried something pleasantly edible in his pockets for his parishioners' pets. Eleanor opened the door and the little dog scrambled in.

As Eleanor was about to follow, Jocelyn sniffed and said in tones of strong disapproval, "Fish and chips. Do get rid of the papers before you get in, Eleanor. The car will stink of frying fish."

Meekly, Eleanor looked round for a litter basket and dropped the papers in. A herring gull promptly swooped down to grab the greasy ball. Flapping off, it was attacked by three more gulls. The papers scattered in tatters.

"So much for Keeping Britain Tidy." Jocelyn changed into first gear and waited for the passing of a sudden stream of traffic, no doubt brought out by the disappearance of the fog. "Tell me about your Boscastle smugglers and your encounter with That Man." She zipped through a gap between two delivery vans to turn right in front of a car pulling a small caravan. "And

221

why are you stranded in Port Isaac?"

Eleanor told her story as they drove up the hill, out of the village, and through rolling farmland. The lane narrowed, winding and occasionally zigging and zagging around ancient field boundaries.

"Bother!" Joce exclaimed, interrupting a description of Eleanor's efforts to prise the locations and secrets of the hidden caves from Abel Tregeddle. "I always forget how hopeless this road is. We should have gone the other way."

"This is definitely the long way round. Never mind, we must be nearly at St. Endellion."

"Yes, here we are," Joce agreed, spotting an outlying bungalow. "How did Tregeddle know about the caves?"

"Passed down through the family, for a couple of centuries, at least."

"Disgraceful!"

"Of course, it must have been someone with similar knowledge who took the Chudasamas to the cave. Always supposing the story is true."

Stopping at the T-junction, Jocelyn turned to stare. "Megan wouldn't lie. Do you think the boy was making it up?" She turned right on the B road.

"No, not making it up. But his physical

condition was pretty bad, and his mental condition may have been, too. Did you call the hospital, by the way?"

"Yes. I said he was one of my husband's parishioners. Much as I object to lying in principle, there are times —"

"When it's necessary to shade the truth for a good cause."

"Timothy and I tried to work out whether Rocky Valley is within his parish boundary. Unfortunately he's mislaid the map. He's quite worried about whether the boy can be considered a parishioner. You know how he is, charity first, then duty, then . . . But finish your story first."

"No, you tell me first how Kalith Chudasama is. Joce, why on earth did you turn right? We're heading south."

"That's part of it," the vicar's wife said, infuriatingly mysterious. "Kalith is still unconscious, I'm afraid."

"Oh dear!"

"He had to have a brain operation, and they're keeping him in a drug-induced coma because . . . Well, I didn't really understand the rest. They're hopeful of complete recovery but they won't know for some time. Go on about Tregeddle, and I'm dying to hear what That Man had to say."

Eleanor continued her story. By the time

she finished with That Man's long-distance order to Megan to sail with the lifeboat and Megan's departure in obedience thereto, they were on the A39, still heading south.

"Joce, where are we going? And why?"

"Truro. It came to me when Timothy was worrying about whether Kalith Chudasama is his parishioner. He'll pray for him anyway, of course, but he wondered whether he ought to go to Plymouth to see him in hospital. It's not only what you might call the geographical confusion over the parish boundaries. Also, he doesn't know whether the boy is an Anglican, or even a Christian at all. What is it proper for him to do if he should be a Hindu or a Mohammedan? I wouldn't say this to anyone else, but I'm afraid Tim is a little vague about doctrinal questions, the dear man."

"Charity first, then duty, and doctrine last." If at all, Eleanor amended silently. "I thoroughly approve. So we're going to Truro to consult the bishop? I'm hardly the right person to take with you. And I shouldn't have thought he'd be willing to discuss the vicar's doubts with his wife, anyway."

"Not the bishop." Jocelyn — remarkably — looked slightly shifty. "I don't imagine you're aware of it, but one of the canons at the cathedral is an Indian from East Africa."

"I remember your mentioning him once."

"The Reverend Dinesh. He came to England a few years ago, when things started getting sticky for Indians. He was personally threatened, I understand. The Church helped him enter the country, so he had no difficulty, but I wondered —"

"Joce! You think he's involved in smuggling people in?"

"Of course not. A clergyman . . . and he's rather quiet and shy. But if it were members of his own congregation . . . Well, you never know, do you? I thought it might be worth talking to him."

Eleanor tried to hide a smile. "Under cover of the vicar's dilemma? Really, Joce, how jesuitical."

"He might merely have heard something useful," Jocelyn said defensively. "Do you think it's a waste of time?"

"No, no, doctrinal doubts must be resolved. Seriously, no, it's not a waste of time when there doesn't seem to be anything else helpful we can do." But she had a niggling sense that there was something she could do, if only she could make the right connections between all the bits and pieces lurking in the murky recesses of her mind. "As you say, you never know."

"Well, then!"

"Isn't it a bit beneath the vicar's dignity to have his wife asking advice for him?"

"My dear Eleanor, surely you realise by now that Tim has absolutely no sense of his own dignity or the dignity of his position. If he did, he would not go buzzing about the countryside on that horrid motor scooter."

"In that case, you wouldn't have a car always available in which to do your own buzzing about the countryside."

Jocelyn sighed. "Very true. I must count my blessings."

"And I'm sure none of his parishioners respect him the less for his humble Vespa. Look, there's the cathedral."

From a distance, the neo-Gothic cathedral dominated the county town of Cornwall. An ancient river port, a city in name if not in size, Truro appeared as a mere backdrop to the three towering spires.

Once they reached the bottom of the hill, crossed a bridge over a tributary of the Truro River, and entered the narrow, cobbled streets, the cathedral seemed less overpowering than ever present. Built at the turn of the century on the site of a previous, much smaller church and a few adjoining buildings, Truro Cathedral had to make do without the spreading lawns of a close. But every side street, every alley between

226

shops, offices, and houses, offered a glimpse of the pale gold Bath stone cladding the Cornish granite bones of the walls and towers.

They were lucky enough to find a place to park in a small cobbled area right in front of the cathedral. As they walked towards the twin-arched porch, several people came out. Jocelyn moved to one side to avoid them and Eleanor veered the other way, so they entered through different arches. Inside the porch, Eleanor was held up by meeting an acquaintance who was giving visitors from the Midlands a tour.

When she managed to get away and go on through one of the doors into the nave, Jocelyn was waiting with an impatiently tapping toe.

"Where *have* you been? I was just about to come and look for you. I was afraid you might have fallen on the cobbles."

"Just because I tripped while running on a rough, rocky path yesterday . . . ! Never mind. Sorry." Eleanor explained the delay. "Now that I'm here, where do we find Canon Dinesh?"

"I asked a verger, who thinks he's in his office. It's not actually in the cathedral. We'll go out by the south door." She led the way into the south aisle.

"Joce, I don't think I ought to be present when you're discussing Timothy's difficulties."

"You're right, it would be awkward. But you'll have to be there to talk about the smuggling. I don't see how we can do them in reverse order."

"As the theological quest is designed to soften him up for the interrogation —"

"Really, Eleanor! And in the cathedral!"

Once again she apologised, adding, "It's true, though; admit it. I'll tell you what, I'll just stay here in the cathedral and try not to be sacrilegious, then come and join you in . . . what? . . . quarter of an hour?"

"All right." Jocelyn explained how to find the cathedral offices and went off.

Eleanor was tempted to take a seat in a pew. She was tired, and she needed to consider how to tackle the clergyman about his possible collusion with smugglers. But the place was quiet, in spite of an unexpected number of people wandering about — holiday makers fleeing the fog on the north coast, perhaps. She was afraid she might fall asleep.

Crossing to the north aisle, she went to visit the ebony Madonna. In the circumstances, the black mother and child seemed appropriate. She bought and lit a candle, not that she expected the gesture to help Kalith, his mother, or the rest of his family, but it couldn't hurt. If a statue of the Buddha had been available, she would have lit incense, or garlanded four-armed Lakshmi with marigolds.

For a minute or two she watched the candle flame flickering in the currents of air as people passed and entrance doors opened and closed. Then she walked on to the Chapel of Unity and Peace.

Here she did sit down to collect her scattered thoughts. She tried to centre her being as she would before starting her Aikido practice, shutting out the world yet conscious of her precise place in it. But tranquillity was hard to achieve. As soon as she closed her eyes, the cathedral, seemingly so quiet just moments ago, echoed with footsteps shuffling, tapping, thudding on the paving stones; though voices were hushed, they were buzzing all about her.

She gave up as the cathedral clock chimed the quarter. Five minutes to get to Canon Dinesh's office and she couldn't remember whether Joce had said to turn left or right when she reached the street.

A helpful verger gave her directions. She went out by the south door. In the short time she had been inside, the sky had filled with mackerel clouds, small, fleecy puffs delightful in themselves but presaging bad weather. If a storm came in, the chances of a continuing search for Kalith's family diminished to the vanishing point.

Eleanor found the cathedral offices. Jocelyn had told the secretary she was expected, and she was ushered straight into Canon Dinesh's room. There was a desk, adorned with a plain gold crucifix and a colour photo of a woman wearing a turquoise sari with a gold border and several gold chains round her neck. However, the canon and Jocelyn were sitting by a small driftwood fire in two of a trio of well-stuffed armchairs, intended, presumably, to make those consulting him more comfortable, less intimidated.

Not that the canon looked intimidating. He was a short, chubby man with a round, solemn face, considerably darker than Kalith, with quite different features. That didn't mean they were not related. But even if he had no connection with the Chudasamas, his own family might have arrived in the country illegally. He just might know something that would lead to the smugglers responsible for Kalith's family's plight.

As he stood to greet Eleanor, the skirts of his black cassock made him look even shorter and tubbier. Jocelyn introduced them and they shook hands.

"Do sit down, Mrs. Trewynn," he said in a soft voice without a distinguishable accent. "Mrs. Stearns tells me you're in no hurry, and I usually take tea at about this time."

The secretary brought in a tray. Jocelyn took it upon herself to do the honours. While she poured, Canon Dinesh said to Eleanor, "I understand you were present when the unfortunate young man was rescued from the sea?"

"Not exactly. I went for help when he was spotted. It's terrible to think he'd have died if we hadn't happened to walk that way and found him just in time."

"But the Good Lord sent you, and I shall pray for his swift recovery."

"I'm so sorry for his family, not knowing where he is." Eleanor accepted a cup of Earl Grey from Jocelyn, declining a bourbon biscuit — not her favourite and she was still full of chips. "Kalith seemed very worried about them, from the little he was able to say. Do you have a family, Canon?"

"Yes, indeed. My wife and children and my wife's sister came from Africa with me, several years ago, before the law was changed. We have no relatives there now, though many in India."

Eleanor continued to probe the subject as

231

far as she decently could, without asking directly whether he was aware of any smuggling. She was pretty sure he wasn't. She would leave it to the police to ask that question if necessary. Jocelyn would kill her if she confronted him and upset him.

The secretary came in to remind the canon of another appointment. They parted with many expressions of mutual esteem and many earnest promises from the Reverend Dinesh to pray for the sufferer and his family.

"Well, what do you think?" asked Jocelyn as they walked back to the car.

"I don't believe he has any personal interest in the Chudasamas, though their situation distresses him."

"He's a gentle soul. I agree, I didn't see the slightest sign that he suspected they might have arrived illegally."

"The trouble is," said Eleanor gloomily, "they might not. Perhaps he simply went for a solo swim and no one has reported him missing because no one was expecting him, and he was raving when he talked to Megan. It's all too plausible. If the authorities decide that's the case . . ."

"Unless Kalith wakes up and clarifi es things, they might stop the search," said Jocelyn. "We can't let them get away with

232

that, when there are — or may be — several lives at stake. Let me think."

In silence they got into the car and Jocelyn negotiated the one-way streets back to the A39.

"Bother," Eleanor said as they left the town behind them. "If I'd known you were going to carry me off to Truro, I could have brought the clothes Megan and Nick borrowed and returned them to Julia and Chaz. They both live near Falmouth, I think."

"But you didn't bring the clothes. I wish I knew who'd make a decision like that. Someone local, or someone in London? Plymouth?"

"I don't know. Is the Coast Guard part of the Navy?"

"I don't think so, but in any case, it's useless to try and influence the military mind. The RNLI, though . . . Their mission is saving lives. If they threaten to quit, the press . . . perhaps the Race Relations Board, though that would probably take too long. And in the end it's always a question of money. Could we persuade them to regard it as a training exercise?"

"Joce, I'm sure they'll keep searching as long as there's the slightest hope."

"I wouldn't count on it. Bureaucracy! The Church will have to get involved. I'm afraid

Canon Dinesh is not a very forceful person."

"What does a canon do?"

"Do you really want to know?" Jocelyn asked ironically.

"Not particularly," Eleanor admitted. "I just don't want to dwell on what Megan and the lifeboat men may be finding. Or not finding."

EIGHTEEN

Megan hung on to a loop of rope as the skipper, at the outboard in the stern, piloted the lifeboat between the quays. Walter and Maggie perched on the sides, facing each other, apparently at ease. The *Belinda* cleared the headlands and swung northward. As soon as they were far enough from shore not to tangle with lobster pot lines, their speed increased. The bow rose at an angle. Spray flew back on either side and spattered Megan's face and helmet.

The sun had sucked up the last wisps of mist. The sea glittered as if a fortune in silver coins miraculously floated on the surface. No wonder seamen always had creases at the corners of their eyes.

Megan reckoned the boat was about sixteen feet end to end, with the covered bow taking up a good chunk and the outboard another. The puffy, inflated sides narrowed the space inside. Gunwales? Perhaps they didn't count as gunwales in an inflatable, if that was the right word to start with. Although she had grown up near Falmouth, Megan's experience of boats was limited to ferries, cross-Channel and otherwise, and a rowboat on the Penryn River as a child.

"Get on the radio, Maggie, and give Falmouth our numbers," said the skipper. "Don't forget to tell them DS Pencarrow's wearing the sixteen."

When Maggie had reported in and signed off, Megan asked her, "What difference do the numbers make?"

"In case of . . . accident. They won't be notifying the wrong family." She shouted backwards, "We're lucky with the weather, Skipper. Couldn't be calmer."

"For the present. Till that front they forecast rolls in." He hoicked a thumb at the western horizon. Megan saw a dark line marking the meeting of sea and sky.

"What about the tide, Skipper?" asked Walter. "On the turn, isn't it?"

"That's why we're in a hurry. Let's hope we make it to Lye Rock while the gut's dry, for a start. I wouldn't want to be caught in there when the current's running."

Megan, out of her element and a trifle shaken by Maggie's explanation of the numbers, said, "What I don't quite under-

236

stand is, if the approach to these caves is so difficult and dangerous, how did the smugglers manage it? Presumably they'd prefer to work under cover of dark nights and stormy weather."

The skipper nodded. "A good question. Familiarity, I suppose. I doubt they'd tackle that area in really bad weather, but at sea a very little light goes a long way because it reflects off the water As well as having experience of safe channels, I imagine they'd use a narrow boat with shallow draught, flat-bottomed, even, and they'd have someone in the bow with a pole to feel for unexpected rocks. As I told you, things move."

"And we don't know where the channels were to start with," Walter pointed out pessimistically.

Maggie jeered, "I swear that load of gloom you carry around is going to sink you one of these days, Walter. That's what we're going to find out."

"I'll have to take you aboard the *Daisy D.*, Sergeant —"

"Megan."

"Megan. To show your map to Tom."

"Tom?"

"Coxswain Kulick, the skipper."

"Kulick? That doesn't sound English."

"He's Polish, or was. He got out of Poland as the Nazis and the Commies moved in, in '39, and joined the Wavy Navy, the RNVR. After the war he went into the Coast Guard. Then, when he retired, he came over to the RNLI. He can explain your map to Jackson, skipper of the *Lucy,* the Bude boat. It has farther to come than we do. You all right, Megan?"

"I think so," Megan said uncertainly. She had been perfectly all right until the boat started skipping across the crests of the waves.

"Watch the horizon," Maggie suggested, pointing westward.

Megan looked, but the sight of the clouds, already a band rather than a line, was not encouraging, so she turned her gaze to the east. The dark band in that direction was cliffs. Unfortunately, they jigged up and down to the motion of the boat. She closed her eyes, but the uneasiness in her middle immediately became queasiness. She'd just have to put up with the sight of the advancing front. It was definitely an improvement on watching the waves go up and down.

By the time they rounded Tintagel Head, some twenty minutes later, Megan was beginning to adjust to the motion. The *Belinda*'s course curved eastward, standing

238

clear of a group of offshore islets Maggie told her were the Sisters.

"And that's Lye Rock," the skipper pointed out. "You can see the cleft separating it from the headland. That's where one of your aunt's caves is supposed to be."

Megan glanced at the narrow "gut," as Aunt Nell's smuggler had called it, but she was more interested in the view ahead, where a black-and-orange ship stood out like a hornet against the speedwell-blue sea.

"The *Daisy D.* Maggie, signal her and tell her we're coming alongside."

Maggie announced their imminent arrival and asked for permission to board, which was duly granted.

To Megan's relief, as they approached the *Daisy D.* it shrunk from a distant monster to quite a small ship. She had envisioned making a fool of herself trying to climb the side of a vessel towering over the tiny inflatable. It turned out to be only about three times the length of the *Belinda,* though much more solid, with a wooden hull and a considerable superstructure, painted orange. Aerials sprouted here and there.

Larkin handed over the controls to Walter, who manoeuvred *Belinda* alongside the all-weather boat. Magically, he held her in position about a foot from the larger boat's side

239

as both rose and fell with the swell. A crewman stood by on the *Daisy D.* — to help
with the crossing, Megan hoped. He wore a
life jacket like those of *Belinda*'s crew but
with yellow waterproof trousers instead of a
dry suit and without a helmet.

"Think you can make it, Megan?" Larkin
asked.

"Yes," said Megan with confidence. She
had forgotten her borrowed garb. It hampered her movements, she lost her balance,
and in spite of a boost from the skipper and
the crewman on the *Daisy D.* grabbing her
arm, she landed on hands and knees on the
deck. Not the dignified appearance she
would have liked to present.

She hoped Coxswain Kulick wasn't watching. If he was sceptical about what Kalith
had said to her and didn't really believe
there was a family in danger, or if he scoffed
at Aunt Nell's map, she needed to present a
competent appearance, cool, calm, and collected, to persuade him.

"All right, miss?" The sailor helped her up
and released her arm.

"Yes, thank you. I'm not really RNLI. I
was lent these clothes and they don't fit.
I'm a copper — Detective Sergeant Pencarrow."

He grinned. "A landlubber, eh? The cox-

240

swain's expecting you, Sergeant. And you, Coxswain Larkin," he added, as the *Belinda*'s skipper swung himself aboard. He waved them towards the wheelhouse at the rear. Stern? Aft?

Larkin led the way, one hand on the safety rail, the other ripping open the Velcroed breast pocket of his jacket and taking out the map and his chart.

"Afternoon, Tom." He handed them over to the *Daisy D.*'s skipper, a grizzled man who looked tired. "This is DS Pencarrow. She'll explain the map to you. I won't stop. We must get going before the tide starts to rise." To Megan, he said, "No sense you coming till we find them."

"I'd only get in your way," she agreed. She stepped into the wheelhouse out of his way, and he went back to the *Belinda*. A moment later, she heard the roar of the outboard.

"Steady as she goes, Gavin," Kulick told the helmsman. Unfolding the map and Larkin's chart, he pinned them up on his chart board and beckoned Megan to join him. "Right, Sergeant, let's hear it." He rolled his *rrr*'s like a Scot, or, Megan supposed, like a Pole.

Megan explained that the arrows on the map showed the locations of the secret caves once used by smugglers. "I gather they can't be seen from offshore, except the middle one, which looks as if it's full of water what ever the tide level." She described the secrets of the three.

"And just how did you happen to find out?"

"My aunt was told by a descendant of a family with a tradition of smuggling in the old days."

"It all sounds pretty unlikely, you must admit. And this story about people being stuck in one of them? The Coast Guard didn't mention hidden caves when we were called out in the middle of the night."

"In the middle of the night? What did they expect you to do in the dark?"

"We have searchlights. We might have found survivors in a small boat. But mostly to be on hand when the inshore boats arrived at dawn. We're considerably slower and had farther to come. We got out of Padstow just before the fog closed down."

"Then they couldn't come out and you couldn't go back."

"Exactly. We've been sitting here since, waiting, so you see why I'm not happy about the unreliability of your information. Not just these mysterious caves; I understand the alarm came from the chap you rescued, who's suffering from concussion."

"Sir, I'm convinced that when he told me he was lucid. What he didn't say was whereabouts on the coast his family is. It's the Coast Guard and your people who pinned it down to Bossiney Cove."

The coxswain sighed. "Well, we're here and we're searching. I just —"

"Skipper," came a shout from the deck, "the *Lucy*'s in sight."

"The Bude boat." The skipper acknowledged the sighting and logged it. A moment later, the *Lucy* was on the radio.

Megan gathered she was going to have to explain everything to yet another sceptical skipper. She needed a break first. "I'm just going to step out and see if I can see what the *Belinda*'s doing."

Kulick nodded consent.

"Here." The helmsman handed her binoculars.

"Thanks!" She went out on deck. Behind her, she heard Kulick reporting by radio to the Falmouth Coast Guard.

It took her a minute to focus the powerful glasses. Then the cliffs sprang to life. At the top, rough turf, gorse, and bracken sloped down steeply to end in a sudden vertical plunge. She saw in minute detail every crack, every seam, every crease and hollow in the rock face. She could almost count

243

the blades of grass where thin soil, no doubt bountifully fertilised by seabirds, had collected on shelves and protuberances. A herring gull perched on one such knob seemed to stare her in the eye.

Sweeping the scene, Megan saw the beach at Bossiney Haven, difficult to get to and exposed only at low tide. All the same, anyone stranded in its well-known, thoroughly explored cave would be able to walk out next time the tide ebbed. Today the fog would have kept away beachgoers.

As she scanned along the ragged white line where sea met land, every indentation in the shoreline seemed to have a black hole at its heart, revealing a cave wherever softer rock had been worn away by pounding waves. Searching all of them would take forever. Now she realised fully the importance of Aunt Nell's discoveries.

Larkin had spoken of trying the Lye Rock gut cave first. She turned the glasses to the southeast end of the cove, and at once the brilliant orange inflatable sprang into view.

It was hard to judge from a distance, but the *Belinda* seemed to be moving slowly, cautiously. Two of the crew — Maggie and Walter, she thought — were in the bow, leaning over to peer into the water. The skipper, at the helm, made constant small course adjustments. Dodging rocks. Here and there, whitecaps marked the presence of obstacles just beneath the surface. At least it was a bright day. With the sun's rays penetrating the water, they should be able to see to quite a depth.

From Megan's position, the gut itself wasn't visible. She wondered how soon the tide would fill it with water.

A buzzing in the background turned into a roar as the Bude lifeboat approached, then dropped to a hum as she drew alongside. Megan lowered the glasses and stood back to let Coxswain Jackson board.

He swung up, nodded to Megan, and went into the wheelhouse. He was all business. Standing in the doorway, she watched and listened as Kulick showed him the map and chart and described the hidden caves. He didn't ask for explanations, just said, "Pete Larkin is over to Lye Rock? *Lucy*'d better tackle the northernmost first, right?"

"Right. Watch out for lobster pots."

Jackson swung back into his inflatable and it buzzed off towards the upper end of the cove.

The radio woke again. After the ritual exchange of boat numbers, Larkin's distorted voice announced, "They've found the cave. No response to shouts. The mouth is dry, but Walter's belaying Maggie's line while she goes in. Hold on . . ." A moment's pause, then, "Bingo! Tom, they hear someone in there all right. Over."

"I'm redirecting *Lucy,* Pete. She'll join you in five minutes or so. Over and out." Kulick spoke to Jackson. Megan saw the Bude inflatable turn, her wake inscribing an arc behind her.

Larkin was back. "Sorry, false alarm. Just an echo. No one there. We'll move on to the middle cave as soon as Walter and Maggie get back aboard."

"Right. Jackson, you hear that?"

"I heard. We're turning north again."

Megan watched *Lucy*'s wake complete the arc. "I should have guessed it wouldn't be the Lye Rock cave," she said to Kulick.

"Why? How could you?"

"It's perfect for smugglers, who can — could — choose when to go there. Access from both the open sea and the cove, isn't there? But the cove end of the gut is dry at low tide, I gather. The refugees, once they realised no one was coming for them, could have walked out to the end and conceivably attracted attention. A lobster fisherman, or someone on the cliffs with binoculars."

"A pretty slim chance, with just a couple of hours once a day."

"But a chance the bastards who marooned them couldn't take."

"You really believe that's what happened?"

"It's the simplest explanation, sir. And we haven't found any other that fits what little we know."

"I was a refugee myself." Kulick was silent for a moment. "I, for one, will keep searching till there's nowhere left to look."

"Believe me, my boss is not going to give up on catching those responsible!"

Stepping outside, Megan focussed the glasses on the *Lucy*. She was approaching with caution an area of ruffled water between the cliff and the offshore Saddle Rocks. There, even at slack tide, the ever-restless sea swirled and broke in white spray.

Presumably Jackson knew what he was doing. She watched apprehensively for a few minutes. The *Lucy* slowed to a crawl and her course zigzagged wildly.

Megan couldn't bear to watch. If they came to grief, she could do nothing to help. She looked for the *Belinda*.

Pete Larkin's boat was also moving slowly, approaching a small cove notched in the cliffs, between two sloping headlands. Though the cove was shadowed, Megan made out within these sheltering arms one of the black holes she had noticed earlier.

Not so sheltering arms, she thought. They hadn't stopped the sea battering the less resistant rock in the middle, digging it out, undermining it.

Undermining — was that the explanation of the northern cave, the one concealed behind a barricade of solid stone? Perhaps, long ago, a slab of rock deprived of support had slid down the face of the cliff, leaving a space between but effectively hiding the entrance to the cave. Other boulders might have fallen at the same time, creating the turbulent area that further blocked access.

Megan swung the glasses back to *Lucy*. She seemed to have stopped moving forward, but it was hard to tell. Amid the white foam, a wake was impossible to detect.

Belinda also was surrounded by whitecaps now. So, come to that, was the *Daisy D.* The tentative breeze that had cleared the fog was blowing in earnest, though still no more than a stiff breeze. The sea was choppy. The motion of the all-weather boat became irregular enough to disturb Megan's insides.

Damn it all, she was not going to give way to seasickness just when she'd attained her sea legs. Mind over matter, she told herself sternly. She concentrated on the now difficult task of finding *Belinda* again through the jerking binoculars.

There she was, framed by the black mouth of the cave.

The radio squawked. "Tom, underwater to the back, as far as we can see. Hope the sergeant's right. We're going in. May lose reception."

"Get it done before the big rollers start coming in."

"We'll try."

As Megan watched, the cave swallowed the inflatable.

"Jackson?"

"Not smooth sailing here, old man. We're considering our options."

"Your decision. Pete?"

Larkin's voice was more distorted than ever, and fainter. "Can just hear you. Nearly . . . By Jerry, it looks . . . sergeant . . . right . . . sort of buttress . . ." He faded out.

"Pete, come in. Pete, can you hear me?" They listened to the hiss of the static. "Lost him. Well, Sergeant, it sounds as if your aunt got a straight story from her smuggler."

"Two out of three."

"So far. But whether —"

"Tom!" Very faintly, then stronger: "Tom, are you there?"

"Here. What's up?"

". . . ten or more, Maggie says. My God! Hold on half a mo . . . One dead, one too

ill to walk. Oh, dear God! We need a chopper."

"Understood. I'll tell Falmouth, Pete, and
send the *Lucy.*"

Ten. Mother, father, uncles, aunts, and
cousins, children . . . Megan hadn't really
believed it. In spite of her insistence on
Kalith Chudasama's lucidity, in spite of her
trust in Aunt Nell, the whole thing had
seemed too far-fetched for credibility. How
she had persuaded her boss and how he had
persuaded the Coast Guard and the RNLI,
she couldn't imagine.

But apparently it was true. And now she
had to put her money where her mouth was.
To collect evidence for what might end up
as a murder trial, she was going to have to
venture into that cave.

NINETEEN

The news that his long vigil had not been for nothing erased the lines of tiredness from Kulick's face and straightened his back. He talked via radio to the Coast Guard and the *Lucy,* then turned to Megan. "So you'll be wanting to look round the scene of the crime, Sergeant?"

"Yes, sir. Though 'wanting' isn't the word I'd choose. I ought to ask a few questions first, though, when they bring them out. Assuming they speak English."

The *Daisy D.*'s skipper shook his head. "That'll have to wait till after. The sooner we get you in and out, the safer."

"Because of the tide?"

"It's turned. And the wind's rising. Once the swells start rolling into the cave, it'll be too dangerous. It's bad enough already for trained personnel. If it wasn't a matter of life and death . . . We're too late for one of the poor devils. You heard?"

"Yes. That's why it's urgent that I see the place. The sooner we get to work, the better chance we'll have of collecting evidence. As far as we're concerned, finding the people is only the first step. Hell, I haven't got a camera, let alone a fingerprint kit!"

"Can't manage the kit, but a camera we can do. Go down and ask one of the chaps in the cabin." He waved to a narrow staircase — companionway — in one corner of the wheelhouse.

"Thanks." Megan had seen two or three crewmen pop up out of nowhere and as many disappear downward but she hadn't paid much attention.

"Gavin, it's time you were spelled. Take the sergeant down, would you? And find the camera for her. You can send Charlie up to take the wheel." Kulick took it over himself in the interim.

"Okay, Skipper." Gavin was a rather weedy young man, with pimples and limp, longish hair, but he couldn't be all bad if he volunteered with the RNLI, and he'd lent her his binoculars, too. "Watch your feet, Sergeant. The steps shouldn't be wet and slippery in these seas, but you never can tell."

The calm sea was definitely becoming agitated. The *Daisy D.* now moved in unpredictable twitches. Megan took an uncertain step towards the companionway.

"Maybe I'd better go first," Gavin said hurriedly, tactful enough not to add that he'd be able to catch her if she fell.

Megan slid her hand along the metal stair rail as she descended, and clung to it for a moment when she reached the bottom, steadying herself. Gavin hadn't touched it on his way down.

The cabin was surprisingly spacious, though gloomy. It even had a tiny galley. A kettle steamed on the gimballed Calor gas stove. A bald, burly man, made burlier by his life jacket, was unwrapping Oxo and chicken soup cubes, popping them into a varying array of mugs. He looked round as Gavin, followed by Megan, arrived below.

"How many are we expecting?"

"Better be ready for a dozen or so. Right, Sergeant?"

"That's what it sounds like. DS Pencarrow," she introduced herself. "Megan."

"I'm Charlie, and that's Charles." He waved at another crewman, who gave a silent nod and went on taking multicoloured blankets out of a locker, piling them on the waterproof-cushioned bench. "Better take a seat, Megan, while you can. Coffee?"

"I'd love some, thanks."

"Charlie, the skipper wants you at the wheel."

"I'll take him up a coffee. Gavin, you take charge here. Rout out a few more mugs. Better not pour till they start coming aboard, though."

Megan warmed her hands on her mug of coffee. She hadn't realised how chilled they were. Charles had closed the locker and replaced its cushion. On top he put the cushion from the next section of bench/locker, which he opened to retrieve more blankets. Megan saw that each cushion had straps on the bottom, so that they could be used as floats in an emergency, if there weren't enough life jackets to go round.

"Okay if I sit here?" she asked him, indicating the lockers on the opposite side of the cabin.

"Be my guest."

She sat down, only to have to move a few minutes later when one of the men whom she'd noticed earlier on deck came down.

"Sorry," he said, opening her seat. "Skipper says they may not be capable of climbing the scramble net and we'll likely need the sling to help 'em up from the inshore."

"Have you got two? The Bude boat . . ."

"Good point. *Lucy* may arrive before we've emptied the *Belinda.*" He went off

254

loaded with tackle, balancing easily as he crossed the tilting floor.

Megan quickly finished her coffee. The smell of Oxo in the enclosed space wasn't helping her nausea. With care, she negotiated the way to the stairs, handing her mug to Gavin as she passed.

He grinned. "You're looking a bit green about the gills. You'll be better in the fresh air."

"I hope so."

"Oops, forgot the camera. There's one in here somewhere. Here you go, and an extra roll of film."

"Terrific, thanks." It was in a waterproof case with a long strap. She looped it over her head and put her arm through, so that it was safe against her side.

At the top of the stairs, she felt better at once in the briny air wafting into the wheelhouse. It wafted with more force than before, she noted, and the bank of clouds in the west hid the sun, though the sky above remained blue. The sea was too ruffled to retain its deep azure, but as far as she could tell, the swells hadn't yet swelled. She hoped she'd make it into the cave and safe out to the *Daisy D.* again before they became breakers.

Charlie, at the wheel, winked at her. Kulick was on the radio, apparently talking to a helicopter pilot. Megan still had the binoculars hung round her neck. She stepped out on deck to see what she could see.

The *Lucy* must have extracted herself from the turbulent area faster than she had edged into it. She was skipping across the waves, more than halfway to the place where the *Belinda* had disappeared. *Belinda* was still out of sight. Megan tried to picture Larkin holding the inflatable steady while Maggie and Walter helped the refugees embark. Women and children first? Or those in worst shape? One too feeble to walk. One dead: Kalith's mother?

Was Kalith still hanging on to life?

Kulick called to her, "The Coast Guard chopper's on its way, Sergeant. I'm taking the *Daisy* a bit farther in, though we'll have to move out again if the wind grows much stronger."

Megan raised her hand in acknowledgement. The note of the engines changed.

As soon as they were under way, the joggling eased. The boat cut through the waves instead of sitting rocking on them. It didn't last long, though. The sound died back to a purr, just as the bright orange of the *Belinda* reappeared.

The contrary motions of the two boats made counting heads impossible at that distance. The inflatable seemed to be crammed full. With any luck, Megan thought, the *Belinda* was carrying at least half of the Indians. In that case, *Lucy* could bring the rest of the ambulatory refugees, so that when *Belinda* took her to the cave it would stay and wait for her, rather than having to return to the *Daisy D.* and come back again to fetch her.

But there was the helicopter to consider, too. Megan had no idea how the lifeboats were going to handle that.

It was their problem, though. Hers was to make sure the Coast Guard understood that both the deceased and the patient were probable crime victims. The former must be autopsied; the latter guarded by the police and questioned as soon as possible.

Reluctantly interrupting her surveillance of the two inshore boats, Megan turned back towards the wheelhouse.

Kulick stood in the doorway, watching the inflatables through binoculars.

"Sir?"

"Yes, Sergeant?" He kept the glasses trained on *Lucy* and *Belinda.*

"I was wondering whether you've made it clear to the Coast Guard that they're picking up victims of crime, not just accident or stupidity."

"They know the police are involved. Your superintendent has talked to them — to HQ in Falmouth, that is, not the crew or the medic. Don't worry, they know how to deal with it."

"The helicopter will take the body as well as the patient?"

"That's their decision, depending on conditions."

"I ought to see it in situ first."

"We'll get you there as soon as we can, Sergeant. But understand, once the helicopter arrives, there'll be no hanging about. Look, *Belinda*'s cleared the headland and *Lucy*'s going in."

The two inshore boats were moving slowly as they passed in opposite directions. Both were outside the shadow of the cliffs, clearly visible. Through the glasses, it looked to Megan as if the skippers were talking to each other. Larkin was probably describing the situation in the cave and perhaps the best way to approach it. Then the *Lucy* went on at low speed into the shadows, while *Belinda* picked up speed, heading for the *Daisy D*.

By then, one of the *Daisy*'s crew was kneeling on the roof of the wheelhouse, with binoculars. "Three kids," he called down, "and three adults. Looks like three women."

With the six extras as well as the three crew members, the inflatable was heavily laden. It seemed to move sluggishly, through the choppy water rather than on top of it. When it came closer, Megan saw that the Indians were huddled on the floor. Larkin was at the helm, while Maggie and Walter sat on the tubular sides, holding on to the loops of rope, swaying as the boat ploughed on. They looked perfectly at ease, though neither they nor the skipper had life jackets.

They must have lent them to the women, as well as a spare. All three and the oldest child were wearing the bulky yellow jackets. Two of the women had their arms round smaller children.

As the *Belinda* pulled alongside the *Daisy D.,* Megan moved to the stern, well out of the way. She watched the two crews work together to lift the children, then the women, from the inshore boat to the deck of the larger boat and help them into the wheelhouse on their way down to the cabin.

Unless Megan hung over the rail — an unwise move for more reasons than one, she felt — she didn't have a very good view. The two younger children seemed lethargic, apathetic, but a boy of ten or so made an effort to pull himself up by the scramble net. Awkward in a life jacket too large for him, he hindered more than he helped as he was hoisted upward in the sling. He was chattering nineteen to the dozen.

The crew's responses suggested he was speaking English, though Megan couldn't make out his words. With any luck, at least some of the adults would be able to answer questions without an interpreter.

The last of them was brought aboard the *Daisy D.* and supported, half carried, into the wheelhouse. Kulick came out and leant over the rail, talking to Larkin.

Megan made her way forward, hanging on to the rail. She heard Kulick say, "The copter should arrive soon after you get back there. Good luck." He turned to her. "Good luck, Sergeant."

The crewman who had helped her earlier, when she bungled her arrival, passed down a rolled-up canvas stretcher to Walter and Maggie. Then he tossed down the borrowed life jackets.

"How are they?" Megan asked him. "Those people . . ."

"Not so hot. Not at death's door, but hungry and cold. They've had nothing to eat for a couple of days, and that's the kids

260

and the one who's expecting. For the rest, it's been more like four or five days."

"Oh Lord! One of the women's pregnant?" No wonder Kalith swam for it.

"Five or six months, I reckon." He threw down a couple of extra life jackets.

Larkin, Walter, and Maggie had all put on their numbered jackets. As Walter stowed the spares, the skipper called, "Megan! If you want to inspect the cave, we need to get a move on."

Even with directions from above and a helping hand below, her descent into the inflatable was not much more graceful than her ascent from it. It didn't help that the two boats were bobbing up and down irregularly, so that the distance between was constantly changing.

But Megan arrived safely, and Larkin at once swung the *Belinda* away from the *Daisy D.* He put on speed, the bow rising.

"How many more people?" Megan shouted to Maggie over the noise of the engine.

"Four men, one woman, and two teenagers in reasonable shape. One old woman who's in pretty bad shape. And an old man who didn't make it. He died just last night, they said. If it wasn't for the fog . . ."

Megan was silent for a moment, then she

261

said, "If we'd got things moving quicker!"

"If wishes were horses!" Walter said roughly. "It was only yesterday you found the bloke drowning, wasn't it?"

"Was it?" She thought back: Rocky Valley, the ambulance, the hospital, Kalith's brief consciousness, a few hours sleep while DI Scumble did his utmost to persuade his superiors to move, then dashing hither and yon, ending with her unexpected embarkation on the lifeboat. "Yes, you're right. It feels like forever."

"There you are, then. You made sure they were found soon as poss, and now you've got to concentrate on nailing the bugger that dumped them."

"They didn't tell you who it was, did they?"

"That'd be too easy."

"We didn't exactly have time for a conversation," said Maggie. "We were too busy sorting out how many we could take and getting them quickly and safely into the boat. The little boy talked a lot, but I can't say I made much sense of what he was saying."

"Too noisy," Walter agreed.

A few minutes later, Larkin cut their speed as they neared the twin headlands. The *Lucy* passed in the opposite direction, the crew waving. Besides the three of them, she carried three men and a boy and girl in their midteens.

The *Belinda* went on, with caution, into the tiny bay. Maggie and Walter, boathooks at the ready, started watching over the sides for rocks. Megan gazed ahead at the black hole of the cave. She really, really didn't want to go inside it. Yet there were people who explored not only caves but potholes for fun! How bad could it be?

"I haven't got a torch!" she realised aloud.

"We do," the skipper told her, "and an electric lamp."

"It's not completely dark in there," said Maggie. "Watch out to port, Skipper. Okay. There's a hole in the roof that lets in a bit of daylight. It must go right up to the top of the cliff, I should think. It's not very wide, and it's crooked, so you can't actually see the sky."

"An old mine shaft, I bet!" Who had mentioned dangerous mine shafts in the cliffs? Probably Julia or Chaz, hikers with an interest in geology. "I shouldn't be surprised if the smugglers used to use it as an alternative access to the cave."

"Damn good thing it's there," Walter grunted. "When they ran out of water, they managed to catch rain running down.

Knocked the top out of an old barrel."

Megan hadn't thought about lack of water. No one could survive long without it, nowhere near as long as without food. "Thank goodness they weren't driven to drinking seawater," she said.

Contemplating the refugees' ordeal, she stopped worrying about her own venture into the bowels of the earth.

The walls of the cave, the curved roof, were about them now. The outboard barely murmuring, the boat proceeded under its existing momentum. The water was calmer than outside, rocking them gently. Walter produced a large rubber torch, clicked it on, and shone it towards the back. Megan saw a small patch of sand and rounded pebbles, sloping up to jumbled boulders, enclosed on three sides by the rocky walls.

"But where — ?"

Walter swung the beam to the right. "You'll see as soon as you get out on the beach."

The *Belinda* grounded gently. "Walter, Maggie, get the stretcher out and the old woman on to it. Megan, I've got to move back into radio reception range. Here's the lamp. You go and do your stuff. I'll be back as soon as the copter arrives."

Megan helped the others unload the

stretcher and a spare life jacket. She grabbed the lamp and, shining it to the right, walked a few steps up the slope. The right-hand wall turned out to be a sort of buttress. Behind it was a narrow gap, about thirty inches wide. The sides looked rough-hewn and the ramp beyond too smooth to be natural.

The lamplight showed a middle-aged Indian man standing at the top. He bowed, palms together. "Namaste."

Megan had forgotten what Aunt Nell had told her the word meant, but it seemed proper to return the greeting.

"My name is Nayak. You have come to help my sister?"

"Yes, sir." She decided explaining that she was a police officer might upset or confuse him. "We've brought a stretcher, and a rescue helicopter should be here any moment."

"I thank you." He turned and led the way into a cavern that seemed quite spacious but must have been a tight fit for a dozen people or so to live in. Carrying the stretcher, Walter and Maggie followed Megan.

Mr. Nayak's sister lay to one side, bundled in rugs. Her eyes were closed, her breathing stertorous. Another woman, his wife, sat cross-legged beside her. On the other side of the cave, the dead man had a single rug pulled up over his face. At the far end was a neat stack of cardboard boxes.

Megan set the lamp on a projecting rock and got out the camera. "Let me take a couple of photos before you move her."

"You are a newspaper reporter?" Nayak asked in alarm.

"No, nothing like that. But the scene has to be documented." She didn't tell him reporters would certainly be waiting when he and his family were landed. She snapped a couple of pictures of the sick woman. "Okay, go ahead."

Maggie and Walter had unrolled the stretcher. While they eased the sick woman on to it, Megan went over to the deceased. She looked to Nayak for permission, and he nodded resignedly. Folding back the rug, she photographed his father's wasted face, then carefully covered it again and stood for a moment with bowed head.

She became aware of a curious, regular thumping noise. Maggie was the first to recognise it. "The helicopter. It sounds weird down here. The noise must be coming down the mine shaft. Come on, Walter, let's go. Mr. and Mrs. Nayak, you'd better come too. Here, put on these life jackets.

Need help?"

"My father . . ."

"We'll be right back for him, don't worry."

Maggie helped the woman into the life jacket while Walter gave her husband a hand with his. With a last glance at his dead father, he followed the stretcher.

Megan took a couple of pictures of the stack of boxes, then went in for close-ups. Almost all were printed with the names of the contents: tinned everything. Tinned peas, salmon, baked beans, tomato soup, sardines, peaches, Spam, corned beef, fruit cocktail, and one box that had contained rye crisp-bread. None of it looked as if it would appeal to Indian tastes. Now all the boxes contained empty tins, washed out — presumably in seawater — and piled up higgledy-piggledy.

She frowned. It must have taken more than one man and a lot of hard work to lug this lot into the cave. Why bother if the people were to be abandoned?

TWENTY

When Jocelyn dropped her and Teazle off outside the LonStar shop in Port Mabyn, on their return from Truro, Eleanor was unhappy.

She felt less and less certain of the value of the information she had gleaned from Abel Tregeddle. Not that he had lied to her, but did it actually have any relevance to Kalith Chudasama's plight? Had Megan correctly interpreted what the young man had said? Or had her favourite niece embarked on a possibly perilous expedition based on a trail of uncertain inferences — or, in colloquial language, a load of codswallop?

Jocelyn's dark forebodings had infected her and she felt in need of an antidote. She went to see Nick. His particular combination of pragmatism and cheerful insouciance was just what she wanted.

"Come on, Teazle, we'll catch him just

before the shop closes."

Nick had turned the sign on the gallery door to CLOSED and was just locking up as they arrived. He turned the key back and opened the door.

"Come on in. Hello, Teazle." He stooped to rub between her ears. "Just let me pull down the blind. There. Cuppa?"

"No thanks, I've just been taking tea with a canon. But don't let me stop you."

"Nothing could. What's wrong, Eleanor?"

"How do you know something's wrong?" she asked crossly.

"I'm an artist. I *see* faces. Come upstairs and sit yourself down."

Nick's flat was one large room, only the bathroom walled off. His bed was unmade, but otherwise it was quite neat. All over the walls were pinned what he called sketches, some at least partly coloured though Eleanor had always thought of a sketch as being black and white. "Ideas, trials, and reminders," he'd once explained to her.

The furniture was sparse, a heterogeneous lot he'd picked up here and there, some from LonStar, some from auctions, whatever caught his eye. The only objects of any value were his collection of LPs and his stereo — or hi-fi, or what ever the latest term was for a gramophone. He had another down in the studio.

He put on a record.

"What's that?"

"Dowland. Lute. Soothing."

Eleanor sank into the chair she found most comfortable. A rocking chair originally upholstered in crimson brocade, it was now a dusty pink except in the cracks, but its springs had held up against the passage of time, perhaps because Nick didn't find it comfortable. Rocking, she poured out her story, her fears and uncertainties, while he heated water on the gas ring by the fireplace and made himself a pot of tea and a couple of boiled eggs.

"I must have missed lunch," he said thoughtfully, as Eleanor finished her tale of woe. "Sure you won't have a cup of tea? There's plenty."

"Yes, perhaps I will. But what do you think, Nick?"

"According to what I've heard, everything's under control."

"Why didn't you say so right away?" she asked, indignant.

"I didn't know what you were worrying about until you told me."

"What did you hear? Who from?"

"That cub reporter of yours. What's his

270

name? The laddie from the *North Cornwall Times.*"

"David Skan? How does he know what's happening? What *is* happening?"

"The press have their ways. He snoops on the police radio and has a pal at Coast Guard HQ in Falmouth, I gather. Megan and the RNLI have found the Indians."

"Oh, thank heavens! What about Kalith's mother?"

"I don't know, Eleanor. He said no names were mentioned. They've sent a helicopter to lift someone out."

Eleanor shivered. The day seemed darker. Not only an emotional reaction, she realised; clouds were rolling in, hiding the sun. Nick lit the gas fire.

"Megan's all right?"

"Nothing's been said about a police officer in difficulties. I'm sure Skan will be back, and you can interrogate him. It was you he wanted to see in the first place."

"Me!"

"Well, you're the one who's getting herself talked about in Boscastle. Apparently half the inhabitants are convinced *you* dived into the sea and single-handed pulled this chappy out. Skan's not so naïve as to believe it, but it does make a better story than a mere police officer — even a woman police officer — performing a daring rescue."

"He wouldn't dare to print that!"

"I wouldn't put it past him. Carefully worded so as not to be downright untruth. You'll probably have to bribe him with a few choice tidbits."

"Oh, Nick! What did you tell him?"

"Me? Nothing!" Nick said innocently. "But when he didn't find you at home, he didn't come straight to me; he went to find Mrs. Stearns."

"Who wasn't in either."

"So he talked to the vicar."

"Oh, no!" Eleanor gasped in horror.

"Who seems to have given him the impression that you'd gone off to Truro to make a citizen's arrest of the bishop —"

The telephone extension rang.

"On what charge, he didn't seem to be certain. Quite puzzled, the poor man, and Skan, too. Though he assumed you'd get the Truro police to do the job, not attempt it yourselves. That'll be Mrs. Stearns, no doubt. Hello? Yes, she is. We were expecting you to ring." He handed the receiver to Eleanor.

"Jocelyn?"

"Have you talked to that newspaperman?"

"No, dear. You know I only came home a few minutes ago."

272

"Home! That's where I first tried to get hold of you."

"Came to Nick's, rather."

"What has Nicholas told him?"

"Nothing, he says."

"He didn't tell him you and I intended to arrest the bishop?"

Nick, who was hovering close, shook his head, grinning.

"Certainly not."

"Then where did Timothy get hold of such a ridiculous notion? The poor man is extremely worried!"

"Joce, what did you tell him — the vicar — about where we were going and what for?"

"I don't recall exactly, but certainly not that . . . I suppose he might have got a little confused. But Eleanor, he says it's going to be in the paper! He's afraid he'll be asked to resign his cure, if not be defrocked! What am I going to do?"

Eleanor covered the receiver and hissed at Nick, "What's a cure?"

"A parish, sort of. If the vicar's talking about it."

"Jocelyn, for pity's sake, they wouldn't print something like that without checking. They don't want to be sued for slander."

"Libel," Nick whispered.

"For libel. I have no doubt whatsoever that Mr. Skan will turn up again on your doorstep or mine to — In fact, Nick's doorbell is ringing. I bet you anything that's him. I'll ring you back. After the weather forecast." Was Megan still at sea, in a gathering storm? Perhaps David Skan would know.

"If it's him, you're prepared to talk to him?" Nick asked.

"Yes. I want to know what he knows — and what he thinks he knows."

Nick went running downstairs, leaving the door at the top open. From below came the jangle of his shop bell as he opened the street door, then two pairs of footsteps ascended the stairs.

Eleanor heard him say firmly, "And you're not to pester her, or you'll be out on your ear!"

"Not to worry," said the jaunty voice of the cub reporter. "It's a good story, whichever way she wants to play it." He appeared at the top, his bush of white-blond hair as vigorous as ever, camera slung round his neck. "Hello, Mrs. Trewynn. I hear your niece is a heroine and you've turned detective again!"

"You've got half of it right, Mr. Skan."

"That's what I thought. Plenty of sources for the lifesaving — though you're the only actual witness I've talked to, Mr. Gresham — but I treat anything the Reverend Stearns tells me with great caution."

"How wise of you," said Nick mockingly. "Have a seat. Tea? Beer?"

"A beer would go down nicely, thanks. Tell me about your visit to Truro, Mrs. Trewynn."

"It was related to church matters. You'd hardly expect Mrs. Stearns to discuss that sort of thing with me. I went along only to keep her company. She picked me up in Port Isaac on her way, you see, after Megan went off in the lifeboat."

Skan pounced. "So DS Pencarrow *did* go out with the lifeboats. Cheers," he added, as Nick handed him an opened bottle.

Bother! Eleanor thought. She must be more careful not to reveal facts he might not already have acquired. Too late to take that one back. "Yes, and I'm very worried about her. It was fine when they left, but it looks now as if a storm is blowing in. Nick, let's listen to the weather."

Nick turned on his transistor just in time to catch the beginning of the weather and shipping forecasts. Skan started to speak, but Eleanor put her finger to her lips and they listened in silence, Nick and the reporter swigging now and then from their

275

bottles. Young people these days didn't seem to bother with glasses.

At the end, Eleanor asked, "We're Lundy, aren't we, Nick?"

"Yes. Wind thirty-five knots with gusts to fifty, heavy seas and squalls expected."

"Don't let it worry you," Skan said cheerfully. "They'll all be on land by the time it starts really blowing. According to my Coast Guard source, the Padstow lifeboat's expected to arrive home between half six and seven, and the other two are already in." He glanced at his watch. "In fact, I'd better get going. I'm supposed to meet the Padstow boat. I'll come back afterwards for a word with you, Mrs. Trewynn. Thanks for the beer, mate. Cheerio!"

He dashed off before Eleanor had a chance to say she was rather tired and would prefer to speak to him tomorrow. "Bother! I know he's inescapable, but I'd have liked to get it over with. Did he tell you, earlier, anything else he'd heard from his Coast Guard source?"

"I refused to describe Megan's gallant rescue until he spilled the beans. He hasn't got on to Julia and Chaz yet, so I was his only source for that, and I didn't give him their surnames. According to him, the lifeboats rescued about a dozen people."

"Thank heaven! I've been so afraid they wouldn't find anyone and we'd never know for sure . . . Or worse, the boy would wake up and confirm what he'd said, and it would be too late . . . What about his mother?"

"I don't know for sure, but as I said, the rescue helicopter winched up someone, a seriously ill woman, and took her to hospital."

"Surely that must be her. I wonder if she's gone to the same hospital as Kalith. Did Mr. Skan tell you where they took her?"

"No. Perhaps he didn't know, but he was holding his cards close to his chest. He wouldn't tell me anything at all until I swore an oath of secrecy."

"Oh dear, then you shouldn't have told me. Though I'm very glad you did."

"Megan's sure to if I don't. Schoolboy stuff, anyway, 'oath of secrecy,' my foot! And idiotic. As if it won't all be common knowledge by the time his paper comes out."

"Writing for a weekly must cramp his style."

"Another thing he didn't mention: I'm not sure whether he knows they're Indian. Or at least that our lad is. If it comes out, the inspector can't blame me."

"What with the ambulance men and the hospital people, not to mention the lifeboat crew, he'll have plenty of possible leaks to blame, though they're not supposed to talk about patients. Perhaps Jocelyn can find out which hospital Mrs. Chudasama was flown to. She's as much a parishioner as Kalith, after all. I wonder whether Joce has thought to ring up and ask how Kalith is doing. I'd better give her a ring and remind her, and ask her to try and find out where his mother —"

"Eleanor, we don't know that it was Kalith's mother. I hate to be the one to break it to you, but Skan said there was a body, too."

"Oh! Oh no!"

"Whisky," said Nick, jumping up and going to the cupboard whence had appeared the beer. "I've got a half-bottle for emergencies."

"I'm perfectly all right."

"No soda, though. But I seem to remember you prefer water?"

"Yes," Eleanor admitted. Whisky was a rare indulgence and she really had felt quite faint for a moment. She pulled herself together, accepting the coffee mug Nick handed her.

"Sorry. I really must buy a few glasses now that I can afford such frivolities."

"There are always some going for practically nothing in the shop." She took a sip. It tasted just the same from a mug. "I'll ask Jocelyn to pick you out a nice matching half dozen. Oh, Nick, I don't think I can cope with Joce again today. Fond of her as I am, she can be quite exhausting. But I said I'd ring her, so I'd better go home and get it over with."

"Be my guest." Nick waved at his phone.

"I don't want to run up your bill."

"There's your excuse for not talking too long."

"All right. Thanks. Do you mind if I tell her what David Skan told you?"

"If a vicar's wife can't be trusted not to spread gossip, who can?" he asked rhetorically.

The vicarage phone rang several times before Timothy Stearns answered, his hesitant voice as always sounding as if he wasn't at all sure that the number he was giving actually corresponded with the one printed on the dial.

"Hello, Vicar. Sorry to bother you. It's Eleanor — Eleanor Trewynn." One could never be too specific with the Reverend Stearns. "May I speak to Jocelyn, please?" She almost added Joce's surname.

"I'm so sorry, she's not here. She just went out. In fact, I thought — Could I be mistaken? — I was under the impression that she said she was coming to see you."

"I expect you're right," Eleanor said, resigned. "No doubt she'll be here in a couple of minutes. Thank you, Vicar. Good-bye." She was always punctilious about saying good-bye to him when she hung up. Otherwise, his devoted spouse had informed her, he was liable to clutch the receiver saying, "Hello? Hello?" in increasingly despondent tones for some time.

"I'll tell her you left," Nick offered.

"You must be mad! She'd go next door and ring my doorbell — and probably go upstairs as I wouldn't be surprised if I forgot to lock up — and when she found I wasn't there, she'd call out the police to search for me. She'd be convinced the smugglers had got me."

He laughed.

"No, seriously," Eleanor assured him. "She was very upset when I went to look for smugglers in Boscastle. She warned me it was dangerous. And now it turns out there really are smugglers prepared to leave all those people to die, she'll be quite sure they're after me."

TWENTY-ONE

The cabin of the *Daisy D.* was not the ideal place for police interviews. However, Coxswain Kulick had told Megan the lifeboat was to be met in Padstow by an ambulance or two and a minibus to bundle everyone off to hospital. After their ordeal, some if not all would need medical attention.

A hospital was a still less hospitable environment for questioning witnesses than a crowded cabin, even though the cabin was pitching and rolling. At least the motion was regular now. Megan was pleased to find it didn't bother her, and most of the Indians seemed able to cope. A lifeboat man was dealing kindly and efficiently with the three who couldn't.

The taciturn Charles had distributed blankets. He and Gavin handed round hot drinks. Megan was glad to warm her hands on a mug of bouillon.

The obvious person to begin with was Mr.

Nayak. For a start, he spoke English. Also, he appeared to have some authority, perhaps as the eldest, as well as having been the one to stay behind to make sure his ailing sister was cared for and to keep watch over the body of his father.

He was between a middle-aged woman and a man of about Megan's own age, perhaps a couple of years younger. The older pair both sat slumped on the bench, scarcely aware of her approach. The young man stood up and came towards her.

"How do you do," he said formally. He sounded more like an English colonial expat than an Indian. "May I introduce myself? I'm Ajay Nayak. You're Miss Pencarrow, I think?"

"Yes," Megan admitted, not sure whether being Miss Pencarrow was a good thing in his eyes or a bad. Had someone told him she was a police officer? She shook hands. "How do you do."

"I'm told you saved my cousin Kalith's life, and so, all of us."

"I got him out of the sea, with a lot of help. Whether I saved his life . . . I haven't heard the latest news. He was pretty ill when I last saw him."

"But thanks to you and to him, the rest of us have been rescued. Except for my grandfather. He chose to stop eating as soon as the shortage of food became obvious, so that the children and my sister could have more."

"He and Kalith are responsible for your survival."

"Kalith is the only one of us able to swim. He used to go swimming with the black children, much to the family's horror, though secretly I envied his boldness."

This was all very well, but it wasn't getting Megan any further. The *Daisy D.* was ploughing steadily towards Padstow. She glanced at the elder Nayak. He had closed his eyes. His son, on the other hand, was alert and seemed cooperative.

"Sir —"

"Please call me Jay."

"I should tell you that I'm a police officer."

"So was I." He grinned sourly. "But they're all African now, except the top brass — white, of course. And I don't suppose they'll be there long, but at least they'll be able to come to Britain when they're kicked out."

"I'm sorry." Megan paused. "But you'll understand why I've got to ask questions, and the sooner the better."

"Yes." He looked around the cabin, where

his family were variously talking, brooding, dozing, or being sick. "Not here."

"Let's see if Coxswain Kulick will let us have a corner of the wheelhouse. I don't fancy out on deck."

"Nor do I." He followed her up the winding stair.

At her request, the skipper waved them over to the chart board. She took out her notebook. "I'm Megan. Also known as DS Pencarrow."

"I was a sergeant. Not detective, but still . . . Do you suppose — No, it's no good trying to guess what will happen to us. At least most of us are alive. You want to know how we came to be in such a mess. I take it you know about the situation in Kenya and Uganda?"

"Roughly."

"My grandfather chose British citizenship for the family, but we didn't come here soon enough and they changed the rules. We didn't have any choice about leaving Africa. I was sacked from the police and we were forced to sell our family business. At a huge loss, of course. Africanisation. We came to Britain, with British passports in our hands. I can show them to you."

"That's all right, I believe you. Though you'll have to produce them sometime, of course."

"For all the use they are," he commented bitterly. "After we were turned away, we tried other places, without success. We were back in Mombasa . . . well, not exactly *in* Mombasa."

"How do you mean?"

"In the harbour, on board a tramp steamer. They wouldn't let us land. A sailor came to us, a lascar, as they call Indian sailors, and told us he'd met a man on shore who had offered to get us into Britain. For a price, naturally. I should say, my grandfather had the foresight to move much of the family's assets abroad before it was too late. We had to leave most of our belongings behind when we were taken, at dead of night, by water to a larger ship. A freighter."

"Its name?" asked Megan, pencil poised.

Jay shook his head. "Everything that might have given it away was covered."

"Damn. An elementary precaution, I suppose. But you must have been on board for some time. Surely —"

"We were taken down to a hold. In one corner, they'd built three rooms out of plywood. Easily dismantled. Electric light. No plumbing, but a cubicle with what you'd call basic facilities. Very decent, really. We managed quite well. That's why I didn't expect and can't understand — Why go to all that trouble?"

"We'll find out," Megan said grimly. "Go on."

"They fed us well enough. We had the same food as the lascar seamen. They told us the purser provided rations for us."

"That suggests everyone aboard knew about your presence."

"Such was my impression, though I never heard anyone say so outright."

"Maybe one of your family did. Did you talk with the lascars in English, or in your own language?"

"They spoke what you might call sailors' English and sailors' Hindi. Our native language is Gujarati. Among us, we have varying abilities in English, Hindi, and Swahili. I myself have little Hindi."

"But excellent English." She smiled at him. "Which is a great help. And luckily Kalith speaks at least enough to bring us looking for you."

"He speaks as well as I. If he was able to tell you so little, he must indeed be in bad shape."

"I'm sorry I can't give you more recent news. Coxswain Kulick might be able to find out." They both looked at the skipper. He was peering into the gloom. The sky had darkened without Megan's noticing, And the *Daisy D.* was definitely tossing about more than she had been. "But on the whole I'd rather not distract him. As soon as we land . . ."

She wondered what they would face when they arrived at Padstow. The promised ambulances would probably take them to the Bodmin hospital, the closest. Would the Bodmin district police be there, or would Scumble manage to wangle his way into staying in charge? Immigration officials? If it came to a battle between the immigration people investigating unlawful entry and the police investigating homicide, who took preference?

Time would tell. And meanwhile, Megan had to make the best of the time left to her.

"Do you know where the ship went after leaving Mombasa, Jay?"

"Through the Suez Canal. That part was obvious from all the stopping and starting, as well as dictated by geography."

Megan tried to picture a map of that area of the world and failed dismally. "The Horn of Africa?" she ventured.

He grinned. "Yes, round it. Gulf of Aden, up the Red Sea and via the canal to the Mediterranean. The ship made several stops. I have no idea where."

"You didn't by any chance count the days between ports of call?"

"I think my uncle did to start with, going by his watch and the arrival of meals. But it began to seem pointless. Day and night were alike. We were never allowed to leave the hold. We could neither see nor hear anything beyond it."

"Any guess at the cargo?"

"Trying to guess was one of our chief entertainments," he said dryly. "I don't know about other holds, but ours was mostly stacks of big hessian bales. They had a sort of greasy, animal smell. We decided, probably wool — unwashed fleeces. Therefore, probably Australia or New Zealand."

Megan perked up. "That gives us somewhere to start! How did you get from the ship to the cave?"

"Hazardously! We were lowered one by one to what I think you'd call a motor yacht. At night, of course."

"With its name carefully hidden, I assume. At sea? In a harbour?"

"At sea."

"City lights on the horizon?"

"Not that I saw. Perhaps on the other side of the ship."

"But you didn't notice the sort of glow in the sky that a big city always makes?"

After a moment's thought, he shook his head. "No."

"Pity. Though it does mean Falmouth isn't ruled out. It's small enough not to have that sort of halo."

"Falmouth?"

"A port in southeast Cornwall. Oh, maybe you don't know, your cave is on the North Coast of Cornwall, which is the southwesterly tip of England. How long were you on the yacht?"

"Through one day and into the next night. Then they anchored. We could hear the chain let down. After a while, they let us all up on the deck. It was very dark, no light but a couple of torches. Two men. They showed us a stack of boxes and told us they contained supplies for us. That was when we found out we were not to be put ashore at a place where we could find our own way inland. The man giving the orders —"

"One of them definitely seemed to be in charge?"

Jay hesitated. "I think so. I had the impression that he was the boss, the captain of the yacht, maybe the owner. He had an educated voice, or so it seemed to me. The other said very little, and his accent was so thick I couldn't understand much of it. A common seaman, I think."

"Foreign or local? Oh, I suppose you wouldn't know. It's too much to hope that you saw their faces."

"They both wore caps — hats — that covered their faces, all but the eyes and mouth."

"Balaclavas. They were well prepared."

"Yes, except . . . But I'll come to that in a minute. The captain explained that it was too dangerous for so large and conspicuous a group to travel together. We were to wait in a safe place for a day or two, then we'd be picked up a few at a time and taken to various nearby harbours."

"He didn't say where? Name any places?"

"No. We and our few suitcases were transferred into a rowboat, two or three at a time along with a couple of crates of supplies in each boatload, and taken to the cave. Kalith and I were last as they needed our help with the last boxes."

"Did both the men appear to know how to get to the cave?"

"I'm not sure. The seaman was rowing. The captain was in the front, directing him, but that could have been so he didn't have to keep looking over his shoulder. Also, the captain had a very powerful torch he turned on when we got close, and a pole he used to fend off from rocks. You went there, didn't you?"

"Yes. Part of my job."

He nodded. "Then you'll understand that we were surprised and alarmed to see where we were expected to wait. But what choice did we have?"

"None, realistically. The men went with you into the cave?"

"The seaman led the way, carrying a box. Kalith and I managed the last one. The captain sent the seaman back to the boat. The women were crying and my children were frightened. My grandfather asked if there was not somewhere more civilised where they, at least, could stay while waiting to be picked up. The captain said — he was sneering — that beggars can't be choosers. My grandfather told him we were not beggars. Perhaps unwisely, but he had dealt honestly with us until that moment, bringing us all the way from Mombasa."

"You're sure he was running the show the whole time?"

"Well, no. I assumed so, but the yacht may have been his only part in it. Anyway, we paid someone extremely well for the journey, and I'm certain he got his share. Everything was well planned, well prepared, as you said. I don't think the plan included demanding more money when we'd so nearly reached our destination. It seemed to me he just decided at that moment, suddenly, he wanted more."

"Why do you think so?"

"The way he looked. There was a paraffin lantern, quite bright. I saw his face change, what I could see of it — his eyes and his mouth. A book we read at school, *Dr. Jekyll and Mr. Hyde* — Do you know it? It was like that. One minute he was helping us, the next he was telling us everything had cost more than expected and he needed more money to pay the man who was to pick us up."

"And again, you had no choice. Would you recognise him? His eyes, his mouth, his voice?"

"If you ever find him, I think so. I'm pretty certain."

"We'll find him. You've given me plenty to start with. My boss, DI Scumble, is bound to come up with a long list of questions I should have asked. One thing I know he'll want is all your names. We'd better begin with your grandfather — I'm very sorry we arrived too late for him."

"He saved my children by giving them his share of the food. His memory will be always honoured."

Megan couldn't think of anything to say

292

that wouldn't sound trite, so she was silent for a moment, as she had been beside the old man's body.

Coxswain Kulick chose the moment to say, "Sergeant, we're going to get pretty busy here shortly, as we turn into Padstow Bay. The storm's coming up fast and will likely hit as we cross Doom Bar into the Camel estuary. The two of you will have to go back to the cabin."

"Yes, sir." To Jay, she said, "That'll work better, actually, because you can point out each person as you give me the names."

They went down. Gavin was stowing the galley equipment. Most of the refugees seemed much revived after the hot drinks, and the little boy, Jay's son, had stopped retching. He ran to Jay, who picked him up and held him as he talked to the family briefly in their own language — Goodge-something? Megan hoped she had written it down.

He included her name and rank, so she assumed he was introducing her. The words "detective sergeant" appeared to excite some consternation. Jay spoke again, soothingly.

Then he went round the cabin giving her all the names and, in English, their relationships. At her request, he also told her which of them spoke English. She scribbled madly, hoping to be able to interpret her notes later, and to find out the proper spellings. An attempt at a family tree might be useful, too.

When Jay finished, Megan felt she ought to make some sort of announcement, but she didn't know what to say. Before the right words came to her, a sudden blast of wind buffeted the *Daisy D.,* nearly knocking her off her feet. Rain rattled on the roof.

"Better sit down," Gavin advised loudly. "Hang on to the kids. Looks like we're in for a proper blow."

It wasn't so much a blow as a series of blows, gusts and squalls that hit unexpectedly, with pauses between. Megan thought they must be more difficult to navigate through than any steady wind, especially as they were getting into the narrowing estuary and then the still narrower River Camel. She tried to suppress thoughts of crossing the bar with the sinister name.

Doom Bar! She shuddered. No one noticed because the lifeboat was shuddering too. Padstow was the skipper's and crew's home port, she reminded herself. They knew what they were doing.

As if at the wave of a wand, the water calmed and the wind gusts nudged instead

294

of striking violently. Doom averted, presumably. They were past the bar, into the tidal estuary between low but sheltering hills. Slow but steady, the *Daisy D.* zigzagged between buoys, then came to a halt with a couple of gentle thumps. The sounds of feet and voices competed with the rattle of rain on the roof of the cabin. A heavy thud suggested the placing of a gangway.

One of the lifeboat crew came down the steps. "Sergeant, you're wanted ashore. The rest of you, stay where you are, please, till we get things sorted out."

As Jay translated for those who had not understood, Megan went up and out on deck.

The air was fresh and clean and wet. Rain dimpled the black water of the harbour. It danced on the stone paving of the quay, slanting down in the pools of light cast by lampposts and the beams of the headlights of a minibus, two ambulances, and two police cars, Megan saw as she climbed the gangway. She'd left the RNLI helmet and life jacket behind. Cold rain streamed through her hair and down her neck.

The tip of the quay, where they were moored, was closed off with steel barricades, manned by two coppers in rain capes.

Bodmin police? Padstow was in Bodmin's district. Was she about to receive retribution for poaching in their territory? She was much too tired to cope with the inevitable ructions. The thought of facing the toadlike Superintendent Egerton made her feel physically sick . . . unless that was just the transition to footing that didn't keep moving beneath her but felt as though it did.

A large man heaved himself out of the nearest panda car and came towards her. The brim of his hat shaded his face, but surely he was not large enough to be Egerton —

She wouldn't have thought it possible to be so happy to see Detective Inspector Scumble.

"So you found 'em, Pencarrow."

"Yes, sir. One dead, one in bad shape, but the children are okay. Three of them. Is Kalith — ?"

"That can wait till tomorrow. You've had quite a day and I've got stuff to take care of here." Turning, he walked her along the quay away from the lifeboat. "We picked up your car in Port Isaac on the way here. Don't make a habit of leaving police cars about the place."

"No, sir. My shoulder bag . . . ?"

"In the car." He opened the passenger-side door and spoke to the uniformed constable at the wheel. "Take DS Pencarrow back to Launceston."

"Yes, sir." The voice was that of PC Dawson, the Speed Demon, Terror of the Highways and Byways. Another terrifying journey — just what she needed.

At least he'd get her home as soon as humanly possible. She couldn't wait to get out of her —

"When you've typed up your report, Pencarrow, you can go home. Be at the nick at eight in the morning."

"Yes, sir." Damn him! She should have known better than to think he sympathised with her "quite a day" to the extent of letting her postpone the reports till tomorrow.

She got into the car. Dawson had already started the engine and before the door had quite clicked shut he started backing at an alarming speed towards the barricade. As they zoomed in reverse through the narrow gap, Megan saw, beneath their uniform sou'westers, the faces of the local sergeant and his sole constable, and next to them a dripping figure in a felt hat and sodden mac, with a camera slung round his neck — David Skan, ace reporter of the *North Cornwall Times*.

"Rain drove off the telly blokes," said

Dawson conversationally, still speeding backwards along the quay, "and the rest of the newspapermen hopped it to the nearest pub. Pity, really. You're quite a sight for sore eyes in them tights, Sarge."

Without much hope, Megan asked, "I don't suppose you picked up my clothes in Port Isaac?"

"In the boot with your bag."

"Thanks." All very well, she thought, but here she was stuck with yet another outfit that had to be returned to its owner.

TWENTY-TWO

Eleanor opened one eye, squinted at the alarm clock, and closed it again. Ten to eight. She was in no rush to get up. The drumming of rain on the slate roof was no incentive to leave the warmth of her bed.

She cast her mind back to last night. Megan had phoned, interrupting Jocelyn in mid-harangue. She had rung up Eleanor's flat first, of course, and then the vicarage, to Timothy's utter bewilderment. Nick's was her last attempt. She had, Nick said later, apologised handsomely for having bitten his nose off earlier, though he was far too much a gentleman, he declared with a laugh, to disclose the reason for their falling out.

Megan was safe. That was all that mattered. Apart, of course, from the rescue of the Indian refugees. Megan had passed on a bit more of the story than David Skan had known — or revealed. It was sad that the old man was dead, but all the rest might have died as well if Eleanor hadn't stuck to her guns about the smugglers' caves.

Nick had called for a celebration and brought out the whisky bottle again. Jocelyn accepted a small tot. Eleanor had already emptied her first glass, but she hadn't refused a second. That must be why she had slept so late —

She sat bolt upright. Twenty to ten, not ten to eight! The phone was ringing downstairs, and, "You must be bursting, Teazle! Past time to go out."

"Wuff," said the little dog hopefully, jumping off the bed.

Eleanor threw back the duvet, reached for her dressing gown, and thrust her feet into her slippers. The phone fell silent.

"Oh bother! Come on, girl."

Teazle scampered down ahead of her. She had just reached the door when the phone resumed its plaintive *ring-ring, ring-ring.* Eleanor grabbed the receiver.

"Sorry, I *must* let the dog out. Back in half a tick."

The flat door opened to stairs going down to a semipublic passage. It was used only when goods arrived to be carried back to the storeroom, though, and by LonStar volunteers going to the loo by the street door. Fortunately, almost all the volunteers

300

were women. All the same, Eleanor belted her dressing gown more securely about her as she followed Teazle to the back door.

She had forgotten to bring the key, but luckily it wasn't locked. Or unluckily, if Jocelyn happened to find out. Today was her day to run the shop, so doubtless she was there now, preparing to open for business.

As Eleanor turned the handle, the door was flung open by a blast of cold wind and rain. It crashed against the wall. Teazle darted out. Eleanor, her dressing gown wet all down the front, battled to close the door. Jocelyn popped out of the stockroom.

"What on earth . . . ? Oh, it's you, Eleanor. Filthy day! But the street is sheltered from that howling gale. I'd go out the front if I were — You're not dressed yet!"

"Teazle had to go out. And someone rang. I asked them to wait and left the receiver off the hook. I must run."

"If that dog has any sense, she'll have done her business and want to come straight back in. I'll help you with the door."

Between them, they managed to open it just far enough for Teazle, already sodden, to zip back in. They slammed it shut and Jocelyn reached towards the keyhole.

"The key must have fallen out." She

scanned the floor.

"It wasn't locked," Eleanor confessed. "Sorry."

Taking her own keys out of her pocket, Joce gave her a look but refrained from comment. She was beginning to resign herself. Eleanor had long since explained that she'd lost the habit of locking up after spending much of her life in places where people's homes had no doors, let alone locks. If she'd ever had the habit. In her childhood, in the country, people didn't —

Teazle shook vigorously, spattering them both. Jocelyn looked down at her clothes — smart as always but not silk today, thank goodness — and pursed her lips.

"It's just water," Eleanor pointed out. "She didn't have time to get muddy."

"You're almost as wet as she is. You'd better go and get dressed. Your caller will have rung off by now." Joce beat a hasty retreat as Teazle braced herself to shake again.

They went back upstairs. Eleanor shut Teazle out on the landing while she went in to fetch the dog towel. The phone had reverted the purr of the dialling tone, so she hung up. It immediately began to ring.

She picked it up. "I really can't talk now. I've got a soaked dog and I'm pretty wet and chilly myself —"

"Aunt Nell!"

"Hello, Megan. Sorry, dear, but —"

"DI Scumble wants to talk to you."

"Tell him I'll ring back in quarter of an hour." Eleanor hung up, picturing with some plea sure the inspector red-faced and spluttering. She hoped he wouldn't be angry with Megan. Oh dear, she had been rather rude. Perhaps . . . She reached out to the phone, but Teazle barked impatiently.

First things first.

Fifteen minutes later, she sat down with a cup of tea, dialled the Launceston police station, and asked for DI Scumble. "This is Mrs. Trewynn. He's expecting my call."

She hoped to speak to Megan first, but she was put straight through to Scumble.

"All dried off, are we?" he said sarcastically. "I take it it's raining on the coast. You'll be glad to hear Launceston is sunny."

"How odd. Nice for you, but —"

"Because I want to see you here, as soon as you can make it, if not sooner."

"Why can't you come here?" Eleanor asked indignantly. "You could get here much quicker than my car can get to you."

"Because I'm extremely busy. I appreciate it's possible you are too, and that your business is more important to you than providing further assistance with the case in which

303

you have already been involved. I can't make you come."

"If there's really something I can do to help . . . All right, I'll come. I hope it's not so urgent that I can't have breakfast first."

"Breakfast!" said Scumble, in the voice of a man who has been up and at work for several hours already.

"And the Incorruptible probably needs petrol," Eleanor thought aloud. "Ummm . . . This may sound silly, Inspector, but I can't remember where I left the car." A wordless explosive sound reached her ear. "Let me see: I drove the Incorruptible to Boscastle, and then went to tell you . . . and Megan drove us both to Port Isaac in a panda car. And then Mrs. Stearns picked me up there." Better not to mention the futile trip to Truro, though it had given her an idea, which she couldn't quite call to mind . . . "So the Incorruptible is still parked in Launceston," she concluded, "unless it's been towed away."

"You win," the inspector conceded bitterly. "I'll send a car to pick you up."

In spite of the police car taking about half as long to cross the moors as the Incorruptible would have, Eleanor had time to feed Teazle and herself and wash up before the street doorbell rang. Peering down through the rain-washed kitchen window, she saw a panda below, parked with two wheels on the pavement, as was necessary to allow other vehicles to negotiate the narrow street.

She clipped Teazle's lead to her collar, gathered up handbag, raincoat, and umbrella — whatever Scumble said about the weather in Launceston, one never could tell — and went down. The uniformed constable awaiting her was the boy who had asked her only yesterday whether she could manage the stairs at the police station.

Blushing, he saluted her. "PC Arden, madam."

"We're ready to go," she said with a smile.

He looked at Teazle, blinked, and opened his mouth. Nothing came out — fortunately, since Eleanor had no intention of leaving the dog behind. She hoped he wouldn't get into trouble with Scumble.

Teazle had no intention of being left behind. As soon as the constable opened the car door, she jumped up on the seat and popped over the gear lever to the back. She sat in the middle, stumpy tail thumping, always happy to go for a ride and unconcerned as to where she was going.

Eleanor, on the other hand, spent the journey wondering just what Scumble expected of her. It seemed most unlike him to actually request her help. She didn't have any further help to offer, now that the Indians had been found and rescued. Was he going to insist on her giving him the name of the fisherman who had told her about the caves? She had promised Abel Tregeddle she'd keep him out of the picture.

What other reason could Scumble have for wanting to talk to her? She worried about it the whole way to Launceston.

It rained until they started down off the moor. The slow-moving storm seemed to have stalled on the heights, as if held at bay by the towering boulders of Brown Willie and Rough Tor. As promised, Launceston itself was bathed in sunlight.

When Eleanor walked into the station, the sergeant on duty smiled at her benevolently. "Mrs. Trewynn, for DI Scumble, right? And how's the pup today?" Teazle wagged her tail but continued to head for the stairs. Picking up his phone, he laughed. "She knows where she's going. I'll let him know you're on your way, Mrs. Trewynn."

Led by Teazle, Eleanor reached Scumble's door just as Megan opened it. "Hello, dear. Good morning, Inspector. I've been think-ing and thinking, and I can't imagine any way I can help you."

"I don't know that you can," he said

306

sourly, "but my superintendent had a call late last night from some VIP at the Commonwealth Relations Office vouching for your credentials."

"Sir Edward Bellowe?"

"That's him. He'd somehow heard your name in connection with this business. Mr. Bentinck assured him we'd paid heed to your suggestions and they had paid off in spades."

"Then what more can Sir Edward possibly expect?"

"It's not just Sir Edward, or even just the Commonwealth people. The super is afraid we're going to have the whole kit and caboodle landing on our doorstep — Immigration, Home Office, Foreign Office, even Scotland Yard all gumming up the works. The Coast Guard already have a finger in the pie."

"And you're hoping to use Sir Edward as a scarecrow?" asked Eleanor, adding a fresh ingredient to the stew of metaphors.

"If we can tell the others that Commonwealth Relations are holding a watching brief, maybe it'll make them think twice about poking their noses in. By what I hear, our relationship with the New Commonwealth isn't too grand just now. And if we're consulting you, we can just about justify claiming we're working with Sir Edward and his lot."

"I suppose so. Would you like me to talk to Sir Edward? He and his wife are good friends of mine."

"Possibly, later. We'll see how things go. I'll tell you something, Mrs. Trewynn, I'm going to collar the villain who left three kids and a pregnant woman to die — not to mention the rest of them! — and I won't stand for any interfering busybodies getting underfoot. Nor anyone holding back pertinent information. So now you're going to give me the name of the man who told you about those caves."

"I promised! If it were a matter of saving lives . . . That's what persuaded him to tell me. But they're safe now."

"And what about the next lot? If we let this bloke get away with it, what's to stop him trying it again? From all I hear, there are plenty of potential victims out there. Not every family can boast of a hero like young Chudasama, and even he was too late for the old man."

"How is he? Do you know?"

" 'Resting comfortably.' Hospital-speak for still in the land of the living. The doctors won't let a copper near him yet, though. Come on, no more messing about, let's have that name."

It wasn't just his usual irritation, Eleanor realised. He was truly angry. Yet a promise is a promise and she still hesitated.

"Sir, I've been thinking —"

"Congratulations, Pencarrow! Don't strain the brain."

Megan ploughed on. "It seems to me we could find the in formant just by going door-to-door in Boscastle. It's not a very big village. I bet everyone knows Aunt Nell, because she collects donations there, and lots of people probably know exactly which houses she called at yesterday morning. Even which was the last house, before she came here to pass on the info."

"You've got a point," the inspector said grudgingly. Eleanor let out a sigh of relief. "We're going to have to do a door-to-door there anyway. If Ajay Nayak — Have I got that right? Assuming he interpreted the sudden change in the 'captain' correctly, the man must have had someone in mind to pick up the Indians."

"The captain?" Eleanor ventured.

"We have to refer to the big boss villain somehow, Mrs. Trewynn."

"Jay Nayak called him the captain, Aunt Nell. He —"

Scumble made an impatient gesture. "If I

may be allowed to continue: Chances are, he'd already sounded out a boatman who knew how to find the caves, and that boatman is likely to be from Boscastle. Makes sense?"

"Yes, sir. Assuming Jay's right. Isn't it possible . . ." She hesitated.

"Spit it out, woman!"

"If Jay's wrong — or even if he's right, come to that — isn't it possible the captain paid a boatman in advance and the failure to pick them up was the boatman's fault, not the captain's?"

"Could be, I suppose. Yes, it's possible."

"And Jay did say the captain claimed he needed more money for the boatman."

"I don't like you calling him Jay, Pencarrow. You're getting too close."

"But most of them are surnamed Nayak. I can't refer to all the men as Mr. Nayak. Besides, he is — or was — a copper. A fellow sergeant, at that."

The inspector snorted but didn't argue.

"Anyway, I can't remember all their christian — their first names. I wish I'd had a chance to talk to some of the others yesterday, about their impressions of the captain, and anything else they might have noticed that Jay missed or didn't think to mention."

"You'll get your chance this afternoon.

Mr. Bentinck fixed it up with Egerton."

"Egerton is the Bodmin superintendent?" Eleanor asked.

"That's right. As a matter of fact, the super said Egerton wouldn't touch it with a barge pole. He's afraid of coming to grief — too many complications. So though they're in Bodmin, they're ours. Or rather, for the moment, your niece's."

"All on her own?"

"Mrs. Trewynn, this isn't the only case I have to deal with. Among others, four tourists were mugged in the fog in Bude, and my other sergeant is helping out there. DC Polmenna — you may remember him — will have to manage the Boscastle door-to-door with a couple of uniforms. I don't want to borrow people from Bodmin if I can help it. Wait a bit!" He snapped his fingers. "Do you speak — What are those languages, Pencarrow?"

"Gujarati is the main one, plus Swahili and Hindi."

"Only a few words of Gujarati. Quite a lot of the others, though I'm a bit rusty. You mean, you want me to go with Megan to interview the Indians?"

"She will ask the questions. But your knowing the lingos gives me an excuse to send you along. That should keep Sir Edward Bellowe happy. He told the super you have a gift for setting people at ease, and these people have got to be in a state of anxiety, so you might even be helpful."

"I'll do my best," said Eleanor.

"Thank you."

"Who's looking after them? Are they still in hospital? They're not in prison, are they?"

"Don't worry, Aunt Nell, they're not in prison. Some are in hospital. Kalith's in Plymouth and the Coast Guard took his mother there, too, when they airlifted her out. The woman who's expecting is in Bodmin Hospital still, and one of the children, with his mother. I can't remember all the relationships. Jay told me, but the boat was tossing about and my notes got a bit muddled."

"Not to say illegible!"

"I can read them, sir. I just . . ."

"Can't make sense of them. That's another thing you'll have to do, get the relationships straight and get the names spelled properly."

"Yes, sir. Social Services is taking care of the rest of them," Megan told Eleanor.

"Another damned interfering government department," Scumble said gloomily.

"They're lucky, they've been put in one of the new council houses in Bodmin. Very cramped, of course, but a sight better than the cave!"

The phone rang, and Megan picked it up. "Pencarrow . . . Who? . . . You're not serious? . . . Yes, just a moment." Looking aghast, she put her hand over the mouthpiece. "Sir, it's . . . it's DS Faraday. Will you take the call? Please?"

"Kenneth Faraday? The Boy Wonder? Scotland Yard? Bloody hell, just what we need!" Scowling, he picked up the receiver of the phone on his desk. "Scumble here. Put him through. Sergeant Faraday? What the devil" — he glanced at Eleanor — "deuce do you want? . . . No, I have not heard from the chief constable . . . For *who*? No, there's no need to repeat yourself . . . Better the devil we know, eh? Well, we don't need your help but I suppose you don't have a choice in the matter . . . All right, all right, someone will meet you at the station . . . Hang on." He covered the mouthpiece. "He wants to know if you'll put him up, Pencarrow."

"What cheek! No, I bloody well won't!"

Scumble spoke into the receiver again. "You're out of luck, Sergeant. I'll have a room booked for you at the White Hart." He hung up.

Megan was bursting with indignation. "What's he coming here for?"

"To keep an eye on things for the Home Office, the Foreign Office, and everyone else under the sun. Could be worse. At least we're spared a representative of each. They're sending him, specifically, because he's already acquainted with the local yokels."

"What! He didn't say —"

"No, no, simmer down. He's cocky but not quite that cocky. That's what it amounts to, though. Ah, well, I expect I can dig up a job of work to keep him out of my hair."

"I hope you don't intend to palm him off on me! Sir."

"No promises, Pencarrow, no promises."

Eleanor was racking her brains. Kenneth Faraday? She recognised the name but couldn't picture the face, which meant she had never met him, as her memory for faces — if not for keys — was excellent.

Scotland Yard? He must have been a colleague of Megan's when she worked in London. It was obvious neither she nor Mr. Scumble liked him.

Megan sighed. "Well, he may be a pain in the neck, but no one can say he isn't a smart detective, as well as being a smart aleck."

TWENTY-THREE

Megan and Eleanor drove south towards Bodmin in pouring rain. The windscreen wipers swished back and forth, back and forth. Eleanor, as she didn't have to concentrate on the road beyond them, found herself involuntarily watching them, her eyes crossing. She blinked and turned towards Megan.

"Miserable weather for driving. But for heaven's sake, remember the Incorruptible is in Launceston and don't drop me off at home on the way back."

Megan laughed. "After hearing what the boss said after you told him, I couldn't possibly forget. Sorry about the language back there. It sort of goes with the job."

"I daresay I heard a mild version, and Mr. Scumble did switch from 'devil' to 'deuce' in my honour. Though why it's acceptable to say 'Better the devil we know' and not 'What the devil,' I never shall understand."

"I expect Mrs. Stearns would be happy to explain."

"I shan't ask her. But there is something I want to ask you, and if you don't want to answer, you may tell me to go to the devil."

"I wouldn't dream of it, Aunt Nell! What is it?"

"I was wondering about Detective Sergeant Kenneth Faraday of Scotland Yard. I know I've heard the name. Isn't he the one who came down about the stolen jewels and went with you to Bristol?"

"That's him."

"Why does Mr. Scumble call him the 'Boy Wonder'?"

"Because he behaves as if he thinks he is. I mean, Ken acts as if he was God's gift to the police. And to women."

"Is he the London boyfriend you told me about?" Eleanor asked tentatively. "The one you said was your reason for coming back to Cornwall? You never mentioned his name. I don't mean to pry, dear, but if there's a chance I might meet him, perhaps I should know."

"Yes, he's the one. You'd think two hundred miles would be enough, but he seems to haunt me. Of course, it's partly the boss's fault. Anytime he needs Scotland Yard's co-operation, he makes me ring Ken, so I suppose it's not surprising he gets the idea I'm still interested. But I'm not. I expect you'll find him charming, because he is. And that's enough of that."

Eleanor quickly changed the subject. "I didn't follow all that Mr. Scumble was saying about the questions you need to ask. Are you allowed to tell me what you found out yesterday?"

"I don't see why not. He shouldn't have sent you with me if he didn't want you to know."

"Why don't you begin at the beginning and tell me as much of their story as you've picked up so far."

"Okay. They were on board a ship in the harbour at Mombasa — That's Kenya, isn't it? That's where they originally sailed from, though I'm not sure whether they started out in Kenya or Uganda."

"They're both expelling Asians."

"Whichever, they weren't allowed to land in Mombasa."

"They have British citizenship?"

"As Jay said, for what it's worth. They'd already been refused entry, here and other places. One of the sailors on their ship met a man ashore who offered to get them into England. You can hardly blame them for jumping at the chance. What else could they do?"

"I don't know, dear. It's an appalling situation. Sooner or later the government will have to relax the restrictions on immigration, but in the meantime . . . So much suffering! So they accepted."

"And paid a stiff price, Jay said. The boss wants to know how they paid, because of what happened later. I mean, were they carrying sufficient cash, or what? They couldn't have written a cheque, or they'd know the man's name."

"Could he describe the man?"

"Never saw him. Unless he was the same bloke that dropped them off in the cave, and he . . . Well, I'll get to that later."

Eleanor smiled at her. "You see how difficult it is to provide the sustained and consecutive narrative the inspector always wants?"

Megan laughed. "I do. I'll never demand it of a witness again. The next thing was, they were transferred at night to a larger freighter."

"Blindfolded?"

"No, the name of the ship was covered up, everything that had it on. Life belts and so on, I suppose. They were taken below, and it certainly sounds as if they weren't

318

the first, judging by the accommodation they found in the hold."

"Wait a bit. Surely you can narrow down what ship it might have been? Every port I've ever been in kept a record of comings and goings. The harbourmaster at Mombasa should be able to tell you what ships were there at the right time. Names and registration, I should think. I assume the family know the date they were there?"

"Aunt Nell, you're a genius! The boss told me to ask for dates, but we never thought of shipping records. At least, if he did, he didn't mention it to me. I wonder whether the harbourmaster would respond to a request from CaRaDoC, though. Damn, we might have to go through the Yard, and that means Ken."

"Suppose I try Sir Edward first? I shouldn't think they'd give him any trouble."

"Good idea, if the super agrees. Blast!" She peered through the windscreen. "It's coming down heavier than ever."

"Just as well my car is in Launceston. The car park at home is probably underwater by now."

"Talking of underwater, that reminds me — I really must find a moment to wrap and post the clothes Julia lent me."

"As I have to go back with you, I'll pick them up and post them from Port Mabyn."

"Thanks. I don't know when I'll be able to get away during post office hours. I bet Nick hasn't sent the stuff he borrowed back to Chaz, either."

"I'd better deal with those, too. I shouldn't think Nick has Chaz's address. I take it you do, and Julia's?"

"They'll be somewhere in the case notes, I'm sure, or their phone numbers, at least. I'll find them. I expect that's what Mr. Scumble and I will be doing all day tomorrow — reading over stacks of reports in hopes of illumination." Megan pulled a face.

"Perhaps you'll find the answer this afternoon," Eleanor consoled her. "Where did the freighter take them to?"

"They don't know. They stopped at sea, at night, and were lowered into a yacht, a motor yacht."

"It must have been quite a big yacht for all of them to fit in!"

"That's what the boss said. He wants to know how big, and how luxurious. If we manage to narrow down where it came from, that could help narrow the choice still further."

"How far did it take them?"

"As far as Bossiney Cove from wherever

they started!"

"Silly question. How long?"

"A whole day and part of two nights. They couldn't see out. The boss says to find out if they noticed whether the engine was going full throttle all the way, because they might have dawdled so as not to arrive in daylight. But they could have gone in circles to make it seem a longer voyage, so I can't see that would help. Anyway, the yacht anchored offshore in the night. Then they were taken by rowboat to the cave. They'd expected to be put ashore at a spot where they could make their own way inland."

"Is that what they were told, or was it an assumption?"

"I don't know. One more question to ask. It had certainly all been set up in advance, presumably by the 'captain,' whether he was captain of the yacht only or of the freighter as well. They were provided with boxes of supplies for a stay in the cave."

"For how long?"

"It looked to me like maybe a week, for that many people. But that's pure guesswork. Once the refugees realised they were running low, and no one came to fetch them, old Mr. Nayak stopped eating so that there would be more for the children and the pregnant woman — Jay's sister. They

321

started rationing the food, but none of them had eaten in a couple of days. We were too late to save the old man. It's touch and go with Kalith's mother."

Not for the first time, Eleanor wondered why she had expected retiring to Cornwall to shield her from contact with the effects of human folly, greed, and cruelty. She had seen too much in too many different parts of the world to believe that any place is immune.

"What was it you were saying about the captain demanding more money at the last minute?"

Megan frowned. "That's the strange part. Jay said it seemed to be a sudden decision. If he brought them all the way from Africa, he could have asked for more up front, or at any point. It does seem to suggest that he wasn't in charge from the beginning, only the yacht part."

"Or the boatman supposed to pick them up really did insist on being better paid and then failed to do what he was paid for." Eleanor frowned in turn. Why should she suddenly recall the man in the telephone box? Should she mention him to Megan? She couldn't see any reason for the unexpected flash of memory.

"So we're back to who was responsible,"

322

Megan said with a sigh, "the captain or the picker-upper. There always seems to be a point in every case where all the evidence takes us round in a circle."

"But you always find the way out."

"Usually." She slowed as they reached the outskirts of Bodmin and turned in at the first pub. "I don't know about you, but I'm starving. Pub grub okay?"

"Of course."

A pasty and a half of cider each later, they returned to the car.

"Now I must concentrate," said Megan, "or we'll be going round in circles in the one-way streets. I've got the directions written down, in my bag. I think I remember, but could you dig it out?"

Eleanor dug and directed. A few minutes later they turned into an estate of semi-detached houses, so new that several were still under construction, parts sheltered by tarpaulins from the relentless rain. Builders' lorries and vans obstructed the streets. Curtains in a few windows and tentative efforts to turn mud into front gardens showed which houses were already occupied.

Megan drove along a row of these and stopped in front of one that had candy-striped sheets roughly hung in place of curtains.

"Everyone who's at home is watching us," said Megan. "I should have asked for a plain car. I'm afraid this, added to the gross overcrowding, will confirm all their prejudices."

"The Nayaks won't have to stay here, stuffed into too small a house, though?"

"No, it's just the best Social Services could do in an emergency. It's the only one finished but empty."

"They were lucky, then."

"Yes. Look at that van — next door still has the plasterers in. Besides, so many people in a two or three bedroom is illegal. The local people have no responsibility to house them, though. I don't know who does, to tell the truth."

"No one. That's the whole trouble, isn't it? They have no place to lay their heads."

"That sounds rather biblical, Aunt Nell. More Mrs. Stearns than you. From what Jay told me, I'd guess they may be able to afford their own housing. Assuming they're allowed to stay."

Eleanor brightened. "I should think they have a better chance of being allowed to stay in Britain if they won't be a charge on the rates."

"That's the way the world wags," Megan agreed. "Come on, let's go and see what we can find out. Teazle had better stay in the car."

"Yip?" After sleeping all the way, Teazle had sat up bright eyed and ready for anything as soon as the car stopped.

"Sorry, girl."

Her ears drooped and she slumped down on the seat.

"If it stops raining, we'll take her for a quick w-a-l-k on the way back," Megan promised.

"It looks as if it's all set to rain for a week. Megan, what do you want me to do in there? Interpret for the ones who don't speak English? Because I'm sure one of them who does would do that better."

"I'm going to interview them in small groups. With any luck, what one person says may spark memories in another. There are four men and four women, if I got it straight, plus the kids. No, two women and one child may still be in the local hospital." She hesitated. "I hate to say this, but given cultural differences, is it fair to assume the women are less likely to speak English and more likely to be nervous?"

"I hate to agree, but in spite of Indira Gandhi, probably."

"Then, if it's all right with them, what I'll do is talk to the men while you chat with the women and make them feel comfortable. Don't worry about trying to get information, just be sympathetic."

A path as much mud as gravel took them to the front door. Megan rang the bell. After a minute, the door was opened a few inches on the chain.

"It is you, Megan. Gopal — my young cousin — said he recognised you. He has been watching the builders opposite, from the landing window. One moment, please." The door closed, then re-opened without the chain. "Come in out of the rain! Perhaps today I should call you 'sergeant'? This is an official visit?" He noticed Eleanor and blinked. "Or perhaps not."

"It is official," Megan said hurriedly, "but by all means call me Megan. Aunt Nell, this is Ajay Nayak. Jay, my aunt, Mrs. Trewynn. She's here in a sort of semi-official capacity, with my inspector's . . . sanction." "Approval" would be stretching the truth. "She speaks . . . Which languages, Aunt Nell?"

Eleanor exchanged proper greetings with the young man before she answered, "I used to speak reasonably good Hindi and Swahili, and a little Gujarati, but I'm rusty. Out of practice."

An older man, Jay's father, came from the room to the left of the tiny hall. Megan propounded her plan, which met with approbation from both Jay, as a policeman, and Mr. Nayak, as head of the family.

Jay ushered Eleanor into the room on the right. It was furnished with three mattresses, three pillows, and quantities of sheets and rugs.

"From the Red Cross," he explained. He introduced his mother, his wife, and his two young children. "My aunt will join you, and Kalith's sister, my cousin."

The little girl performed a creditable namaste. Her younger brother sucked his thumb and stared.

"I am sorry we have no chair for you," their mother said in fluent though accented English.

Eleanor smiled at her. "Don't worry. I'm quite good at sitting cross-legged." Though not quite as good as she had been a few years ago. The Aikido exercises kept her limber, so getting down was not a problem, but staying in that position for long became uncomfortable, and then getting up was difficult. She'd cross that bridge when she came to it. "I'm glad your little boy didn't have to stay in hospital."

"He is well. They taught me what to give him to eat to make him strong again. The Red Cross gave us food, also, but it is strange, not what we are used to. My husband's sister is still in hospital." She made a gesture indicating pregnancy. "They want to keep an eye on her. Luckily she speaks English, and we may visit this evening."

Another woman and a girl of seventeen or so came in and were introduced as a third Mrs. Nayak and Naima Chudasama.

Naima shyly asked after her mother and her brother.

Before Eleanor could answer, a teenage boy shoved a younger boy, perhaps ten or eleven, into the room by the scruff of his neck. They both spoke at once in Gujarati, the older ordering, the younger obviously protesting. Eleanor understood enough to guess a good translation of the protest might be, "I am *too* a man!"

Jay's aunt (if Eleanor was keeping them straight) spoke sharply to them. The elder disappeared, presumably to join the men, and the younger, looking sulky, bowed to Eleanor and sat down, as far from the two smaller children as he could get.

"My aunt apologises for the behaviour of her sons," Jay's wife said. "Gopal can't wait to be old enough to sit with the men. Can you tell us if my aunt Chudasama and my cousin Kalith are well?"

"I can't tell you much, I'm afraid. The

hospital says they are resting comfortably."

"Jay said the lady sergeant saved Kalith," said Mrs. Jay. "She is your niece?"

"Please, madam," Gopal interrupted eagerly, "tell us how the lady sergeant saved Kalith."

So Eleanor told the story, in several languages at once, and in return they told her about their long journey. Gopal kept trying to interrupt, but he was firmly shushed by his mother.

"Pal," said Mrs. Jay at one point, "when we are finished, you may speak."

After that he sat mum, though bouncing impatiently on his bit of mattress. At first the women were hesitant, but once they warmed up they sometimes interrupted each other, sometimes paused in painful silence when no one wanted to put a difficult passage into words. At last they ended with their arrival at the house in Bodmin. A longer silence seemed to Eleanor to hold a sense of relief, of release. Simply talking about their ordeal had brought a degree of comfort.

"I'm sorry," Eleanor said into the silence.

"Now it's my turn," Gopal announced. He stood up, at attention. "Madam, they say we were not allowed to go up on the deck of the ship. But I went. The sailors did not see me. I went everywhere on that ship. Upstairs and downstairs and everywhere. I did not tell anyone, not even my brother. They would have said I must not."

"And what did you see, Pal?" Eleanor asked with a frisson of excitement.

"I saw the captain," he said importantly.

"Did you really? What did he look like?"

"He was big, bigger than the sailors. I thought he would wear a smart uniform, but his clothes were ordinary, except for his hat. That had gold on it. He was a white man. Except, his face was red."

"Did you see the colour of his hair? Of his eyes?" She remembered she wasn't supposed to be asking questions. They knew she wasn't a police officer, though, so surely she couldn't get into trouble for impersonating one?

"I saw his hair once. He took off his hat to scratch his head. He was . . . He had no hair in the middle?"

"Bald?"

"Yes, bald in the middle. The hair round the edge was the colour of straw."

"You're very observant, Pal. Good at noticing. What about his eyes? I don't suppose you had a chance to see them close."

"I did!" the boy said triumphantly. "Not on the big ship, but when we got off the little ship. He was wearing a funny sort of hat that covered almost all his head, but I saw his eyes when the torch crossed his face. They were grey. Pale grey, with lines at the corners."

"The man on the yacht was the captain of the big ship? You're sure?"

"Yes, madam, of course. I am very observant. And I heard the other man on the . . . the yacht call him 'cap'n,' like 'captain' without a *t*. And he called the man Lenny."

Eleanor decided it was time to get Megan in on the act. Who could guess what else the boy might reveal?

TWENTY-FOUR

With reluctance, Eleanor lowered herself to the mattress again. It had been quite a struggle getting up from it, requiring a helping hand from Mrs. Jay.

The room had a new cast of characters: Eleanor, Megan, Gopal, and the boy's parents, Jay's uncle and aunt. Megan had insisted on the parents being present, one or both of them, but made them promise not to interrupt. She invited Gopal to sit beside her, opposite his parents, but he chose to stand in front of her at attention, as he had with Eleanor. She assumed it had been required at the school that had taught him such excellent English.

"I hear you're a very observant young man," said Megan.

"Yes," he agreed complacently, then hesitated. "Shall I call you madam or sergeant?"

"Sergeant will do nicely. All right, tell me again what you told Mrs. Trewynn."

He did so, avoiding any temptation to embroider with a wart or two or a missing finger. Eleanor thought he would make a good witness. But were ten-year-olds allowed to give evidence in court?

"You're quite sure it was the same man, Pal?" Megan asked. "On the big ship and the yacht?"

"Yes. If not, I would not say it."

"And you're certain Lenny was the boatman's name? You couldn't have mistaken some other word the captain used — 'many,' for instance? Even 'plenty' or 'twenty'?"

"No. He spoke clearly, not like the boatman. I couldn't understand what the boatman said, except 'cap'n.' And the way he said it: 'Lenny, you've got matches for the lamp?' It must be his name."

"Why do you think no one else heard?"

"He spoke quietly, and no one else was near them. My father was on the deck, but he was talking to my uncle and my grandfather. Everyone else was still in the cabin, packing the suitcases. That is when I saw the captain's eyes, when the light of Lenny's torch crossed his face. And I saw something else, too," he added.

"The name of the yacht? Or the ship? Did you see either?"

Gopal shook his head sadly. "No. It was

always night when I went out. But there was a light . . . I heard Uncle Jay — He is not really my uncle but I have to call him uncle because he's old —" His mother caught Eleanor's eye. Half smiling, she was obviously thinking the same thing: Jay would not appreciate that aside. The boy went on, "I heard him tell you there was no light in the sky when we got off the big ship onto the yacht. But I went round the other side of the ship, and I saw a flashing light, a long, long way away."

"A lighthouse!" Megan's back straightened. "Can you describe it? I mean, how often it flashed?"

"I have no watch." He cast an accusing glance back at his parents. "I counted a minute, but my teacher said counting is not accurate."

"Tell me anyway."

"It flashed four times."

"We'll have to find out what lighthouse has that pattern. I bet it's St. Anthony's. That may be very helpful, Pal."

He beamed, bright as a lighthouse. "I, too, am going to be a policeman when I grow up," he announced. "A detective."

"Good for you. Have you anything else to report?"

"I cannot think of anything," he said regretfully.

"Well, keep thinking. Thank you for your assistance."

"Please, Sergeant . . ."

"Yes?"

"I saw a dog in the police car. Is it a police dog?"

"No. She's just a little dog. She belongs to Mrs. Trewynn, and her name is Teazle."

"Can I . . . Please, may I talk to it?" He turned to Eleanor. "Please, madam?"

"Yes, of course."

Eleanor smiled at him, then caught sight of his mother's dismayed face. She understood English quite well though she spoke only a few words. She said something in Gujarati of which Eleanor understood only "wet." Though the hanging sheet completely covered the window, the gurgle of water in the downspouts was only too plain. It must still be raining heavily. They wouldn't have raincoats — or much of anything else. She'd have to set Jocelyn to work finding suitable clothes for them.

But Pal was looking at her pleadingly.

"If I go and get the dog and carry her in, and she stays in the hall with all the doors closed, just for a few minutes, would that be all right, Mrs. Nayak?"

Her husband answered. "The boy has had

335

little play for a long time. It will do no harm."

"While you're playing, Aunt Nell," Megan said with a grin, "I'll talk to the ladies."

Teazle was delighted to be released from the car. Before Eleanor could stop her, she made a dash for a clump of grass the builders hadn't yet ground into mud. Better there than inside, Eleanor thought philosophically, picking up the damp dog. There wasn't much she could do about it except blot her with a handkerchief. The Indians certainly wouldn't have a towel to spare. Perhaps Megan had an extra hankie.

When she returned to the house, Pal eagerly opened the door. He had been joined by his younger cousins, Jay's children.

The little ones were a bit nervous until they saw how small Teazle was. Then all three were down on the floor with the dog, disregarding her dampness in the joy of petting her. She rolled over to let them have a go at her tummy.

The older boy, the one who had turfed Pal in among the women, came into the hall. He watched for a minute, then disappeared through another door, only to return with a bag of Quavers, a bright orange snack Eleanor had seen on the newsagent's shelves but never encountered at closer quarters. Doubtless some kindly Red Cross soul considered them a nice treat for the children.

Eleanor wasn't so sure they were actually edible, in either human or canine terms.

"May your dog have some?" the boy asked.

They probably wouldn't do Teazle much good. She might be sick in the police car on the way back. But on the other hand, as Pal's father had said, the children had had so little fun for so long.

They had plenty now, and so did Teazle, catching, chasing, hunting the cheesy-smelling bits of nothing much. In the small space, chaos reigned for several minutes. Eleanor stood out of the way, in a corner, and enjoyed the sight.

The teenager was teasing Teazle with the last scrap, held just beyond her reach as she danced on her back feet, when the doorbell rang. Pal opened the door. There on the step stood David Skan, his bush of blond hair unflattened by the rain.

"Good afternoon. Ah, there you are, Mrs. Trewynn. I've run you to earth."

"Now what makes me think it wasn't me you were looking for, Mr. Skan? It's not my house, and I can't invite you in." A brain-wave struck Eleanor. What was the power of

337

the Commonwealth Relations Office compared to the power of the press? "But let me just see whether the residents are interested in talking to you."

"You're not going to make me stand here dripping while you . . ."

"Please come in, sir," said Pal.

Eleanor looked to the teenager.

"Mr. Skan is a friend of yours, Mrs. Trewynn?" he asked.

"Mostly." She remembered the wonderful article he had written boosting the LonStar shop.

As if reading her mind, Skan said, "Persuade them, and I'll play it any way you want it, Mrs. T."

"Well, yes, you could say he's a friend."

"Please, sir, step inside while I ask my uncle."

Skan was already scribbling in his notebook as he stepped over the threshold. Eleanor hoped he was noting how polite the young refugees were. Pal closed the door behind him.

Abandoning the reporter to Teazle, Pal, and the little girl and boy, Eleanor followed the older boy. She had to explain to the elder Mr. Nayak — Jay's father — that Skan, though her friend, was a reporter in search of a story.

Jay, his father and uncle, and his sister's husband listened to Eleanor with doubt on each face. She explained that Skan had promised to write a sympathetic article, and she trusted him — within limits — but had no control over him.

"I'll leave you to talk about it," she said. "I'd better get back to the children and the dog."

As she entered the hall from one side, Megan erupted from the other.

"I thought I heard — What the h . . . heck do you think you're doing here, Skan?"

He gave her an insouciant smile. "My job, Sergeant. You're lucky there aren't hordes on the doorstep. That storm last night cut the dramatic potential for the telly crowd."

"I can't let you talk to —"

"You can't stop me."

"If you compromise our investigation —"

"Aha, so this is a criminal investigation?" Megan glared at him.

"Look here," he said in a more conciliatory tone, "I have no desire to mess up a police case nor to get into trouble with my editor. Nor to get you into trouble with DI Scumble, come to that. I've already got a nice piece with you as heroine."

"Bribery?" said Megan dryly.

He grinned. "You could call it that, except

339

there's no way my editor's not going to run with that one. I'm willing to let . . . no, not Scumble . . . Superintendent Bentinck look at what I write and I'll pass on his remarks to my editor. If there's anything that really would compromise your investigation, between them they'll cut it out."

"I suppose . . ."

"Besides, Mrs. T's going to sit in on my interviews. She'll keep me in line."

"Aunt Nell!"

"I just said I'd ask the Nayaks whether they're willing to talk to Mr. Skan. It's a wonderful opportunity for the world to hear their side of the story —"

"For North Cornwall . . ."

"I'm thinking of the nationals," said Skan. "The *Guardian* will pick it up like a shot if it's drawn to their attention, and after that, well, you never know."

Megan groaned. "Just what we need!"

"I'm thinking of what the Nayaks need, dear. A nice loud public outcry could make the difference between their being allowed to stay and their being shipped off to nowhere again."

"Well . . . all right. I can't stop them talking if they want to. But I'm finished here. I've got to get back to the nick and report, so you can't stay, Aunt Nell."

"I expect Mr. Skan will take me home."

"Of course. Be happy to."

"*Not* home. Your car is in Launceston, remember?"

"Oh, yes! How lucky you reminded me."

"Even easier," said Skan. "That's where I'll be heading anyway."

"And don't forget Teazle."

"Oh dear, I did for a moment." Teazle was sitting on the floor amid the three cross-legged children, all of them petting her at once. "Do you mind a dog in your car? She should be completely dry by then."

Skan laughed. "You've obviously never seen my car. It's more a matter of will she deign to honour it?"

Megan sighed. "I hope it holds together till you get back. Give me a minute before you barge in, would you." She went to take her leave of the men.

"Barge in!" Skan said indignantly. "They haven't even said yet that they're willing to talk to me."

"Reporters aren't known for their retiring natures," Eleanor retorted.

Pal stood up. "I will talk to you, sir," he said eagerly.

"Sorry, mate. I'm not supposed to talk to kids without their parents' permission."

The dog also stood up. She retched, her

341

stomach heaving. The children drew back in alarm. As Teazle stumbled stiff-legged towards the front door, Eleanor sprang to open it. Teazle made a staggering dash for the patch of green and was thoroughly sick.

Skan looked aghast.

"Don't worry," said Eleanor, "just something she ate. Be glad she didn't wait to get rid of it till we'd set off in your car."

The rain had slackened and in the south-western sky was a patch of blue big enough to make a sailor a pair of trousers. Did sailors wear blue trousers these days?

The lifeboat crew hadn't. Their black tights would have made a traditional blue bell-bottomed sailor blush. The man in the telephone box hadn't, in spite of his nautical cap and pea-jacket. His grey trousers had looked more like the lower half of a business suit, and he'd been wearing a white shirt and tie to go with them.

A sunbeam broke through and gilded the puddle from which Teazle was thirstily lapping.

Gold, like the gold braid Pal had described on the freighter captain's cap. Had the man in the telephone box been gold-braided? Eleanor couldn't remember, nor the colour of his hair when he strode into the hotel, surely removing his headgear in gentlemanly fashion. It was odd that his image had otherwise remained so clear in her mind, and odder that it kept recurring to her.

Surely the two men couldn't be one and the same? But suppose they were, what would it mean?

Eleanor frowned.

TWENTY-FIVE

"She did *what*?" Scumble howled. "And you let her?"

"How could I stop her, sir? It was the boy who asked him in, not my aunt. And she'd already persuaded them to talk to him before I realised he was there. I really don't see that there was much I could do about it."

"There must have been something!"

"I did get him to promise the super could see his article before it's published."

"That's better than nothing, I suppose, though we can't hold him to it. We'll have to get cracking, though, and work out what we want Mr. Bentinck to ask them to hold back."

"Shall I type my report?"

"No, it can wait. I don't want the whole story at this point. We'll do that when the team gets back from Boscastle. Tell me the bits that are going to help us collar the villain of the piece."

Megan had thought about nothing else on her drive back from Bodmin. "Well, first of all, one of them saw the captain of the freighter. He swears he would recognise him, and he identified the same man as captain of the yacht. The trouble is, he's a ten-year-old."

"You believe him?"

"Oh yes, sir. He's bright and observant. His account was very credible, confident and precise, with no contradictions and nothing impossible for an active and ingenious boy. In excellent English, too. I took down exactly what he said, so I can write up a verbatim statement. His father was present and is willing to sign it, as well as the boy, of course."

"But the courts are funny about children as witnesses," Scumble said flatly. "Let's hope he won't have to be called. Not to mention that we have to find this captain first. No name, I assume."

"No, sir. Not his, nor either ship's."

"What else, then?"

"The freighter picked them up in Mombasa, and I have the date. The harbourmaster there should be able to tell us what ships called on that date."

"And the names of their masters, I

shouldn't wonder. But it may take a while. Better get on to it right away." He picked up the phone. "Overseas cable," he said. "To the harbourmaster at Mombasa . . ." He looked at Megan.

"Kenya, sir."

"Mombasa, Kenya." He dictated the telegram, including the date Megan supplied, and adding the word "urgent" to his request. "Sign Superintendent Bentinck's name and rank, and Constabulary of the Royal Duchy of Cornwall, in full. Read it back to me . . . Right . . . Thank you." He hung up.

"Taking the super's name in vain, sir?"

"He had to go to a meeting in Truro. He told me to do what ever was necessary. And with luck the Royal bit will impress someone at the other end."

"But can we do that — request information from other countries, I mean — without going through channels? Protocol," Megan added vaguely.

"I don't give an effing tinker's curse for protocol. They can't hang me. Go on."

"The boy again: When they transferred from the freighter to the yacht, he slipped away from the group and went exploring round the other side of the ship. He saw what must have been the beam of a lighthouse. He couldn't time it precisely, but he counted and he thinks it flashed four times in a minute. Every fifteen seconds, that is. Judging by how long it took the yacht to get to Bossiney Cove, it may have been St. Anthony's light, at Falmouth."

"In which case, Falmouth was very likely the freighter's destination, and possibly its home port."

"That's my feeling, sir."

Scumble picked up the phone again. This time he had to hold for a minute before it was answered. He drummed his fingers on the desk, saying to Megan, "What the hell is Polmenna doing in Boscastle? He ought to be back by now. We need — Hello? Get me a list of the flashing period — whatever it's called, you know what I mean — of all the lighthouses in Cornwall. Better make it Devon, too . . . Then ring the local library! It shouldn't be beyond their powers."

"Coast Guard," Megan suggested.

"And if it *is* beyond their powers, ring the Coast Guard." Hanging up, he turned back to Megan. "Any more?"

"The Nayaks — I'll call them that for convenience, though there's a sprinkling of other surnames. They seem pretty sure the cargo was wool, in the hold they were in, at least. It smelled, apparently. They were able to walk about in narrow aisles between stacks of bales wrapped in hessian tied with twine."

"Wool. Australia or New Zealand."

"Almost certainly. Jay, the ex-copper, noticed the bales were marked. He remembers a couple of the marks, two or three capital letters. We may be able to trace the cargo and pinpoint the ship that way, if the other stuff doesn't pan out."

"Unless you have some idea of how to start on that, we'll hold it in reserve. Go on."

"I can't think of anything else that would help with the investigation. It's more stuff that will be needed in court. But let me look through my notes." She skimmed through. "Something else the boy said —"

"What's his name, this infant prodigy who has the makings of a detective?"

"Gopal Nayak. Known as Pal. He's the son of Jay's uncle. I tend to see them all in relation to Jay."

"So what else did your Pal say?"

"He heard the captain address the yacht's crewman as Lenny. Presumably Leonard, though it could be something else, I suppose."

"That's not much use till we find the yacht."

"I agree, sir. He also heard Lenny address the captain as 'cap'n,' but he couldn't understand anything else the man said. It sounds to me as if Lenny is a Cornishman, or possibly a native of Devon, who speaks with a pronounced local accent. I find some of them pretty hard to understand, even though I grew up in Cornwall. So if the captain could understand him —"

"He's likely a Cornishman. Or must at least have spent a lot of time in Cornwall, consorting with the natives. Good. Anything else about the yacht itself?"

"There's this: It's pretty luxurious. Fancy fittings, I mean, besides the cabin being big enough to cram them all in."

"So we have the captain of a freighter who had the use of a fancy motor yacht. One that can be handled by two men. At least, they didn't mention any other crew?"

"No, sir. I didn't ask."

"You should have, Pencarrow, you should have."

"Yes, sir. Though I do think they'd have said if they'd seen or heard more than the two."

Scumble grunted. "You finished?"

"I think so." She flipped through the last few pages. "Yes, that's it. I didn't get anything new from the women, except that

Kalith's sister confirmed the marks on the wool bales that Jay reported. Oh, and she'd noticed one he hadn't."

"With any luck at all, we won't have to try to trace them. Right, I have a few questions arising from what ex-Sergeant Nayak told you yesterday. If you can't give me the answers, write down the questions for next time. For a start, this . . . what is it? . . . lascar who set up the trip in the first place, the go-between, what do we know about him?"

"Nothing, sir. I did ask. The old man, the one who died, is the only person he dealt with. The others never caught more than a glimpse of him."

"Not even your Pal?"

"Not even Pal. They don't know whether he was a member of the crew of the ship they were on, or the freighter, or possibly someone hanging about in the port waiting for a berth. The old man seems to have been decidedly secretive about it."

"Hmm. Doubtless he handled the payment, too. I wonder how he managed that, unless they had a suitcase full of large-denomination notes."

"They say not. There's an account at a London bank. Mr. Nayak, the present head of the family, says they transferred money by wire to the branch in Mombasa, but he doesn't know how, as the old man couldn't go ashore."

"Well, I can't see that it matters much, at least for the present. What's more important is how they paid the sudden last-minute demand. Didn't they tell you?"

"Gold jewellery. Apparently, it's traditional for Indian women to buy it as a form of savings. The captain took the lot. Jay suspects he suddenly noticed it when he went into the cave. It was the first time he'd seen them in a decent light."

"Now we're getting somewhere! I assume you got a description of what was taken?"

"I gave them some paper and a biro — they have *nothing.* When I left, the women were writing out a list. My aunt said she'd bring it here."

"That's good of her," Scumble said grudgingly. "Wait a minute, her car's here in Launceston and you drove her to Bodmin, so how is she getting back? No, don't tell me." He groaned. "Skan's bringing her."

"I'm afraid so, sir. She didn't want to leave, and I thought you'd want me to report as quickly as —"

"All right, all right. There can't be much she hasn't already told him. When she gets here, we'll circulate the description of the stuff — if she hasn't mislaid it — to jewellers and pawnbrokers. Cornwall and Devon to start with. Let's pray that we don't have to go as far afield as London to find it. Which reminds me, the Boy Wonder's arriving on the next train. What the hell are we going to do with him?"

"He might be helpful if we have to circulate the list nationally," Megan suggested with reluctance. "And if we have to dig into the bank business." To give Ken his due, he was a good detective.

"I hope he won't be here that long! Now, back to the robbery. It sounds as if it wasn't planned?"

"That's Jay's impression, sir, and from what he and the rest said about it, I'd agree."

"What about his crew? Did the man show surprise? If they could tell, with those damn balaclavas."

"He wasn't present. Jay told me the captain sent the crewman back to the boat, out of view and out of hearing, before he made his new demand. Lenny can't have been fully in his confidence."

"Unplanned. So it didn't originate with whoever was supposed to pick them up. Where does that get us? Think, Pencarrow!"

"Ummm . . . I'm not sure, sir," Megan admitted.

"For a start, it suggests the original intention was as they were told, to land them inconspicuously in a place or places where it wouldn't be too difficult to make their way to wherever they intended to go. I'm wondering what sort of arrangements the captain had made with the . . . let's call him X. Presuming he had made arrangements."

"If his intentions were originally good, I can't believe he'd leave it to chance to find someone willing."

"He'd have to give at least a down payment, with a promise of the rest. I doubt he'd pay in advance the full amount agreed on. The question is, did X decide to make do with what he had rather than take the risk of picking up the Nayaks?"

"Do you think the captain would have been able to tell X in advance when the Nayaks would be there to be picked up?"

"Good point. Probably not." He scribbled a note to himself. "We'll have to talk to some shipping people about freighter schedules, if any. Let's say, having robbed his passengers, the captain decided it was best if they quietly disappeared."

"It's so horribly cold-blooded!" Megan exclaimed. "What could they have done about the robbery, being here in England illegally?"

"So far all we've got is guesswork based on assumptions and beliefs, Pencarrow. Don't get your knickers in a twist till we know what really happened. Let's hope Polmenna has found X, though I doubt it, with just two uniforms to help him. They should have picked up some hints, though, as to who knows about the caves. You may have to go over tomorrow and talk to a few people. Or Eliot, if he finishes in Bude. But he's not up to speed with this business."

"Sir, it seems pretty obvious that X must be a Boscastle boatman. But if he'd landed the Nayaks in Boscastle, how would they get any farther? I wouldn't have said there's anywhere along the North Coast that's easy to get away from unless you have a car, particularly if you don't know the area."

Scumble frowned. "True. Even if they were told where and when to catch a bus, they'd be conspicuous waiting for it. Which makes me think they must have expected to be picked up. Do they have any relatives in this country?"

"Yes, sir. They refused to give me details for fear of getting them into trouble."

"Understandable, if irritating. *I* don't think Dr. Prthnavi knew anything about it. *You* don't think the restaurant people in Camelford or Bodmin knew anything about it. In fact, the only person I can think of who's sympathetic to refugees and keeps popping up all over this case is your auntie. And I wouldn't put it past her."

TWENTY-SIX

Once again, Eleanor trudged wearily into the Launceston police station. Teazle, recovered and full of energy, bounced at her feet.

"This is for Mr. Scumble," she told the duty sergeant, handing him the three pages torn from Megan's notebook, now covered with Jay's wife's neat writing. "I'd like to have a quick word with DS Pencarrow, if possible."

"Right you are, Mrs. Trewynn. I'll give her a buzz, ask her to pop down."

Eleanor subsided onto a bench against the wall. She let Teazle wander and sniff, as the sergeant made no objection. On a nearby corkboard, notices about sheep dip and foot-and-mouth disease kept uneasy company with a few blurry photos of missing and wanted persons.

"Mrs. Trewynn, DI Scumble would be grateful if you wouldn't mind stepping upstairs."

She did mind, but she wasn't going to deliberately provoke Scumble. "All right. Thank you. Come, Teazle."

"I'll send up a nice cuppa," the sergeant said sympathetically. "Here, you can deliver these papers yourself."

The stairs seemed steeper than before. She couldn't believe she'd ever bounded up them, just to show a young policeman she wasn't as decrepit as he assumed. She plodded up, envying the way Teazle's short legs propelled her vigorously from step to step.

As Teazle reached Scumble's door, well ahead of Eleanor, it was opened by DC Polmenna. He stooped to scratch her head and beamed at Eleanor.

"Nice to see you again, Mrs. Trewynn. Come in."

"Hello, Mr. Polmenna." She was happy to see he'd forgiven her for bamboozling him that time . . . "Good afternoon, Inspector. Megan dear —"

"Hello, Aunt Nell." Megan's smile had a tinge of apprehension.

Eleanor knew better than to go and give her a hug in the presence of her colleagues, but Teazle had no such inhibitions. She scurried over to Megan, delighted to see her again.

Leaving it to her niece to deal with the

357

dog, Eleanor turned to Scumble. "Here's the list of jewellery Megan asked me to bring you."

"Thank you, Mrs. Trewynn. Please sit down." He pointed at the chair facing him across his desk. He looked and sounded grim, but that was nothing out of the ordinary.

She sat, turning the chair sideways a bit so that she could see Megan. She hoped the sergeant would hurry with the tea and Scumble wouldn't have too many questions. "I doubt I have any information about the Nayaks that Megan hasn't already given you," she said.

"So do I. I just hope that reporter hasn't got the lot."

Of course, that was what was bothering him. "I don't think so. The Nayaks told him just the bare bones of their ordeal, and I didn't add to it. It's quite harrowing enough without elaboration."

"Hmm. You'll be glad to hear Polmenna found your smuggler, without you needing to break your word. Seems half the population of Boscastle knew which houses you'd visited and which was the last you called at."

"That's good. I suppose. You did tell him I didn't give him away?" she asked Polmenna anxiously.

"Oh yes, I made sure of that."

"Thank you. Was he helpful?"

"He made a useful suggestion," said Scumble. He didn't seem inclined to be more specific.

Polmenna, however, was eager to elucidate. "He said the people who know about the caves are all old Boscastle families, who've lived there for generations. So I —"

"That'll do, Constable." But having cut him short, Scumble himself became communicative. "The end result is, Polmenna found a lobster fisherman who admitted taking money, a down payment, to bring some people ashore from the cave. He was to be notified when the moment came. That's the last he heard, and all he knows, or so he claims. He denies knowing who the money came from. He's downstairs waiting to have a little chat with me."

At a nod from the inspector, Megan, looking unhappy, said, "He's been given an outline of what happened to the Nayaks — the old man's death and Kalith and Mrs. Chudasama's possible deaths."

" 'In the valley of the shadow . . . ,' " Eleanor murmured, thinking of Jocelyn, wondering whether she had extracted any news from the hospital.

"He's been told about the children. He has kids of his own. He's been cautioned. And he's been left to think about it."

"He's been arrested?"

"No. Not yet. We can hold him overnight if necessary without charging him."

Scumble took over again. "If he can satisfy me that he didn't find out the Indians had arrived until it became public knowledge, he could still be charged with conspiracy to contravene the immigration laws. One thing that's puzzling us —"

He was interrupted by the arrival of Constable Arden with a tray of tea: three thick white china mugs, for the detectives, and a flowery cup and saucer for Eleanor. They all contained the same muddy brew, however. It tasted pretty foul, but Eleanor drank it thirstily. And quickly. Scumble wasn't hiding his impatience under a show of patience, for once.

As she returned her cup to the tray, he reiterated, "One thing that's puzzling us is how, if our lobsterman had picked them up, the Nayaks expected or were expected to travel onwards. None of the small harbours in the area have convenient public transport." He paused.

"I see what you mean," said Eleanor. "Can't you just ask them?"

"We will. But in the meantime, I wondered whether you could shed any light on the subject?"

"Me! I'm sure you can come up with more possibilities than I can."

"The obvious answer is that someone was going to pick them up by car. It would have to be someone local. Were you, by any chance, approached and asked to help?"

Eleanor looked him straight in the eye. "No. But if I had been, I would have."

He sighed. "Naturally. I would expect nothing else of you. Where —" He was interrupted again, by the phone this time.

Exasperated, he gestured to Polmenna, who picked it up.

Eleanor suddenly remembered how upset Lois Prthnavi had been at the plight of Kalith and his family, even before anyone was certain of the family's existence. Was it possible that Lois, without Rajendra's knowledge, had been expecting them? Had she agreed to pick them up and drive them inland?

It was a wild speculation Eleanor intended to keep to herself.

"The super's back, sir," said Polmenna. "He wants to see you right away."

"Tell him I'm on my way." He stood up, leaning with both fists on the desk. "Where are you off to next, Mrs. Trewynn? I'd prefer you to stay within reach."

"I'm going home, and I have no intention of going anywhere tomorrow."

"Good. Don't leave the county, in case I need to talk to you again. Please," he added as an afterthought, turning away in dismissal. To Megan, he said, "Now that we have the list from the library and the reports from Boscastle, you can start going over the lot again, see if you come up with any bright ideas. When I'm done with Mr. Bentinck, we'll go and talk to chummie downstairs. Polmenna, you'd better read everything, too. Oh, and Pencarrow, send young Arden to meet the . . . DS Faraday. Unless you'd rather fetch him yourself?"

"No, thanks, sir."

"No use telling him we'll expect him tomorrow morning at nine, I suppose?"

"Not when he's staying at the White Hart just across the square. He's not that sort of copper."

"I was afraid not." Scumble turned to leave and saw Eleanor. "Still here, Mrs. Trewynn? Changed your mind about coming clean?"

"Certainly not. That is, I have nothing to come clean about, Inspector. I'd like just a quick word with my niece."

He shrugged and went out.

"What is it, Aunt Nell?"

"The things that nice child Julia lent you — I expect you've been too busy to parcel them up and post them back to her. As I'm here, I could pick them up from your flat and deal with them when I get home."

"I haven't washed the shirt yet."

"I'll do it. It will dry overnight in the airing cupboard."

"Thanks. Ask my landlady for the key. And *please*, Aunt Nell, remember to lock the door and give it back to her."

"Of course, dear."

Polmenna, already studiously bent over a stack of papers, looked round and gave her a wink.

The sun shone down on Bodmin Moor. Eleanor knew the ground would be soggy after the heavy rain, so she took Teazle to the old airfield near Davidstow for a short walk. Teazle arrived back at the car with a muddy tummy anyway. Luckily, Eleanor had remembered to put the dog's towel back in the boot after washing it.

When they reached Port Mabyn, Eleanor parked at the top of the hill. The car park at the bottom was probably soggy if not actually flooded, and though the sun still shone, she didn't trust it. She didn't want to find herself unable to get the Incorruptible out of its shed tomorrow. She'd told Scumble she wasn't going anywhere, but one never knew . . .

She nearly stopped at the vicarage on the way down, to ask Jocelyn whether she had rung the Plymouth hospital to ask after Kalith and his mother. Then she remembered it was Joce's day for the LonStar shop. It was nearly closing time. She'd be packing up for the day.

And thinking of closing time, Eleanor hadn't shopped for supper. She didn't feel like cooking. Baked beans on toast it would have to be. She was sure she had a tin of beans, less sure whether there was any bread left. She was nearly home by this time, so she popped into the bakery opposite. The only wholemeal loaf they had left was Hovis, which she didn't much care for. She bought it anyway.

Working out who was responsible for the Nayaks' plight would be much simpler, she thought crossly, if one didn't also have to shop and cook and dust and hoover and wash clothes and . . .

Oh, botheration! She'd left Julia's clothes in the car.

As she was crossing the street, two volunteers came out of the shop. They exchanged greetings, and Eleanor and Teazle went on into the shop. Jocelyn locked the door behind her, turning the sign to CLOSED.

"Did you find time to ring Plymouth?" Eleanor asked. "The hospital?"

"Yes," Jocelyn said grumpily. "All they'd say is that Kalith and his mother are both resting comfortably. It could mean they're on the road to recovery or on their last legs."

"That's what they told the police, too. It must mean Kalith hasn't been able to talk yet, don't you think? or someone from Launceston would have gone to see him. I've been —"

"Eleanor, I've got to check the receipts, and Timothy and I have an early meeting this evening."

"Let me know when you're ready to leave. I'll walk up the hill with you."

She went out through the stockroom and up to her flat, leaving her door open. The taste of police tea lingered in her mouth, so she put on the kettle. But just as she poured the boiling water into the pot, Jocelyn called up the stairs.

By the time Eleanor got back, the tea would be as stewed as the muck she had been served in Launceston.

"Coming!" She clipped Teazle's lead on

again. Teazle, of course, was delighted.

"Did you bring your keys?" Jocelyn asked as they went out through the street door. She had her own keys in her hand ready to lock it.

"No, I —"

"Oh, Eleanor, I wish you'd try to remember! It's the shop's security, as well as your flat."

"I'll only be gone a few minutes. Come on! I left something in the car up at the top."

"Your keys, no doubt."

"No, actually. You *are* in a mood."

"Sorry to snap. Mrs. Davies isn't feeling well and can't come in tomorrow, so I'll have to. It's really very inconvenient. I wish you'd learn to operate the cash register."

"It was you who banned me from touching it. But I must say I'm glad you'll be in the shop tomorrow."

"What!"

"That is, I'm sorry you have to give up your day and I'm sorry Mrs. Davies is ill, but I'm glad I won't have to deal with her." Mrs. Davies, the chapel minister's wife, had a permanent grievance because the vicar's wife was in overall charge of the shop.

They had reached the vicarage. Jocelyn paused with her hand on the gate. "What ever do you mean? Why would you have to deal with her?"

"Joce, the Nayaks have practically nothing. I'm sure the Red Cross people have done their best, but they need . . . Well, it would be much easier to list what they do have. I was thinking, if you'd pick out as much stuff from the shop as you can in the morning, I could deliver it in the afternoon. If you think the donors would object, I'll pay for it."

"I'll worry about that later. What do they already have?"

It didn't take long to tell her. "You'll help?" Eleanor asked.

Jocelyn bridled. "Need you ask? I'll see what I can do. You'd better take my car. You can fit more in."

"*Thank* you, my dear. I'd like to tell you more about them. I won't keep you now, Joce, but can you come to lunch tomorrow? Leave something cold for Timothy for once."

"He gets in such a fuss if I'm not there. Or he forgets to eat. Why don't you come and have lunch with us. He'll be interested, too."

"All right. Thanks." After baked beans for supper, Eleanor wasn't going to turn down an invitation to a good lunch.

"I'll tell you what, I'll ring Mrs. Plover
—"

"Who?"

"The wife of the vicar of St. Petroc's in Bodmin. She can mobilise her forces to do something for the Indians this evening."

"Thank you, Joce. It would relieve my mind."

Eleanor fetched Julia's shirt and pullover from the car. The woollie would have to make do with a thorough airing, or she wouldn't be able to post it tomorrow. She washed the scarlet poloneck and hung it over the bath to drip dry, hoping it wouldn't need ironing. What ever it said on the label, you could never tell, and she did dislike ironing.

She fed Teazle and ate her baked beans with Hovis toast and a grated carrot and apple salad. Then she went next door to see Nick.

He opened the door looking gloomy. "Hello, Eleanor. Come in."

"What's wrong?"

"The painting I've been sweating over for two days isn't working."

"Oh dear." If it wasn't working, it must be one of the kind of pictures she didn't understand, because he could paint a tourist landscape with both eyes closed and one hand tied behind his back. "I wish I could help."

Nick was already heading back to his studio, so she closed the shop door and followed. He stood scowling at the canvas on one of his easels. "*Isle of the Dead.* The trouble is, it's based on music that is based on a painting, and I can't get the original painting out of my head."

Eleanor ventured to take a peek. She couldn't make head or tail of it, except that it was sort of mysterious and vaguely sinister. "This may be a silly idea, but could you call it something else?"

He grinned at her. "You never know. What would you suggest?"

"Ummm . . . *Valley of the Shadow?*"

"Why not? You're thinking of Rocky Valley, aren't you? That's what inspired me in the first place. Have you heard how Kalith is doing?"

"He's still alive, or was last I heard. The hospital's being very cagy, even with the police. Or with CaRaDoC, at least. The Plymouth police — Oh, Nick, are you busy this evening? I don't want to distract you from rethinking your picture, but I absolutely must talk about everything or I'll burst. Jocelyn has one of those blasted parish meetings."

"Come on up. We'll have a . . . Did we finish off the whisky?"

"Not before I left!"

"Then you can have a tot and I'll have a beer. All right, spill the beans."

Eleanor told him everything, including Scumble's suspicions of her being involved in the final stage of the plot, though not her own about Lois Prthnavi. "The thing is, I would have been if I'd been asked."

"But you weren't," Nick said firmly. "And if you had been, you still wouldn't have actually done anything to break the law, any more than that unfortunate fisherman. I'd have thought the police had far too much on their plates finding the real villain to worry about prosecuting the poor chap for conspiracy, if that's the idea. They don't seem to have much in the way of clues."

"They know more than I do, and I have a feeling I just need to put the pieces together in the right order to make sense of it all."

"Are you sure that isn't just the whisky speaking?"

"Really, Nick! I wish you'd put your mind to it and help me think it through."

"Then let's start at the beginning, with Megan rescuing Kalith. Is there anything in that? Could there be something fishy in Julia and Chaz turning up so opportunely?

Hardly. No one could predict Kalith's taking to the water, nor when and where he'd end up."

"No." So much had happened since then that Eleanor hadn't taken it into consideration. Now she remembered: "But Julia told me Chaz's family is in shipping."

"The Averys? I didn't —"

"Avery? Is that his surname? Oh, yes, he told the inspector. How odd! The man in the phone box was Mr. Avery. Can it be a coincidence?"

"Seems highly unlikely. One of the kids did say Chaz's father was going to pick them up from Boscastle the next day."

"Julia said his father isn't in the shipping business. A solicitor? Something like — Oh, an architect, I think. A very rude man."

"Or a man too worried about what the shipping side of the family was up to to care about politeness?" Nick proposed.

"He was oddly dressed, almost like a halfhearted attempt at a disguise. And Abel Tregeddle mentioned a man trying to pump the boatmen in Boscastle harbour about smuggling, who wasn't interested in history."

They looked at each other.

"I haven't yet returned Chaz's clothes to him."

"I promised Megan to get Julia's back to her. I was going to post them, but I've got to drive to Bodmin tomorrow anyway . . . It'll have to be after lunch."

"Suits me," said Nick.

TWENTY-SEVEN

DS Kenneth Faraday of Scotland Yard, alias the Boy Wonder, was waiting when Megan and Scumble went back upstairs after interviewing the Boscastle fisherman. Though "waiting" was too passive a word: Sitting at Megan's desk, he had appropriated the reports on the case and was already halfway through them.

He stood up, good-looking as ever in his unobtrusive Savile Row suit. "Good evening, sir. Hello, Megan."

"Evening, Sergeant." Scumble sat down at his desk.

"Hello, Ken." Megan was dismayed to find that, though she had long ago got over her infatuation, he still made her feel inadequate.

He smiled at her as if he knew. "Anything new, sir?"

"No. Just that we're ninety-nine percent certain the original intention was not to maroon the family. Arrangements had been made to have them picked up."

"Made by whom, sir?"

"That's what we're trying to find out!" Scumble snapped. "The boatman can't tell us. Accommodation address in Plymouth — which may not be London but is a sizeable city, an international port with a shifting population. Payment made by giro from the main Plymouth post office. We let him go. He's a Boscastle native. He's not going anywhere. Pencarrow, get me Plymouth and let's hope to God the bloody-minded super I talked to before is off duty tonight! Faraday, finish up that lot so you know what we're talking about."

Ken pushed the phone across the desk to Megan. It took her several minutes to get put through to a chief inspector, who said the superintendent was unavailable. "Can I help, Sergeant?"

"Just a moment, sir," she told Scumble, who picked up his phone, happy not to have to deal with the obstructive super.

"Megan," said Ken in a low voice, "I've got a couple of questions."

"Ask away."

"You've given up trying to get the names of their relatives already in this country?"

"The boss says it's not really our business

— so far, at least. If some other agency wants to follow it up, that's up to them."

He nodded. "Reasonable. And the relatives will lie low of course, especially once it gets into the press. I haven't seen any news items, papers or on the box, by the way, and this all started two or three days ago."

"It'll break tomorrow, when the local paper comes out. I couldn't prevent their cub reporter interviewing the Nayaks. The telly missed it because they came ashore in filthy weather and the cameramen had all retired to the nearest pub."

"You did a good job there, pulling this chap out."

"All in a day's work," said Megan, blushing, "though as a matter of fact, I was off duty at the time. Any more questions?"

"Yes. Is it certain that the bloke you call the 'captain' knew how to get to the cave, or could it have been his crewman leading the way?"

"Good point. Jay — Ajay Nayak, the ex-copper — was in the last boatload, so he wouldn't have seen. I ought to have asked someone from the first load."

"Can't think of everything. You seem to have covered it pretty thoroughly."

Scumble put down the phone. "Now that's a man I wouldn't mind working with!

He's sending a man right away to the accommodation address."

"Newsagent's," Megan murmured to Ken.

"The post office will have to wait till the morning. He'll send someone first thing, when they open. Not that there's much chance of getting a description of whoever set it up, at this stage. It couldn't very well have been the captain, as he was at sea. Probably Lenny. If we can find him, the post office or newsagent people may be able to identify him."

"Lenny's the man who crewed on the yacht?" Ken asked.

"That's right, according to Gopal Nayak. What I want to know, Sergeant, is where you come into all this business?"

"In the end, sir, the agencies concerned decided they couldn't begin to deal with the illegal entry of these people until the criminal investigation is completed. So my instructions are to help you in any way possible."

"And report back."

"Well, naturally, sir, I'm expected to turn in a report."

"Huh. You'd better go to Falmouth with Pencarrow tomorrow. You may conceivably be of some use to her. Know anything about shipping?"

"No, sir, afraid not."

"Pity. You'll be questioning the harbour-master, and it always helps to know what you're talking about, especially as we haven't much to go on beyond a youngster's memory of a flashing lighthouse. You have an appointment at half two. A busy man, apparently." The phone rang. "Damn, what now?"

Megan got it. A smile spread across her face as she listened. "Thank you, sir, thank you very much." She hung up. "The Plymouth chief inspector, sir. Kalith Chudasama has come round and the doctor says we can probably talk to him tomorrow, after ten a.m., if the consultant says he's well enough."

Scumble actually smiled. "Well done, Pencarrow. You —" *Brrr-brrr.* "Dammit, what *now*?" Impatiently, he grabbed his own phone. His face darkened. "All right, Eliot, I'll be with you in . . . half an hour. Switchboard, get me a driver." He slammed down the receiver and stood up. "I suppose it'll be Dawson," he said gloomily to Megan.

"What's gone wrong, sir?"

"Eliot ran the mugger to earth. He's holed up with his girlfriend and baby and threatening to set fire to the place if they try to arrest him. You can go home now, Pencarrow. Tomorrow: Plymouth, Bodmin, Falmouth. I hope you know what to do. I'm off." He strode out.

"Fire engines," said Ken wistfully, "sirens, ambulances. It's a pity to miss the excitement. Hospital and harbourmaster sound awfully dull in comparison. Come on. I'm going to take these reports with me and reread them to night, but I'll buy you dinner first. White Hart any good?"

"Typical provincial hotel fare. It'll do. We'll go dutch."

"Independent, that's what I've always liked about you, Meggie — Megan." But it didn't stop him liking long-legged blond models better. "You buy me a drink, and I'll spring for dinner."

Dinner at the White Hart would put a hole in Megan's budget. They might have the same rank, but London pay was better, and Ken had private means as well. Besides, she was too tired to argue, and starving. Had she eaten lunch? She couldn't remember. "Okay. Thanks."

"You can pay me back by telling me all the bits that didn't make it into the official reports."

"Sing for my supper. All right. You never know what might help tomorrow."

They managed to get a table in a corner

378

of the dining room. Over excellent roast beef and Yorkshire pudding, she filled in the story, in a low voice. She couldn't avoid talking about Aunt Nell's part in the investigation, which was embarrassing and, she found out too late, unnecessary, as he hadn't recognised the name Eleanor Trewynn. He thought it was very funny.

"Don't worry, I won't tell the world your aunt is turning into a second Miss Marple. She was mixed up in the jewel theft business, wasn't she? It sounds a bit risky, though, sending her to find your smuggler."

"We didn't send her," Megan said indignantly. "It was entirely her own idea. And what's more, she's probably the only person who could have done it, the only person the original informant would have talked to."

"I must say, Boscastle sounds like a hotbed of villainy."

"It's always had a bit of a reputation. I read a history — Oh hell!" The words escaped rather louder than she had intended. She ignored the disapproving glances cast her way but lowered her voice again. "Avery. Chaz. I knew there was something!"

"Chaz Avery? The laddie who helped to pull you out? Would you mind explaining these oracular utterances?"

"I read a history of Boscastle. Avery owned most if not all of it in the first half of the last century. He was the squire and a magistrate, but by all accounts he was a first-rate villain. He had a finger — or a fist — in every available pie: buying and selling, fishing, mining, smuggling, even wrecking. And shipbuilding."

"And Chaz is a descendant?"

"Don't you think? Must be on the wrong side of the blanket. Avery never married, but he was a womaniser and one of his women could have taken his name. Chaz's family is in shipping. He lives in Falmouth."

"So knowledge of the caves might have been passed down, along with a tradition of shipbuilding, or involvement with ships. It's pretty persuasive."

"And gives us a whole lot more to present to the harbourmaster! It's a nuisance that the local directory doesn't cover that area. We'll — I'll have to go back to the nick —"

"Not on your nelly. Relax, Megan. It can wait till morning. You look fagged out."

"Thanks a lot!"

"In a charming way. Pudding? I'm going for apple tart with clotted cream."

When Megan reached the nick next morning, the duty sergeant told her Scumble had

380

talked the mugger out of his hole in the early hours of the morning. "No damage done," he said cheerfully, "except having been all sweet reason there, he came back in a tearing temper. But he won't be in till after lunch and you'll be well away. He said you're to go ahead with yesterday's orders. Report in when you can."

"Plymouth, Bodmin, Falmouth. We've got directories upstairs, but can you round me up a street map of Plymouth, Sarge?"

"Sure thing, Sarge." He grinned at her. "Taking the boyfriend with you, are you?"

"He's not my boyfriend." Megan tried to say it lightly. "I worked with him in London."

"Odd how he keeps getting himself sent down here."

"Didn't you hear? After two visits, his superiors consider him an expert in the ways of the local yokels in this uncivilised corner of the country. Any coffee going?"

He glanced into his own mug, half full of cold, muddy liquid. "I'll have young Arden make some fresh. He'll bring it up, and the map."

"Ta, Sarge."

"Oh, by the way, you seen the paper this morning?"

"The local rag? No." She hurried on her

way before he could tell her about it.

Ken arrived before the coffee. He slung a couple of newspapers on the desk in front of her, the front page of the *North Cornwall Times* and the *Guardian* folded back to an inner page.

The local paper's headline blared, "Heroic Rescue by Local Cop." Beneath it was a head-and-shoulders photo of Megan, looking particularly po-faced, perhaps because it had been cut from the one taken when she'd had to escort her aunt down the hill in Port Mabyn in the course of her duties. Below the fold was a picture of the Rocky Valley inlet, taken in stormy weather with waves breaking against the cliff in showers of spray.

"You dived into *that*?" said Ken.

"It was calm that day," Megan said defensively, turning to the inner page.

A smaller headline read, " 'My cousin saved us,' says Gopal Nayak." There was a photo of the three Nayak children, two solemn, wide-eyed little ones and Pal with his enchanting grin. For some reason, it made her want to cry. She hurriedly folded the papers and put the Falmouth district directory on top.

"I've found several Averys," she said. "Rupert Avery, architect. That would be

Chaz's father. Business address in Falmouth, home address in Flushing — Mr.
and Mrs. Rupert Avery."

"Flushing? Isn't that in the Netherlands?"

"Maybe it was founded by Dutch traders?
It's across the Penryn River from Falmouth,
and it's where Victorian merchants and
ship's captains built their mansions."

"Aha!"

"Paul Avery, same address. Perran Avery,
same address. They all have separate phone
numbers, though."

"One big happy family? Or not, as the case
may be."

"Perran must be Chaz's grandfather."

"Why?"

"Just a guess, but Perran's an old Cornish
name. Rupert, Paul, and Charles —"

"Point taken. That's it?"

"In the family mansion. But there's Avery
Maritime, Worldwide Freight Shipping, with
an office on Duchy Wharf."

"Bingo!"

PC Arden came in with a mug of coffee
and the Plymouth map. "Coffee for you,
Sergeant?" he asked Ken.

"No, thanks."

"It's no worse than the muck at the Yard,"
said Megan, sipping.

"But I just had a splendid breakfast at the

White Hart. Let's have a dekko at that street map."

They pored over it. "Here's Greenbank Hospital." Megan put her finger on it. "Now we just have to hope they haven't changed the one-way streets again since this was printed." She glanced at her watch. "It's much too early to ring the Plymouth nick about the post office and newsagent's."

"Might as well drop in while we're there."

"Yes. I'll leave a message in case they ring here." She gulped down the last of the coffee. "You ready to go?"

Megan at the wheel of the unmarked car, they drove south in hazy sunshine, for the most part through rolling farmland, and across the Tamar Bridge. The hospital was easy to find, a vast Victorian spread with wings branching in every direction. She pulled into a spot in the car park with five minutes to spare.

"Your driving is much improved," said Ken as they got out and started towards the building.

"I do a lot here. I never got much practice in London."

"Megan, you ought to come back. You're wasted here. And we make a good team."

"We're not doing this interview as a team, though. Apart from the doctor not allowing more than one visitor at a time, Kalith doesn't need your intimidating presence."

"Me! Intimidating!" He sounded injured. "You're thinking of your boss."

"Not your manner, idiot, though I know you can put it on with the best. But white, male, stranger, police."

"You're white and police, and the chances of him remembering you after what he's been through are slight, if you ask me. But you're right." He sighed. "The doctor's unlikely to let us both see him. You're the obvious choice."

"Besides, I'm authorised to be here. You, I suspect, are not."

"Plymouth? Oh hell, Devon. Yes, I've got clearance only for Cornwall. It's all yours."

"Do you want to go for a walk?"

"No. We've no idea how long this is going to take."

It took them some time to find the right ward. Then they were told the consultant had had an emergency case and hadn't yet finished his rounds. The empty waiting room was dingy, hung with pallid watercolours of rural scenes, evoking the stillness of death rather than any sense of peace and comfort.

"What they need is to liven up the place with a few of Nick's brightest landscapes,"

385

Megan said tartly.

"Nick?" Ken was investigating a pair of urns. "Tepid tea or tepid coffee?"

"No, thanks."

"Just what I was thinking. Twin hearts that beat as one. Why don't you come back, Megan? We had a good thing going."

" 'Had' being the operative word."

"You're the one who left for the outer reaches of the kingdom."

"You're the one who moved out. And moved in with someone else."

"Yes, well, we all make mistakes."

"And go on making them, from what I hear."

"Only because you aren't there."

"Nor am I going to be there."

"Is there someone else? Who's this Nick? Not that artist bloke who was involved in — ?"

He *would* remember! "My aunt's neighbour, that's all," Megan said firmly. "You'd better stop this, Ken. We're about to quarrel and we've got to work together for the rest of —"

"DS Pencarrow?"

"Yes, Sister." Relieved to get away, Megan followed the nurse.

"Mr. Chudasama's going to pull through," she said, leading the way, "but it's been touch-and-go. You know what happened to him?"

"Pretty much. I . . . I was there when he was rescued."

"Pencarrow! You're the one who pulled him out! I thought it sounded familiar, but all these Cornish names sound the same to me." She turned and looked Megan up and down. "Pleased to meet you. That was a job well done. Here we are." Her hand on a doorknob, she went on, "Doctor says just five minutes, and I'm to stay. You needn't worry, I won't repeat anything I hear."

They went in. It was a two-bed side ward, the second bed empty. The head of Kalith's bed was raised, a refinement not available in Bodmin Hospital. A breathing machine — ventilator — and an IV apparatus stood beside it, though he wasn't using either at present. His head was bandaged, and a pillow on each side prevented much movement. His eyes were closed. In spite of the contrast of his dark skin with the white bandage and bedding, he managed to look pale, and alarmingly frail.

"Kalith." She ought to call him Mr. Chudasama, but she'd been thinking of him as Kalith.

He opened his eyes.

"Mr. Chudasama, this is the lady who

saved you from the sea. She wants to ask you a few questions."

There was no recognition in the dark eyes. "My sister?" he asked in a croaking whisper.

"She's safe and well. I talked to her yesterday."

Tears appeared and trickled sideways down his thin cheeks. Sister tut-tutted and wiped them away.

"Kalith, what do you remember? About how you got here?"

"Everything . . . from Mombasa . . . to the cave. I tried to . . . swim for help."

"You succeeded!"

"Cold water . . . then nothing . . . until here."

"But you remember the journey."

He remembered the journey. In the brief time available, Megan managed to elicit the fact that he was aware of Gopal's forays above deck on the freighter. So Pal wasn't romancing. He hadn't told Kalith much about what he saw, but at least the boy hadn't invented the whole story.

"Time's up," said Sister.

"Wait!" Kalith reached out towards Megan, then let his hand drop. "My sister . . . may visit me? And my cousin Ajay?"

"I'll see what I can do," Megan promised. Outside the room, she said to Sister, "He didn't ask after his mother."

"He was worrying, and Doctor said it was best to break it to him: Mrs. Chudasama died early this morning."

TWENTY-EIGHT

Eleanor had the *North County Times* delivered. Having let Teazle out of the back door, she went to the front door to pick up the paper. Two copies had been shoved through the letterbox. In the top left corner of one, someone — presumably Mr. Irvin, the newsagent — had drawn a red star in felt-tip pen, with an arrow leading down to a photo of Megan.

As though she could possibly miss it! It was a rotten photo. Her niece had a slight frown and slightly pursed lips. The headline almost made up for it, though: "Heroic Rescue by Local Cop."

With one copy under her arm, reading the other, she returned along the passage to the open back door. Teazle was sniffing about under the gorse and blackthorn bushes on the other side of the path. The morning was misty and chilly, and Eleanor was in her dressing gown, so she called the dog in.

"It looks as if David Skan has done us proud," she said as they went upstairs. "Thank goodness he hasn't put me on the front page. I hope he's managed to leave me out altogether, as I asked him."

She fed Teazle but postponed her own breakfast in favour of reading the complete article. The photo on the inside page delighted her. "If that doesn't touch a few hearts, I don't know what will," she told Teazle, who wagged her tail and curled up on her bed for a nice after-breakfast nap.

The paper had no picture of Kalith, of course, but Skan had written about his heroism as equal to Megan's, or more so, as he had no idea where he was going. Altogether, although she was briefly mentioned near the end, Eleanor thought he and his editor had done a wonderful job.

And he'd got the story into the *Guardian* too, though only a couple of paragraphs. With any luck, they'd follow it up, and other nationals would join in. Not that she was greedy for glory for Megan, but anything to illuminate the plight of people forced by hard-hearted governments into the Nayaks' situation . . .

Her mind wandered to their present situation. She could go downstairs and help Jocelyn sort out household stuff for them.

Joce was unlikely to appreciate the offer. Or she could go out on one of her donation-collecting trips. If anyone offered something that would be useful to the Nayaks, she could ask if they'd mind it going to the Indian refugees rather than the LonStar shop. She would take the local paper with her, folded open to show the picture of the children.

After breakfast and a bath, she and Teazle headed Otterham way. Inland the sun shone; the hedges were aflutter with birds squabbling over scarlet hips and crimson haws.

They called at tiny hamlets and farm houses tucked into valleys on the edge of the moors: Trevilla Down, Penhale, Cairo, Kernick, Cardew, Trelash, Tredarrup Cross, Penwenham. Bits and pieces accumulated, but the prize was a floor lamp, perfect for the Nayaks. The donor was happy to agree to let them have it. The only problem was fitting it into the car. They took off the shade, and Eleanor folded down the passenger seat, and with a struggle they manoeuvred it in. The dog wasn't happy, and Eleanor knocked her elbow against it every time she changed gear. They turned homeward.

They arrived back in still misty Port

Mabyn just in time for lunch at the vicarage.

Jocelyn greeted Eleanor with the news that
she had rung up the Plymouth hospital
again. "And this time I spoke to someone
less close-mouthed. Kalith is expected to
recover."

"Oh, wonderful!"

"Unhappily, his mother died this morning."

Timothy said gently that he would pray
for Mrs. Chudasama, then was lost in silent
reflection. Jocelyn, serving a delicious-
smelling casserole that had been simmering
in the oven all morning, told Eleanor what
had been collected for the Nayaks. St. Petroc's congregation and the Bodmin Wom-
ens Institute, some of them also Red Cross
volunteers, had already provided a kitchen
table, some chairs, and other necessary odds
and ends. Most of what Jocelyn had gathered from the shop was small stuff, kitchen
equipment and linens.

"That's lucky," said Eleanor, "because I
picked up a rather large lamp this morning
and the donor particularly wants it to go to
the Nayaks, but it only just fitted in the car."

"Then it had better stay there," Jocelyn
said firmly. "You can deliver it to them
another day. I have to get back to the shop

393

and everything is already loaded in my car. We can't possibly rearrange it now."

Nick drove, Eleanor beside him with Teazle on her lap, to avoid getting dog hair on the sheets, pillowcases, towels, blankets, and eiderdowns piled high on the backseat. Nick hadn't seen the paper. Eleanor told him about Skan's article and pictures, and Jocelyn's news of Kalith and his mother.

"She didn't find out about Jay's sister, though, the pregnant one they kept in hospital in Bodmin. I do hope she's all right."

"We'll soon find out. Jay's the policeman? Perhaps we ought to take him with us to see the Averys. He might notice something we'd miss," Nick suggested.

"Better not. He has no official standing here. It would be terrible if he got into trouble for impersonating a police officer."

"I wasn't proposing that he should try to make an arrest."

"All the same, if the Averys actually were involved, seeing him would alert them to our suspicions."

"Which could surprise an admission out of them, or could make them flee. No, you're right," he conceded. "A confrontation might work, but that's up to the police. Too much risk of it turning nasty. As it is,

Chaz's clothes give us a perfect excuse to call."

"Julia first," said Eleanor. "I telephoned to tell her we were coming and she said she'll be in all afternoon. She'll be able to tell us more about the Averys before we go on there."

"Don't mention them to the Nayaks."

"Of course not."

The Nayaks were delighted to see Eleanor and to meet Nick, whom she introduced as having helped to save Kalith. They had heard about Kalith's improvement and his mother's death from Megan. Apparently she and another detective had turned up that morning to ask more questions. While the children fussed over Teazle, Eleanor asked after Jay's sister. She was being kept in hospital only because of the crowded conditions in the council house.

"Soon the Borough Council will find us a second house," the senior Mr. Nayak said.

"The new houses are being built for people from London," Jay explained. "Officially, 'Metropolitan overspill relocation from the Greater London Council.' Otherwise known as slum clearance, they say. The local people seem to prefer us, at least for the present."

"Everyone is being most kind," said his father.

With many hands to help, Jocelyn's car was quickly emptied, but Mrs. Nayak senior's pressing invitation — relayed by her daughter-in-law — to stay for a cup of tea could not be turned down. Eleanor and Nick left later than they had intended.

"I hope you know how to find Mabe Burnt house," said Nick. "What an extraordinary name for a village."

"I looked at the map, and Julia gave me directions. Don't get confused if you see a sign to just plain Burnt house, though. There's another one a few miles away."

"An epidemic of arson?"

"And another Mabe, as well."

Nick groaned.

However, they quite easily found the village and Julia's house, a modern bungalow with a garden still ablaze with roses. Apart from Merlin, her large but mellow dog, she was alone at home, packing to go back to Exeter University and happy to have an excuse for a break. She thanked Eleanor for returning her clothes.

"I was hoping to get them back in time to pack. Tea?" she offered, "or a beer? Or I could pinch some of Dad's sherry. And water for Teazle, of course."

Though Eleanor felt she had drunk enough tea for the afternoon, refusing offered hospitality was no way to get someone talking and she could hardly condone petty larceny, even from a parent. Nick opted for beer.

"D'you mind the kitchen? I always slop stuff all over the place when I carry a tray through to the lounge. Mum despairs of me."

"The kitchen is fine," said Eleanor.

When they were sitting at the kitchen table, Nick said, "We're taking Chaz's stuff back, too. I hope he hasn't already gone off to Exeter, but we can always leave it with his family. Flushing, isn't it? We hoped you could tell us how to find the Averys' house."

"You can hardly miss it. It's one of the big ones, right on the water, just west of the village, the last or next to last before Trefusis Point. White, with a slate roof and lots of gables. It's the family mansion. They all live together, under his grandfather's thumb."

"All?" asked Eleanor.

"Sounds claustrophobic, doesn't it? Grandfather, who runs the family business. He's a widower, I think. At least, Chaz never talks about his gran. Chaz's dad and mum — He escaped from the shipping business. He's an architect, and Mrs. Avery runs a boutique or something, but I suppose they like the mansion life. Chaz's sister, who's at boarding school, and his uncle Paul, who's divorced and his wife took their kids. I don't blame her; he's never at home."

Julia had the makings of a first-rate gossip. Nick hardly needed to encourage her. "Never?"

"He's a ship's captain, you see, one of the Avery Line ships. They go all over the world. Chaz says he used to like it when he was young, but now he's fed up and wants to take over running the business."

"That sounds reasonable," said Eleanor, trying not to meet Nick's eyes. So the uncle was a ship's captain, was he? "Isn't Chaz's grandfather about ready to retire?"

"Well, all I know is what Chaz tells me. He says his uncle Paul is a good seaman, but whenever he gets into port he goes on a bender. Not just booze, apparently; he's into gambling, too. As soon as he gets home, he goes off to horse races and blows all his money. There was a huge row a couple of years ago, when the old man had to bail him out." Julia's voice dropped to a dramatic whisper. "Chaz said the bookies were after him!"

"I can see why his father doesn't want to hand over the reins, then," said Nick.

"Uncle Paul doesn't exactly sound trust-worthy."

"Didn't you say Chaz isn't your boy-friend?" Eleanor was beginning to feel some qualms — though, given the situation, not many. "He seems to have confided a lot of the family's dirty linen."

"He's *not* my boyfriend. He was boasting, not confiding. He thinks his uncle is ter-rific. It's from him he learnt that racialist stuff he spouted when we helped to rescue the Indian. A lot of Uncle Paul's crew are Indian, apparently, and he despises them. At least, Chaz says those things without thinking." Her brow wrinkled. "I rather gather his uncle means it. But his grand-father gets on well with the common sailors, white or brown. When *he* was a captain, before *his* father retired, when his ship called at Falmouth he always had a party for his crew at the house."

Eleanor glanced at Nick, who looked as puzzled as she felt. The head of Avery Ship-ping liked Indians. Captain Paul Avery disliked Indians. Mr. Rupert Avery, archi-tect, had been questioning Boscastle fisher-men about smugglers, thinly disguised as a sailor and in a state of high anxiety. How on earth did these pieces fit together, and where did the Nayaks' voyage and misadventures come in?

Obviously, Julia wouldn't know. Chaz almost certainly hadn't known when Megan pulled Kalith from the sea. He might know now, though. Whether he'd talk about it was another matter, but he hadn't been exactly reticent about family affairs with Julia.

Eleanor looked at her watch. "Good heavens, it's later than I thought. We'd better be moving on now." She stood up. "Thank you so much for the tea, Julia. It was very kind of you."

"Do you know how to get to Flushing? You can drive round the long way, or cross over from Falmouth on the ferry. No, I'll tell you what. I'd love to take you across in our boat. I'm dying for an excuse to go out on the water one more time before term starts. *Calliope*'s just a little sailing dinghy, but there's plenty of room for three and the dog. Teazle, not Merlin. Let's go quickly, before Mum and Dad come home. I'll leave a note."

"Sailing?" said Nick. "There doesn't seem to be much wind."

Julia laughed. "Don't worry, we'll use the outboard, though with the river current and the tide going down, we'll hardly need it."

"No wind, calm water?" Eleanor said hopefully.

"Yes, and there won't be much traffic — most people have laid up their boats for the winter. We can go ashore right at the Averys' place."

The boat was moored at Penryn harbour, just a few minutes' drive away. Eleanor was relieved to see steps going down to a wooden pontoon — she didn't feel like performing acrobatics to board. It took Julia several attempts to start the outboard; she swore it was just because it was cold, it wasn't going to strand them in midriver.

As promised, the engine, the current, and the ebbing tide carried them swiftly downstream between rows of buoys and occasional moored vessels. Huge puffs of cloud drifted overhead, the sun breaking through at intervals; swirls of mist rose from the water. At first, the river twisted between low green hills, dotted with occasional houses. Then Falmouth town and harbour spread along the southern bank, and the village of Flushing appeared straight ahead on the north bank.

Instead of making straight towards Flushing, Julia steered the little boat round the last bend. The Penryn River widened dramatically. In front of them now were the Falmouth docks, with several large ships moored at the quays.

Eleanor wondered whether one of them had brought the Nayaks all the way from Mombasa.

Their course curved to the left. Mudflats interspersed with patches of sand and seaweed lined the river's edge, below a high, clifflike bank splotched with red valerian. Here and there, small boats were pulled up on the beach, and moored offshore floated a motor launch and a couple of yachts.

Along the top of the bank stood a few large houses, well spaced, each with a long flight of steps down to the beach. Behind them rose a smooth, steep hill. Eleanor would have noticed the Averys' mansion at once, even if they had not been heading directly towards it. White and many gabled, as Julia had described it, it had the grandest staircase leading up to it.

"This is theirs," said Julia, slowing as she steered close to the nearest yacht. The *Andromeda,* anchored at the bow, seemed huge compared to the sailing dinghy. "Isn't she beautiful?"

Another piece of the puzzle clicked into place.

"Very nice," said Nick.

"I've been out on her a couple of times, but Chaz isn't allowed to take her out without a proper crewman, though in a pinch one person can handle her in good weather if you don't raise sail."

Easy for two, then, Eleanor thought, exchanging a glance with Nick. Captain Paul Avery and his henchman Lenny? It seemed more and more likely.

Julia cut the engine, tilted it forward over the back of the boat, and beached the *Calliope* on a patch of sand. Nick had already taken off his shoes and rolled up the legs of his jeans. They both hauled it a few feet farther up, then Nick handed Eleanor out. A rowboat lay on the sand nearby, tethered to a half-buried post at the base of the cliff.

"Chaz has his own sailing dinghy, like *Calliope* only fancier, with a bigger outboard. In the boathouse, I expect." Julia pointed to a small building with wide doors opening onto the beach. "With their speedboat."

Nick and Eleanor were more interested in the stairs leading up to the house, between hedges of scarlet and purple fuchsia.

"Might have been better to drive round," Nick muttered. "Do you think you can make it?"

"Of course. Though I'll admit I'd rather not have to. Just don't rush me."

She made it to the top, happy to note that Nick and Julia were also slightly out of breath. French windows looked out over a granite-paved terrace with a low parapet, to the river and the docks beyond. From the house, the Averys could keep an eye on their ships when they were in port.

"We'd better go round to the front door," Julia said, but someone had spotted them through the window, and Chaz came out.

"Hello, Mrs. Trewynn, Julia, Nick."

"I'm returning your things." Nick handed over the polythene bag of clothes. "With many thanks for the loan."

"Oh, thanks."

"I brought them down the river," said Julia. "That's why we're on the terrace."

"That's okay." Chaz seemed jittery. "Umm, will you come in for a drink, Mrs. Trewynn? If you're not in a hurry. Actually, my grandfather and Dad would like to meet you."

Eleanor managed not to look at Nick. Was it a perfect opportunity or a case of *Won't you come into my parlour . . . ?* The former, she hoped, as she said, "Thank you, Chaz, I'd like to meet them."

The long, high-ceilinged room was comfortably furnished and decorated with bits and pieces from all over the world. The parquet floor was spread with beautiful oriental rugs. Eleanor recognised a Maori mask and an East African ancestor statue

— and the large man who came to greet her, though he wasn't wearing a reefer jacket and nautical cap now.

Rupert Avery didn't appear to recognise her. He introduced himself and his father, Captain Avery, a tall, lean man with silver hair, who rose from his chair with the aid of a stick and limped forward.

Provided with a sherry from a locked cabinet, Eleanor sat by a driftwood fire with the two elder Averys, each with whisky and soda. Julia chose a bitter lemon, Nick and Chaz beer, and the younger trio drifted to the far end of the room.

On the small table at Rupert's elbow was a copy of the latest *North Cornwall Times*. Normally, it circulated no farther south than St. Austell.

Captain Avery opened the proceedings, the interrogation, explanation, defence, or obfuscation, what ever was to come. "Charles told us about your part, and Mr. Gresham's, in saving the unfortunate young man who nearly drowned in Rocky Valley," he said. His eyes wary, he gestured at the newspaper. "We've been reading about this dreadful affair. I've done considerable business with the Nayak family, and in my travelling days, they were most hospitable when my ship called in Mombasa. I'm desperately sorry for their plight."

Rupert broke in. "My father would like to do something for these people, though I understand the . . . er . . . gentleman he used to deal with . . . er . . . died in the course of their journey and he's not personally acquainted with any of the others. We thought you might be able to suggest a way to help them."

Interesting! Eleanor thought. David Skan's article hadn't squeezed in either her connection with the LonStar shop or her lifelong connection with the worldwide charity. She was pretty sure neither Julia nor Chaz had been within hearing of any mention of her work. Had the Averys been investigating her background, and — presumably — Nick's after Chaz told them about Kalith's rescue? Chaz must surely have revealed then that Megan was a police officer.

"It would probably be best to wait a few days and see what the Nayaks need," she said. "One can't say they're comfortable, exactly, but they're no longer in a desperate state."

"You're in touch with them, then?" Captain Avery asked eagerly.

"Oh yes. I'm sorry to have to tell you that there's been another death — Mrs. Chudasama, mother of the young man who was pulled from the sea."

The old man groaned.

"Have they told you how they reached England," Rupert asked, "and came to be stranded in the cave?"

"Certainly."

"And the police as well, I suppose." Rupert glanced at his father, who looked ill.

"Of course. The Nayaks couldn't provide any names, but even the tiniest clues just may help. With two dead, the police have to regard it as —"

"Police!" The howl burst from a huge man who rushed into the room, wildly waving a scimitar.

Or, in the context, probably a cutlass. The irrelevant thought flitted across Eleanor's mind as she realised he was focussing on her. She sprang to her feet.

This she could cope with, in spite of the climb up the stairs. She had practised the sequence of moves appropriate for such a situation so often as to make it virtually instinctive. Not that she had expected ever to have to use it in earnest . . .

He swung the sword as if to cleave her head in half, but the blade sliced only air.

Without conscious intent, Eleanor had ducked under her attacker's arm. She pivoted lightly, placing one hand on the back of his upper arm, the other on the forearm. A nudge of her hip sent him sprawling facedown, as if he'd caught his foot on the edge of the rug. The weapon flew from his grasp.

It was just a matter of using his own momentum against him. She hoped it had happened so fast the onlookers failed to grasp that she had assisted his fall.

The others, aghast, had been slow to react, apart from a horrified gasp, "Paul!" from his father, and Teazle's furious barking — from a safe distance.

Shouting incoherently, Paul was already struggling up from the floor. Rupert put his foot on the cutlass. Nick grabbed Eleanor's hand.

"Run!"

Julia on their heels, they made for the stairs down to the river.

Nick shepherded the women ahead, Julia first. Halfway down, Eleanor's knees went wobbly. She absolutely had to stand still for a moment. A commotion above drew her attention. At the top of the stairs, Rupert and Chaz were grappling with Paul.

Nick glanced back. "Keep moving."

"Come on!" urged Julia.

Teazle had already reached the beach. Eleanor set off downward again.

At the bottom, Nick dodged past her and ran to drop the dog into the dinghy and help Julia launch it. Eleanor looked up again, just in time to see Chaz fall over backwards on the terrace. A moment later, with a cry of terror, Rupert came tumbling down the bank. Paul started down the steps.

Rupert's fall was stopped by a large ceanothus. Eleanor turned back to go and try to help him, but Nick swooped upon her, picked her up, and carried her through knee-deep water to the boat. Julia already had the outboard in place. It started easily now it was warmed up. They moved away from the beach, the propeller stirring up mud.

Paul seemed to be treading cautiously, as if he were dizzy, but he soon reached the bottom. With the strength of a madman, he wrestled the rowboat into the water.

"He'll never catch us in that," said Eleanor.

"No," Julia agreed, "but he's rowing to the yacht. *Andromeda* can do double our max speed, or more."

"At least he's left the cutlass behind."

"Bloody lucky you ducked so fast and he tripped on the rug!" said Nick. "I thought for a moment you were done for, Eleanor. But he'll find something on the yacht. A boathook or a marlinspike, what ever that may be."

"We have a boathook too," Julia pointed out as, fighting tide and current, *Calliope* chugged upstream into the misty gloom. "Not that it's much comfort. All he has to do is run us down."

TWENTY-NINE

The Falmouth harbourmaster, Captain Edwards, had kept Megan and Ken waiting. His secretary, a steel-haired woman wearing steel pince-nez, told them there was a problem with the papers of a foreign-registered ship calling at the port. Captain Edwards had had to go on board to examine them. She didn't know how long it would take to resolve.

"Liberian," she said with a sniff. "Their paperwork is more often out of order than not."

"Perhaps you may be able to help us, Miss Lewis," Megan suggested, reading the nameplate on her desk. This was no totty from the typing pool.

"Well," she said doubtfully, "if you'll tell me what you want, I'll see what I can do."

"First, we need the names of ships — freighters — arriving in Falmouth during these few days." She reached for a convenient memo pad, wrote down the dates, and pushed it back.

"That's easy enough."

"And where they sailed from?" Ken offered his most charming smile.

Uncharmed, Miss Lewis frowned at him. "The last port of call is the best I can do without authorisation. Excuse me." She went through to the harbourmaster's office.

Megan caught a glimpse of wide windows on three sides, offering a view of the entire waterfront.

"Man-eater," Ken whispered. "You'll definitely do better with her than I would."

"Yet the Met still won't give women detective rank."

"It's coming. When it happens, will you come back?"

"I'll be past retirement age, I expect."

"In the next year or two. The rear guard is steadily losing ground. There's a black woman officer now, and I've heard there's an Indian woman recruit in training."

"I bet they have a hell of a time of it, poor things."

"So I hear, but it is progress, you must admit."

"I wonder whether CaRaDoC is ready for an Indian officer."

"Jay Nayak? You think they'll stay in Cornwall?"

"I have no idea. It was just a thought. Hush."

Miss Lewis returned, memo pad in hand. Pointedly ignoring Ken, she handed it to Megan, who thanked her.

The top page named the *British Destiny* and listed the shipping line — BP, country of registration — Britain, home port, the last port of call, and the captain's name. Megan flipped through. Five or six pages were filled with Miss Lewis's neat handwriting. She tore them off and returned the pad.

"Anything clsc I can help with, Officer? I do have work waiting for my attention."

"My colleague and I will just take a look at these. We can't really decide what further information we need until we see what we have here."

They retired to the window, which had a limited and extremely dull view of several utilitarian concrete and metal buildings. Megan shuffled the first page to the back, and after a quick glance, the second.

Avery Shipping sprang out at her from the third.

"Ha!" she said softly.

"Got it?"

She showed him: SS *Pendennis Point,*

413

Avery Shipping, Britain, Falmouth, last call Gibraltar, Acting Captain . . . "Acting Captain Stuart Vandon — Damn!"

"That's what we want," said Ken. "The captain was on the yacht, remember, not on the ship, at least according to the child. Go and ask the man-eater —"

"I'd rather she didn't know that's the one we're interested in."

"Then ask her something about one of the others, as well."

Megan nodded and went over to the desk. "I'm sorry to interrupt, but could you tell me what BP stands for? BP Shipping, here."

"That's British Petroleum. Oil tankers and such."

"And what exactly does 'Acting Captain' mean?"

"It could mean the captain fell overboard en route and the first officer took over. Sometimes if the ship doesn't call at her home port, the captain will have a tender take him off as they pass and leave the mate to bring her in to her destination. In this case — That's the *Pendennis Point* you're talking about? That would be Captain Avery, a local gentleman. Avery Shipping, you'll have noticed. He lives just across the river. He probably went ashore as soon as they docked and left his first mate to complete the formalities."

Or perhaps he was met by his yacht in mid-Channel and went aboard along with a company of refugees. "Is Stuart Vandon a local resident?"

"I couldn't say, I'm sure. Avery Shipping will have his address, of course."

"Yes, of course. Thanks." Megan went back to Ken. "You heard? Any more questions will confirm her suspicion it's the Averys we're after."

Miss Lewis was watching them. "Is there anything else I can do for you, Officer? If not, there's a coffee machine downstairs while you're waiting for the harbourmaster. I'll let you know as soon as he's able to see you."

Ignominiously dismissed, they went downstairs and found the machine. A shilling or five new pence bought a plastic cup of coffee, tea, or hot chocolate, all dispensed through the same nozzle. Megan had chocolate, knowing from experience that it best disguised the taste of the others. She let Ken get his coffee first.

He took a sip and grimaced. "I sometimes think the worst thing about being a copper is the amount of truly disgusting coffee and tea we drink."

"I dunno. It's cheering in a way to find

415

that so many other people are stuck with coffee just as bad as we get at the nick."

They took their drinks outside, to stand in the sun where they could see the big ships and therefore, presumably, the harbourmaster on his return.

"Don't you think we have enough information already to tackle the Averys directly?" Ken proposed.

"I'd say yes if it wasn't that we have a very good chance of getting more soon and quite easily. Where the *Pendennis Point* had been, for instance, and whether it stopped at Mombasa on the way back."

"She. Aren't ships always *she*?"

"I simply can't seriously talk about the *Pendennis Point* as if it was female. A confirmation that *it* carried wool would be useful, specially if Captain Edwards can tell us how to find out about the marks on the bales that Jay and the others noticed. We may be able to persuade him to tell us a bit more about Captain Avery and the rest of the family. If Chaz is a typical example, I'm not impressed."

"Edwards may be a friend of the family, in a place like this."

"But we have to ask," Megan insisted.

"It's your case."

They finished the drinks and bunged the

cups in a litter bin. The sunny afternoon was clouding over and held an autumnal chill. They decided to walk towards the wharves, hoping to meet the harbourmaster. Several ships of varying sizes were berthed there. Men and cranes were at work loading two and unloading another as lorries came and went. A third ship was being painted. The farthest away, Megan guessed, was the one having trouble with its papers. There were also two in dry dock, one being built, one repaired, as far as she could make out.

At last a man in navy blue approached them, a sheaf of papers in his hand. The sleeves of his reefer jacket had gold stripes at the wrists and his cap had a badge with a gold oak wreath and crown, reminding Megan of Pal's description of the captain of the freighter.

She stepped forwards. "Captain Edwards?"

"Yes?"

"We're police detectives, sir. We have an appointment with you. I'm DS Pencarrow, and this is my colleague, DS Faraday."

He was obviously disconcerted to be faced with a woman detective. "Ah, indeed, I'm sorry to have kept you waiting. Let's go up to my office." He fell into step beside Ken, and as they walked, complained to him about the difficulty of dealing with ships registered under flags of convenience, usually Liberia or Panama.

Ken made polite, noncommittal noises. Megan wondered whether she ought to leave the coming interview to him, given the harbourmaster's obvious preference. But as Ken said, it was her case. Though he'd read the reports and talked it over with her, he couldn't possibly be as much in command of all the ins and outs as she was.

Entering Edwards's office, Megan studiously avoided admiring the view, which he'd probably regard as a typical feminine distraction. When he waved them to seats in front of his desk, backs to the windows, Ken cooperated by moving his chair farther to one side and to the rear. He took out his notebook. She threw him a grateful glance and dived in.

"Captain, we're investigating a serious crime. Two people are dead. I hope we can count on your cooperation."

"Of course, of course, though I can't imagine how I can possibly help you."

"That's for us to find out, sir." Go for the simple, unfraught stuff first. "Your secretary has kindly given us a list of the ships in port at the relevant time, including previous port of call. Do you keep records of where they started out from, where they called on the way, and their cargoes?"

"Only the origin of any freight unloaded here, and what it consisted of. I take it you're interested in one particular vessel, not the whole list Miss Lewis supplied?"

"The *Pendennis Point,* sir."

He frowned. "The Averys' ship. Under Captain Paul Avery's command."

"Yes, sir, but we understand Captain Avery was not aboard when it . . . she arrived in Falmouth."

"Ah, yes. He ought to have gone through the formalities, but an old local family, you know . . . No doubt one of them came across the river and picked him up when they docked."

"Perhaps."

"You're suggesting he left sooner?" Edwards shifted uneasily. "The pilot will know, of course, and the records will tell you which pilot brought her in."

"We'll need to take a look at those records, sir."

"If you must." He spoke to Miss Lewis on his intercom, asking her to bring the relevant file, then turned to Ken and asked, slightly plaintively, "What on earth is this all about, eh? Has that rascally crew of lascars they insist on employing been smuggling drugs? They should stick with British seamen."

Ken refrained from pointing out that British seamen were quite as adept at drug smuggling as lascars. "I'm afraid I can't say, sir." He looked at Megan, firmly returning the ball to her.

"An old local family, you say, sir. Can you tell me a bit about the Averys, please?"

"Good heavens, surely you're not suggesting —"

"I'm not making any suggestions, sir, I'm asking for information. I can undoubtedly get it elsewhere, but since we're here —" She stopped as Miss Lewis came in with a manila folder. When she held out her hand for it, the secretary automatically gave it to her. She passed it to Ken. He'd be able to dig out the details they wanted and listen at the same time.

Miss Lewis left.

"The Averys, sir?"

"Yes, well . . . They go back at least to the middle of the last century, you know. Started out in shipbuilding, quite successfully, then turned to running their own fleet. With equal success, to all appearances."

"How big a fleet?"

"Five middle-size freighters, all named after local headlands. They go all over the world, but they're not tramp steamers, picking up a load here and there. Everything's planned. Captain Avery — Captain Perran Avery — served his time on the ships, as Captain Paul is doing now, but he's a very shrewd businessman." The harbourmaster's lips folded in disapproval, unconscious, Megan thought.

Disapproval of shrewdness in business? Or of Captain Paul Avery? Captain Edwards seemed disinclined to elucidate.

"Captain Paul will take over the business side sooner or later?"

"Doubtless."

Megan changed tack. "Are the Averys friends of yours, sir?"

"I'm a local man myself. I've known *of* them all my life, seen them out and about, and since I've been harbourmaster I've come to know them quite well. Captain Avery comes in on business, and of course I see Captain Paul every time his ship comes or goes. I've been invited to their house a number of times."

"Is that where they keep the yacht?"

"*Andromeda*? They have a mooring just offshore."

"Then they must have a dinghy to get to it . . . her."

"Yes, a rowboat. They have a speedboat,

too, and the boy has his own outboard sailing dinghy."

"Ah yes, the boy. That would be Chaz? I've met him." Given her profession, Megan's pause lent significance to the words. She hoped the harbourmaster knew Chaz smoked pot. It wouldn't hurt to mislead him a little, let him believe it was Chaz they were interested in, especially after he himself had introduced the topic of drugs. "Captain Paul is his uncle, is that right?"

"Yes, but he wouldn't have anything to do with the stuff. With drugs. I'd've said his choice of poison is alcohol. I mean . . . I don't mean to say he drinks on the job, mind. A boozy skipper can be a nightmare, a horrible accident waiting to happen, unless he has a competent mate who's willing to take the responsibility without the perks and . . . well . . ."

"Cover up for him? But you say that's not the case with Captain Paul?"

"Absolutely not!" Edwards became confidential. "You won't spread it about, of course, but what I hear is, he goes completely off course when he comes home."

"Off course, sir?"

"On the spree. More like a proper bender, you might say. Booze and the gee-gees. Last time, Captain Avery rescued him from some nasty types — bookies . . . Daresay you know all about that sort of thing. Mr. Rupert had to go and fetch him from Newmarket and there was a pretty penny paid out, I gather. Chap doesn't seem able to control himself. Jolly poor show."

"So you're saying, on shore Captain Paul is impulsive, shows poor judgment, and is inclined to get into debt?"

"Well, it sounds rather bad when you put it like that. Pity. He's an excellent shipmaster. All the same, it's not surprising Captain Avery doesn't want to give up the helm — of the company, that is."

"It wouldn't surprise you, then, if Captain Paul, after — what? weeks? months? — without drinking or gambling, was unable to resist the impulse to go on a binge regardless of the consequences?" Was she pressing too hard? The harbourmaster was turning out to be a goldmine.

"Er . . . hmm . . . Two deaths, you mentioned? I wouldn't be talking to you like this if you hadn't said . . ."

"I can't tell you any more about that, sir, but you may see something on the television news this evening." If Skan's article had been picked up. But Dave Skan knew nothing yet about the Averys, or so Megan hoped.

Captain Edwards sighed unhappily. "Who knows what a chap like that will do? Even the best families —"

His intercom intercepted the inevitable "black sheep." Miss Lewis announced the arrival of a Mr. Lloyd, with whom he had an appointment.

"Yes, yes, I'll be with him in a minute." He clicked off the machine and stood up. Megan and Ken likewise rose to their feet. "I can't spare you any more time, I'm afraid. If there's anything more, Miss Lewis can help you, no doubt. Er . . . You won't mention to Captain Avery that you've been talking to me about his family?"

"I don't foresee the necessity, sir." Megan decided thanking him for being helpful would only worry him. "We're grateful for your time. Sergeant Faraday, have you got any quick questions?"

"Just one." Ken laid the folder on Edwards's desk. "Is Captain Paul's ship in port at present or is he on his way to the far side of the world?"

"Damn!" said Megan, as they walked to the car, "I should have thought of that."

"Well, yes, but you didn't miss much. You

424

can always go back if it seems necessary. In the end, I think he spoke more freely to you than he would have to me."

"Because he doesn't take women seriously. Anything you say to them goes straight through their pretty little heads and out the other side, so why worry? No need to mind your tongue. By the way, you did a good job of disappearing in there."

"It's a useful talent at times. We're lucky Paul hasn't sailed yet."

"Very. I'd hate to have to tell the boss we've got to call in Interpol." They reached the car and got in, Megan behind the wheel. "Speaking of whom, I ought to check in. But we're probably out of Launceston's radio area. I don't want to go through the local cop shop and I don't want to go looking for a public phone."

"Any excuse . . . !"

"To the Averys' house now, don't you think?"

"Yes. There's a lot of sheer slog left, collecting the details, but we know where to dig. I for one am now convinced we have our sights on the right man."

"It does look like it. Car or foot ferry, or drive the long way round?"

It was knocking-off time, and they got caught up in a stream of cars and bikes leaving the docks.

"Drive round," said Ken. "Though the ferry's tempting, in this traffic there'll be a long queue, I expect. We might want the car. It doesn't seem likely we'll be ready to invite him to the Falmouth nick to answer Twenty Questions, but you never know. I can't see bringing him over on foot on a public ferry."

"Not on your life! Have we got enough on him to caution him?"

"Let's put it all together and see. For a start, according to the bumf in that folder, the *Pendennis Point* had one hold full of wool from New Zealand and picked up a load of ivory in Mombasa."

"You don't say!"

They discussed how the harbourmaster's revelations fitted with all the information previously gathered, as Megan drove through Falmouth and Penryn and turned down the narrow road leading to Flushing.

Miss Lewis had given them directions to the Averys' house. Beyond the village, the road narrowed to a lane serving only a few large houses surrounded by trees, lawns, and shrubbery. Between the trees, Megan glimpsed the river, with a veil of mist now rising from the surface. When they reached the white house with multiple gables, she turned into the drive and parked well to one side, out of the way of the multivehicle garage. They walked down to the front door and Ken rang the bell.

They heard it ringing, but no one came. After waiting a minute, he pushed the button again, holding it for a few seconds.

Still no one responded.

"Let's go round the side," said Megan. "Maybe there's a kitchen door where we can attract someone's attention."

They had just spotted a promising door when a confused uproar came from the rear of the house, a yell followed by incoherent shouting. They both brokc into a run.

Rounding the corner ahead of Ken, Megan saw Chaz flat on his back on the stone terrace. As she ran to him, he rolled over, groaning, and felt the back of his head.

"Chaz, what happened?"

"My uncle . . ." He struggled to rise to his hands and knees.

Megan and Ken helped him up, till he was sitting back on his heels, blinking dizzily.

"Your uncle?" Ken prompted.

"He's gone mad!" He started to turn, desisting with a yelp of pain. "Where's my father? Dad!" he shouted, and clutched his head.

"Help!" came a voice from beyond the

parapet.

"Dad! Megan — Sergeant, help him!"

Ken was already dashing over to look down the slope.

At the same time, an old man came out of the house and hurried towards Chaz and Megan, both still kneeling. "I've rung for an ambulance. Charles, my dear boy, are you all right? Who — ?"

"Police," Megan said curtly, standing up. "Keep an eye on Chaz." She ran over to Ken.

The old man called after her, "Paul's not responsible! He's not in his right mind!"

Halfway down the steep bank, a man was sprawled amid bushes that stopped him falling farther. His face was twisted in an expression of agony.

"Rupert Avery," said Ken. "He's put his back out and daren't move. I don't know whether we dare move him."

"There's an ambulance on the way, Mr. Avery," Megan called down to him.

Captain Avery joined them, followed by Chaz, both looking shaky.

"Dad, are you okay?"

"No!"

"They're sending a lifeboat, Rupert. Just a few minutes and we'll have you —"

A clanking noise drew the attention of all

428

four on the terrace to the river below.

"The anchor! Uncle Paul's winching up the anchor."

"That's your yacht?" Megan asked.

"He's escaping!" Ken exclaimed.

"Or going after Julia and the others," Chaz said grimly. "He's mad — crazy and angry! And the yacht's much faster. Come on, Megan, we'll take the speedboat." He started down the steps to the river.

Explanations could wait. Megan followed him, close at his heels in case he had a dizzy spell, but the prospect of action seemed to have cleared his head. She heard Ken pounding after them.

The yacht's engine roared to life and she swung out into the centre of the river, heading upstream.

THIRTY

Julia's little boat struggled against the current and the ebbing tide. The banks moved past with agonising slowness. Eleanor leant forward, as though that would help the *Calliope* along, as she often did when coaxing the Incorruptible up a hill.

Teazle had already lost interest. She was stretched out on the planking, asleep, toes twitching as she chased dream rabbits. So much for dogs sensing their owners' agitation.

Nick was gazing backwards. "You're right, Julia, he's coming after us. How about heading for the other side, where there are plenty of people about?"

"What if no one's about who can stop him? He's gone crazy! I've seen him pretty sozzled once or twice, but never like that. He's scary."

"He's a big man," said Eleanor. "We might just put other people in danger without being out of danger ourselves. Besides, at this time most people are probably indoors, getting supper or watching the news."

They passed round the bend where the river narrowed. The yacht was out of sight for the moment.

"How fast is *Andromeda*?" Nick asked in a conversational tone. "Compared to *Calliope*?"

"At least twice as fast. More, against the current."

"Can we get ashore and hide before he comes round and spots us?"

"Not a hope. But I've got an idea. That's not the only difference between the boats. If he's really lost his mind . . ."

"DTs," said Nick.

"What?"

"Delirium tremens."

Julia looked blank.

"Seeing pink elephants," Nick explained.

"You told us he's a heavy drinker," Eleanor reminded her, thinking that Nick might very well have hit the nail on the head.

"You mean when he looks at *Calliope,* he thinks she's a pink elephant? But it all started in the Averys' sitting room. When Mrs. Trewynn said 'police,' remember?"

"Hallucinations are just one of the possible symptoms. Unreasoning rage is an-

431

other. A mate of mine —"

"Never mind now, you can explain later." Julia glanced back. "Here' he comes. Now I've got to concentrate."

Eleanor watched *Andromeda* closing the gap between them. For a man in the grip of DTs, Chaz's uncle was steering a pretty steady course between the buoys, when by cutting across an arc he'd catch up with *Calliope* quicker. Perhaps deference to buoys became instinctive in a ship's captain, as it seemed to be with Julia, a mere recreational boater. But with delirium tremens, almost anything was possible. Eleanor had seen a few Empire builders who had succumbed to a steady diet of gin and tonic. One part of Paul Avery's mind might follow ingrained rules while another part behaved like a ravening beast. He might even have forgotten that he was after them.

Too much to hope for. Whatever Julia's plan was, it had better work. Soon.

"Hold on, I'm changing course."

Teazle gave a startled yip as Nick grabbed her collar. With his other hand he hung on to the side of the boat, and Eleanor gripped the bench with both hands. *Calliope* heeled over alarmingly as she swerved to the right. Disregarding the channel-marker buoys, she cut between two of them.

Eleanor couldn't work out what Julia was trying to do. The way the river curved at that point, she wasn't cutting across a bend. The flat green meadow on the bank was devoid of hiding places.

"He's still following," Nick reported.

"Good!"

Eleanor glanced back. *Andromeda* was close enough now for her to make out a shadowy figure behind the glass. Gradually the yacht closed in until all she could see was the bow looming over the dinghy.

Megan hung on to the side of the speedboat, wishing it wasn't under the control of a pallid youth who was more than likely suffering from concussion. The wake creamed back on either side until they picked up enough speed for the bow to rise out of the water, flinging up spray behind them.

The roar of the motor made speech impossible, but while they were getting the boat out of the boathouse and down the slipway, Chaz had talked. His uncle had come home the day before, irritable, and taciturn except to say that he'd been to the races in Ayr and Doncaster and for God's sake to leave him alone. Then he had gone to bed.

Chaz's father and grandfather had obviously been worried sick. They'd gone into a

433

conclave that excluded Chaz.

Uncle Paul had not come down next morning. His snores assured anyone who paused outside his bedroom door that he was still in the land of the living, and Granddad had said to let him sleep it off.

He still hadn't appeared when Julia arrived, bringing Nick Gresham, who was returning Chaz's borrowed clothes, and Mrs. Trewynn —

"Aunt Nell!" Megan had exclaimed.

So now they were racing up the river in pursuit of Captain Paul Avery, who was in full cry after Aunt Nell, Nick, and Julia, presumably with fell intent. All Megan could do was hold on and hope: that they'd be in time to save Aunt Nell, that behind them a lifeboat crew was rescuing Rupert Avery, and most immediately, that Chaz was fit to drive a boat at what felt like ninety miles an hour up an ever narrowing river.

The yacht had disappeared round a bend as they launched the speedboat. It hove into view again as they followed, but river mist, overcast sky, and encroaching dusk made it hard to see what was going on ahead. Julia's dinghy was no more than a blob. Megan couldn't even be sure whether it was moving.

Ken leant over and bellowed in her ear,

". . . plan . . . catch them?"

She shook her head. What would they do when they caught up? She had no idea.

He shrugged. Moving with care, he shuffled to the stern and yelled something in Chaz's ear. Chaz nodded, wincing, and gingerly touched the back of his head. Whether he understood, had a plan of his own, or was agreeing to something proposed by Ken remained a mystery to Megan.

The distances between the three boats rapidly lessened. Soon Megan could make out three figures in the dinghy, Aunt Nell's white hair standing out like a halo. The speedboat was no more than a hundred yards behind the yacht when the dinghy suddenly veered to the right, heeling over alarmingly.

But it righted itself with its occupants still aboard. The yacht swung after it, bearing down on it. As he followed, Chaz had to throttle back. The bow sank and the noise decreased to a bearable level.

"What shall I do now?" he shouted.

The yacht blocked their view of the dinghy.

"Get alongside so we can see!" Megan shouted back.

Clouds of mud suddenly swirled to the surface behind the yacht. It slowed. Chaz

435

moved up next to it, a dozen feet away, and Megan saw the dinghy pulling ahead, Nick's and Aunt Nell's pale faces turned to look back.

The yacht came to a standstill. Its motor rose in pitch, choked, and cut off. And slowly, slowly, it listed to the right.

"Oh, well done, Julia!" Chaz cried.

"What did she do?" asked Ken, baffled.

"Led him on to a sandbank. The yacht's draft is about six feet. *Calliope* — her dinghy — is more like two feet, with three adults aboard. She knows the river like the back of her hand! Brilliant! But I bet *Andromeda*'s engine is ruined."

Megan watched the dinghy circle and come back towards them. "Aunt Nell, are you all right?" she called.

But her aunt, Nick, and — she realised — Ken all had their eyes fixed on the yacht. Megan followed their gaze. Paul Avery was crawling headfirst out of the wheelhouse on to the narrow strip of canted deck. His face was blotchy, his eyes blank, and he kept stopping to brush with one hand at such parts of his body as he could reach.

"The creepy-crawlies," said Ken. "DTs. I thought so. Chaz, can you get close to the side of the yacht?"

"Yes." He looked almost as bad as his

436

uncle, his face sweaty and very pale. "I hope she's stuck tight, or we'll be underneath when she goes over." But he moved forward under low power and came round almost touching the yacht, just below Paul.

By that time, the captain was slumped with his feet still inside, one shoulder hung up on a rail-post. Mechanically, he started to try to crawl again. His feet came out and he slithered round until he was caught by the waist on the flimsy-looking post, his head and legs dangling over the edge.

"Hell, I'll have to go up there." Ken gripped the boarding ladder, tilted over them, and hauled himself up.

He had to squeeze past Paul. Momentarily roused, the captain started flailing his arms. He caught Ken a wallop on the shoulder, but Ken gained the shelter of the wheel-house and the captain lapsed into apathy again, but for the ceaseless brushing motions.

Megan thought she heard him mumble, "Get them off me. Get them off me."

Now Ken hung out of the wheelhouse as Paul had before. "Ready, Megan? For Pete's sake, hold her steady, Chaz." Bracing himself with one hand, he grasped Paul's collar and started to work the big man round so that his upper body was back on the deck.

"Been lifting weights, have you?" Megan kidded, her mouth dry.

"Get them off me . . ." But it was a passive mutter. The captain didn't struggle. He slid down into her arms and they collapsed together in the bottom of the boat.

Which rocked, stalled, and started to drift away from the yacht.

Captain Paul lay there twitching like a stranded starfish. Megan extricated herself from the heap, but there was nothing she could do to help Chaz start the engine.

Julia's dinghy slipped into the growing space between the speedboat and the yacht. She held *Calliope* steady beneath the ladder.

Grinning up at Ken, Nick grasped a rung and asked, "Need a hand, old chap?"

Through the darkening dusk, Megan watched as Ken twisted round and lowered himself into the dinghy, with a steadying hand from Nick.

And then Falmouth's all-weather lifeboat arrived, with floodlights and grappling hooks and life jackets . . .

THIRTY-ONE

The phone rang just as Eleanor was thinking about making a cup of coffee for elevenses.

"Eleanor, it's Nick. Listen, I've got Avery here, Captain Avery."

"Not Captain Paul!"

"No, no, Chaz's grandfather. He wants to talk to you."

"Then why didn't he ring up? Or come here?"

"I gather he has more to say to you than he cares to confide on the phone. He was afraid you might not hear him out. And he wanted to apologise to me, too, for Captain Paul running amok, and he didn't want to alarm you by turning up on your doorstep unannounced."

Eleanor blinked as she assimilated the list. "I suppose that's reasonable, added up. I'm just putting coffee on. He's welcome to join me. The street door's not locked."

"I'll tell him. See you later."

The doorbell's ring came a few minutes later, and she opened the door to Captain Avery. Grey faced and weary looking, almost haggard, he said, "I beg your pardon for this intrusion, Mrs. Trewynn. I've heard a bit about you since . . . in the past couple of days, and I'd be very grateful for a chance to talk to you."

Invited in and provided with a cup of coffee and a digestive biscuit, he sank into a chair. He didn't seem to know where to start.

"You've been under a good deal of strain for some time, I think," said Eleanor.

"I've been half out of my mind with worry! Paul's cut loose before, but . . . He's ill. I should have realised sooner it wasn't just overindulgence. He's in hospital now, you know. With a policeman on duty outside the door. I can't begin to tell you how sorry I am that he attacked you and young Julia and Mr. Gresham. Thank God you got away."

"Thank Julia!"

He managed a small smile. "She's quite a girl, isn't she? Good for my grandson, but they're not interested in each other romantically, I'm afraid."

"A good friend is worth a great deal."

"Yes. Batuk Nayak was my friend. We met many years ago, when he was finding his feet in his family's export-import business and I was third mate in one of our ships. My first time in Africa — I was bewitched and baffled, and Batuk introduced me to the Mombasa beyond the yacht club and the sailors' taverns. We remained good friends even after I stopped going to sea. You can't imagine how it pains me that my son caused his death, and his daughter's." He sank his head between his hands.

"No, I can't imagine," Eleanor said frankly.

"I want to explain to you how it came about. I hope — I know your niece is a police officer, but I hope you won't feel obliged to report everything to her. I shan't ask for a promise. It's for you to decide, if you'll hear me out."

"I suspect the police know and guess more than you think."

"You've probably guessed yourself. It was I who arranged to bring Batuk and his family to Britain. He wrote to me in great distress from one of the ports where they were denied entry. I hadn't realised the situation had become so disastrous after our government's disgraceful about-face on British citizenship. I didn't, and don't, consider breaking such a law to be wrong."

Eleanor smiled at him. "No more do I. I would have been happy to help. The plan to smuggle them into the country was yours?"

"But I left it to Paul to implement. I found out, through my extensive contacts in the business, when our *Pendennis Point* would be in the same port as the Nayaks and I told him to go ahead and pick them up. I told him not to charge them for the passage. That was where he first went astray. The tentacles of the gambling fever reached out from England, I suppose."

"Horse racing, Chaz told Julia."

Avery shrugged helplessly. "I don't understand it. He's not in the least interested in roulette or vingt-et-un, or what ever else people bet on. It's the horses or nothing. There seems to be a meeting somewhere in the country almost all the time. In the past, he'd return from a voyage, spend a few days at home, and then go off to the races for a couple of weeks, till it was time to ship out again. I can't blame my former daughter-in-law for leaving him."

"This time, you didn't expect him when the ship came in?"

"No. I knew he had the yacht and was taking the Nayaks to the secret cave. He came back at night, left *Andromeda* at anchor, sneaked into the house without waking anyone, picked up some clothes, and left without a word or a note. That was when I started worrying. When I'd still heard nothing from him after ten days or so, I sent Rupert to try to find out who had picked them up — Paul hadn't told me — and whether they had been spotted coming ashore in Boscastle, or Port Mabyn, or Port Isaac."

"I saw him in Boscastle."

"Yes, and he asked me to apologise for his rudeness. He was reporting to me, when you saw him telephoning. We were both getting a bit frantic by then."

"He's all right? I should have asked sooner. And Chaz?"

"A day in bed in a darkened room with his mother cooing over him was enough to send Chaz rocketing back to Exeter," Avery said dryly. "Rupert's back is an old problem that's flared up. He's lying down, taking pills, and hoping he won't have to have an operation. Doing as well as can be expected, if not quite resting comfortably."

"We — Julia, Nick, and I — have both of them to thank for giving us time to get away. Did Captain Paul have anything to say about his decision to rob the Nayaks and his failure to arrange for their rescue? I'm sorry to put it so bluntly . . ."

"How else could you put it? No. We didn't know then about the robbery. When he came home I demanded to know about . . . about the other." Avery closed his eyes. "He said he'd been in a hurry and it had slipped his mind. I'm sorry, I can't . . . I don't know what else to say."

Eleanor had no comfort to offer. After a moment's silence to let him pull himself together, she asked, "How much of this do the Nayaks know?"

"I haven't contacted them. I haven't been able to face them. But I must. That's really the favour I wanted to ask of you: Would you be prepared to approach them on my behalf and find out if they're willing to see me? I'll return all the money Paul took from them, of course, and the value of the jewellery. I don't know whether I can help them with immigration, since I've already blotted my copybook in that regard. What I can't do is give them back Batuk and his daughter."

Eleanor's sitting room was crowded. It was just as well Julia and Chaz's term had started and DS Ken Faraday had gone back to London. DI Scumble, though declining the invitation, had allowed Megan to borrow a police car and she came via Bodmin, picking up Jay and Mrs. Jay, and Kalith and his sister Naima. Jocelyn was present. She'd been rather peeved to have missed most of the excitement.

Though it was Eleanor's sitting room, Nick was in a sense the host. He was feeling rich because Captain Avery had bought *Valley of the Shadow* — to which Nick had added a small patch of blue sky and a patch of vivid green sunlit foliage on the edge of the rocks, after Jocelyn told him it was too gloomy.

"The whole point," she had told him severely, "is that there is hope even in the valley of the shadow of death."

Captain Avery had said it perfectly expressed his feelings, and he didn't blink at the price.

So Nick had ordered Chin's Chinese takeaway for everyone. He and Jay fetched it, as Kalith was still a bit pale and limp. Kalith was settled in one armchair, the other three being occupied by Jocelyn, Mrs. Jay, and Eleanor. Megan and Naima sat at the kitchen table, upon which the feast was spread, and Nick and Jay made do on the floor, where they had to fend off Teazle as they ate.

When the plates and most of the little

boxes were empty, Mrs. Jay and Naima insisted on doing the washing up. Megan moved to Mrs. Jay's chair.

"Police report first," said Nick. "Please, Megan. Bring us up to date, as much as you're allowed to tell us."

Megan looked at Eleanor, who said, "Yes, do, dear."

"Well, then, Paul Avery was arrested, as I expect you all know. We've come up with more than enough hard evidence to prosecute, but they haven't decided yet exactly what the charge will be. The boatman who crewed the Averys' yacht and rowed the dinghy to the cave is a family employee. He's not quite an idiot, but pretty dim. We have no evidence that he knew what Paul was up to. I doubt he'll be charged."

"And Captain Avery?" Jay asked.

"That's out of local hands. It's up to the Home Office so I can't say for sure, but I gather he's unlikely to go to prison. They're finding it hard to believe that none of your family knew he was responsible for bringing you here."

"None but my grandfather," said Jay. "He told my father he knew who had set up the whole business. The more people who knew, he said, the more danger our benefactor would run. Even at the end, when he knew he was dying, he refused to tell my father. It is as well. We can't be called to give evidence against Captain Avery. He has paid back every penny Captain Paul took from us, you know. He wouldn't accept any payment for our passage."

"And we have our jewellery!" Naima exclaimed, her dark eyes as bright as the multifaceted gold studs in her ears. "Most of it. Sergeant Megan found it for us."

"Not personally," Megan said hastily. "We circulated descriptions. The stuff was picked up at jewellers and pawnshops in every city between here and Ayr, or just about, wherever Paul had disposed of it. Apparently he bet every penny he had in his pockets at Ayr and won a bit, then went and blew the lot at the Doncaster races. Nothing we can do about that."

"It has always surprised me," said Jocelyn, "that the good Lord didn't give Moses a commandment against gambling."

"I expect he thought ten was as many as most mortals could cope with," Eleanor suggested. "In fact, rather more. Now, *I* have some news. My friend at the Commonwealth Relations Office, Sir Edward Bellowe, tells me that the government is being forced to increase the number of special residency vouchers available to Asians from

Kenya and Uganda. He's going to make sure you and all your family are able to stay in Britain."

Naima and Mrs. Jay started crying, their arms around each other. Kalith was speechless. Jay, beaming hugely, shook hands with Eleanor, Nick, Megan, and even Jocelyn, and then shook hands again, venting his feelings in a mixture of English and Gujarati.

Nick, warned in advance by Eleanor that emotions might get out of hand, unfolded his long length from the floor and produced a bottle of cognac. He poured a little into each of the mismatched collection of glasses Eleanor had gathered and handed them round.

"I'm driving," Megan objected in a low voice.

"Come on, it's just a drop. You can't miss this. A toast to Kalith," he said.

Kalith's thin cheeks flushed as they all raised their glasses to him. Slightly unsteady, he rose to his feet. "To Megan," he proposed, and added, displaying an unexpected sense of humour, "because if she hadn't jumped in after me, I'd still be swimming."

"And Nick," said Megan, grinning. "Because if he hadn't pulled us both out, we'd both still be swimming."

"And Eleanor," said Nick. "Because if she hadn't — Well, for any number of reasons, so let's just say because."

ABOUT THE AUTHOR

Carola Dunn is the author of numerous books, including *Manna from Hades* and *A Colourful Death,* the two previous books featuring Eleanor Trewynn. Born and raised in England, she lives in Eugene, Oregon.